Kickapoo Creek

Kickapoo Creek
By
Brett Shayler

BRETT SHAYLER

Dedication

I dedicate this book to the resilient spirits of the Lipan Apache people, whose rich history and unwavering strength continue to inspire. Their deep-rooted kinship to the land, their intricate social structures, and their enduring cultural traditions testify to the power of community and the importance of preserving heritage in the face of adversity. The story of "Kickapoo Creek" is a small tribute to their living memory, a glimpse into the complexities of their lives and their enduring struggle for survival and identity in a transforming world.

I also dedicate this work to the courageous individuals who, throughout history, have dared to cross-cultural boundaries, forging unlikely alliances and challenging societal norms. The characters within these pages, both fictional and inspired by real individuals, embody the spirit of reconciliation, the power of understanding, and the potential for love to blossom even amidst conflict and misunderstanding. Their journeys highlight the enduring power of empathy, the necessity of confronting prejudice, and the possibility for even the most unlikely groups to discover common ground and create a shared future.

I dedicate this book to the countless unsung heroes of the American West, the trailblazers, cowboys, and settlers who met the hardships of frontier life with unwavering courage and resilience. who braved the harsh realities of frontier life. They shaped the nation's landscape and left an indelible mark on its history. Their stories, both triumphs and tragedies, deserve to be remembered and understood, as they provide a crucial context for understanding the complex tapestry of the American experience.

To those who endeavor to grasp and cherish history's complexities, its beauty and brutality, I dedicate this book. May the following pages encourage contemplation, promote understanding, and deepen your appreciation for the intertwined histories of the American West and its indigenous peoples. This story should remind us of our shared history, the lessons we learned, and the future we can create together.

Chapter 1: The Trail Boss Journey

The air hung thick, a shimmering haze of red dust rising from the parched earth. Cole squinted, his eyes shielded by the brim of his worn Stetson. The sun beat down, baking the land into a seemingly endless expanse of prickly pear cacti and scrub brush. Kickapoo Creek, the destination of his arduous cattle drive, was within sight—a thin, silver ribbon snaking through the arid landscape, promising respite from the relentless Texas heat. He'd been riding hard for weeks, pushing his herd across miles of unforgiving terrain, the weight of the journey pressing down on him as heavily as the saddle on his weary horse.

The cattle drive had been brutal. He'd lost several head to stampedes, to illness, and to the thieving hands of opportunistic rustlers. The constant vigilance, the endless sun, and the dust that coated everything had taken their toll. But more than the physical strain, Cole carried a burden that haunted him, whispering doubts and regrets into the silence of the plains. He'd left behind a life he no longer recognized, a life marred by mistakes he couldn't undo, hoping that the sprawling Texas cattle industry would offer him the anonymity and the fresh start he craved. This raw, untamed territory seemed to mirror his internal turmoil.

As he approached the creek, the landscape subtly shifted. A cluster of teepees, visible against the ochre earth, came into view. The Lipan Apache village nestled beside the creek, starkly contrasting with the desolate beauty of the surrounding plains. Cole's heart pounded a hesitant rhythm against his ribs. He had heard tales about the Lipan, whispers of their fierce independence and deep-rooted kinship to this land. He knew little about their customs, beliefs, and ways—only that they were a proud people fiercely protective of their territory. His initial encounters with them were tense, negotiated steps on precarious ground.

He dismounted slowly, his hand resting on the worn leather of his holstered Colt Peacemaker. The action felt instinctive, a reaction to a lifetime lacking trust. He watched the village from a distance, his keen eyes scanning the movements of figures as they went about their daily lives. Women drew water from the creek, their movements graceful and fluid; children played amidst the teepees, their laughter echoing across the quiet landscape; warriors sharpened their weapons, their focus unwavering. He was an outsider, an intruder in their world. Yet, he needed water for his weary herd and himself. He had to cross the invisible line that separated his world from theirs.

Approaching the village felt like stepping into a different era. The air hummed with a unique energy, one less hurried and driven than the clamor of Fort Worth or the relentless pace of the cattle trails. Cole could feel a quiet dignity in how the Lipan Indians carried themselves, a rooted kinship to the land even through his apprehension. Their eyes met his with a mixture of curiosity and suspicion. Their gaze was piercing, assessing, calculating the potential threat he represented. He understood their wariness. He remained an outsider, a representative of a culture that had invaded their land and threatened their existence.

Cole's throat was dry, and his tongue felt thick and useless as he considered his next move. He knew he couldn't turn back, and the creek was his only hope for survival. With a deep breath, he started forward, his boots stirring up small dust clouds with each step. He kept his hands relaxed at his sides, his eyes fixed on the village, and his mind alert for any signs of aggression or welcome. As he drew closer, the sounds of the town became more apparent: the murmur of women's voices, the high-pitched laughter of children, and the sharp ring of metal on stone as the warriors worked. Cooking fires filled the air with their scent, and low-hanging smoke added to the day's haze. He stopped at what he assumed was the customary distance, waiting, hoping for some acknowledgment. A sudden movement caught his eye, and he turned to see a tall and proud warrior striding towards him.

The man's expression showed no emotion; his dark eyes gave nothing away. Cole held his ground, his heart hammering in his chest, as the warrior stopped a respectful distance away. He unholstered his rifle, laying it on the ground, offering goodwill, a symbol of his intention to cause no harm.

This was a calculated risk; offering a weapon to show good faith was an unorthodox approach. He made a point of having his hands visible and empty, showing that he held no immediate hostile intentions. He knew that any sudden movements, any hint of aggression, could escalate the situation far beyond a simple interaction.

The scent of woodsmoke and roasting meat hung heavy in the air, a primal and welcoming aroma. He could hear the rhythmic beat of a drum, a low thrumming that resonated deep within his chest. It was a foreign and familiar sound, drawing him in even as a part of him screamed to retreat to maintain the distance of an outsider. The music spoke of a deep-rooted history that far predated his own, a culture that had endured despite civilization's unstoppable progress. The village's beauty, intricate teepees, powerful sense of community: a life simpler yet more complex than his own. He was a stranger; survival, integration, and becoming part of this new world were necessary for a fresh start. His past mistakes, the weight of his troubled history, felt miles away, less substantial than the raw beauty and mystery surrounding him.

The warrior's gaze remained fixed on Cole, and their tension hung heavy, a tangible force in the air. Cole's gaze remained fixed on the man; he breathed shallowly. In a slow, deliberate movement, the warrior raised a hand, palm facing out, a silent command to wait. With a brief nod, Cole acknowledged the gesture, his hands remaining relaxed at his sides. With graceful, confident strides, the warrior turned back towards the village. Cole watched him go, his body coiled tight, ready for any sign of a potential threat. As the warrior reached the village, Cole saw a brief exchange of words with one of the women. Seeing Cole, curiosity and worry showed on the woman's face. The warrior heard her words, answered, then disappeared into the teepees. Cole was alone again.

He shifted his stance, stirring dust at his feet as he waited. Minutes ticked by. The sound of approaching footsteps broke the quiet. Cole tensed, his hand hovering near his holster, as the warrior reappeared, accompanied by an older man. A weathered face and intelligent eyes marked the warrior. Cole's instinctive wariness softened as he sensed a similar air of authority and experience in the older man.

Observing the Lipan Apache Indians for days, he studied their customs, interactions, and daily routines. Watching them hunt, he saw their skills honed to perfection; He observed their respect for their elders, deference to their leaders, and fierce loyalty to one another. It contrasted the cattle trade's individualistic, often ruthless nature and the rough-and-tumble life he'd known. This profound, rooted kinship to the land, and each other offered him a fresh start; however, this new life caused him to shed his hardened exterior. He recognized the beauty in their communal existence and the profound, rooted kinship they shared with their heritage.

Cautious observation, a delicate dance of mutual suspicion and distrust, marked his initial days. The Lipan Indians were wary of him, their eyes never far from him, their movements suggesting they were ever ready to defend themselves should the need arise. But as they watched him and witnessed his respect for their customs, their apprehension eased. There were brief exchanges, gestures, and nods, the slow unfolding of mutual understanding. He learned some basic phrases in their language, a slow and laborious process that helped break down the language barrier and, more importantly, build trust.

The water he sought was more than survival; it was a step towards integration. By sharing a common need, he created a fragile bridge of rooted kinship. As the days blended into one another, his presence became familiar. His resilience, quiet strength, and clear commitment to his survival against the vastness of the Texas landscape earned him a cautious respect. He saw beyond the initial fear and suspicion to glimpse the kindness, warmth, and strength of their people. The land seemed to become his ally, shaping his perception of his identity and place within this unforgiving world. The dust, the sun, and the isolation became a shared experience, a shared reality. A tentative understanding, a subtle shift in the atmosphere, replaced the initial tense silence.

The landscape whispered secrets of the past, revealing the history embedded in the soil and the struggles of people striving to maintain their heritage. The endless expanse of the plains mirrored the vastness of their history and the resilience of their spirit. Their strength, he perceived, lay not only in arms but also in their way of life, their community, and their deep roots in the land. His strength and resilience were being tested and reinforced within this new context. His arrival was an unexpected turning point. The journey had just begun, and he found that his purpose, like the surrounding landscape, stretched out before him, boundless and unpredictable.

Chapter 2: Meeting Tala

The sun dipped below the horizon, casting long shadows across the Lipan Indian village. The scent of roasting meat and wood smoke lingered in the air, cooling as nightfall approached. Having secured permission to draw water for his thirsty herd, Cole found himself drawn to the creek's edge, the rhythmic pulse of the drum still echoing in the twilight. It was then that he saw her.

She emerged from behind a cluster of teepees, her silhouette stark against the fiery hues of the setting sun. Effortless grace marked her movement; her fluidity revealed a life harmonious with the land. Even from a distance, Cole could discern the details—the intricate braids that adorned her dark hair, the turquoise beads that glinted around her neck, the simple yet elegant lines of her buckskin dress. Her presence mirrored the rugged beauty of the land—striking, grounded, and self-assured. It defied the delicate, almost fragile femininity he had encountered in the saloons and dance halls of Fort Worth.

She carried a water jug on her shoulder, balanced with an ease that hinted at her strength. Her gaze was direct and unwavering, meeting his with an intensity that took him aback. Her demeanor was not one of shyness or timidity, but a quiet self-assurance that impressed him. She was unlike any woman he had ever met—fiercely independent, wonderful, and captivating. He felt something unfamiliar, akin to awe, washing over him.

They exchanged their first words in broken phrases, a mixture of gestures and rudimentary Lipan Indian learned through patient observation and tentative interactions. He asked permission to draw water, his words hesitant but laced with respect. She responded with a single nod, her expression unreadable, a subtle flicker of something he couldn't quite decipher crossing her features. It could have been suspicion, curiosity, or something else. The language barrier was like a frustrating game of deciphering unspoken signals.

The brief encounter left Cole breathless. As she walked back towards the village, he watched her. The image of her walking away, her silhouette graceful and proud, remained etched in his mind. The rhythmic beat of the drum seemed to intensify, a primal pulse that echoed the strange mixture of apprehension and desire stirring within him. He felt a surprising certainty: this woman, this influential, mysterious figure, had irrevocably changed his life. He did not know her name, yet he felt a profound pull toward a life he had never expected.

The days that followed were a delicate dance between cultures. Cole learned more of the Lipan Indian ways, his previous prejudices eroding as he witnessed the richness of their society, the strength of their community, and the profound, rooted kinship they shared with their land. He watched the women weave intricate designs into their baskets, their deft hands moving with a practiced grace that spoke of generations of tradition. He saw the men teach their sons the ways of the hunt, their skills honed to perfection through years of practice. The harmony between the people and their land impressed him; he marveled at their deep understanding and respect for the delicate balance of nature.

He learned her name from one of the younger children, Tala. The name, barely audible, resembled wind sighing through tall grass, a gentle ripple disturbing the creek's surface. It evoked images of the untamed landscape, the unyielding spirit of the Lipan Indian people, and the interesting force that had drawn him into their world. It was a name that resonated with a mystical power, as evocative as the sun-drenched plains of Texas and as mysterious as the swirling clouds overhead.

His interactions with Tala remained cautious and measured. The language barrier still hindered their communication, yet a subtle understanding developed between them — a silent acknowledgment of their mutual respect. He sought her out, his eyes scanning the village, his heart beating a little faster whenever he saw her.

He learned Tala was beautiful, intelligent, and fiercely independent. Her archery skills exceeded those of many male hunters. She was a gifted healer, and her knowledge of herbal remedies was extensive and impressive. Her eyes, the color of dark chocolate, held a depth of understanding and a strength that belied her youth. She was the antithesis of the women he'd known in Fort Worth—strong, self-sufficient, unconcerned with the social expectations that defined women's lives in his world.

Though limited by language, moments of shared understanding punctuated their conversations. He would gesture towards the herd, explaining his need for water and rest. She would point to the land, animals, and natural rhythms, conveying her profound, rooted kinship to the environment. Looking into her eyes, he would see a reflection of their shared isolation and the vast land that united them despite their cultural differences.

One evening, as the sun cast a golden glow over the creek, he found Tala alone, sketching intricate patterns in the sand with a stick. He sat beside her, and the silence between them was comfortable. He watched her work, mesmerized by the effortless grace of her movements and the concentration in her dark eyes. Sensing a vulnerability within her, he perceived something hidden beneath her strong exterior. There was a profound melancholy in her he understood—melancholy stemming from a dying culture on the edge of extinction, threatened by the unrelenting advance of a society that neither appreciated nor understood its value.

He reached for her hand, offering a tentative touch. She didn't pull away. Her fingers, cool and smooth, brushed against his. A current of electricity surged between them, a spark transcending language, culture, and the differences that had separated them. In that shared moment, beneath the vast Texas sky, the unspoken promise of something new, powerful, and forbidden blossomed between them. Initial mistrust, cultural differences, and risks proved insignificant compared to a growing attraction defying all logic. It was a moment of profound, rooted kinship, a tentative step toward an uncertain future, yet one that brimmed with the possibility of something extraordinary. The dance had only just begun. The music played, the journey unfinished.

Chapter 3: Life in the Lipan Indian Village

The days unfolded like a slow, deliberate dance, each movement measured, each step contemplated. The rhythmic pulse of life captivated Cole, a man accustomed to the frenetic energy of cattle drives and the boisterous revelry of Fort Worth saloons, within the Lipan Indian village. It was a life lived in harmony with the natural world, a stark contrast to the relentless expansion and exploitation he had witnessed elsewhere.

The women, their faces etched with the wisdom of generations, moved with a quiet grace as they prepared the evening meal. The air filled with the rich aroma of roasting venison, mingling with the earthy scents of herbs and wood smoke. He observed the intricate process of preparing the food, handpicking ingredients, and the precise techniques that had been handed down through countless generations. It was a communal effort, a shared experience that strengthened the thread of trusts between the village members. Each task, from gathering firewood to grinding corn, was imbued with a sense of purpose, a rooted kinship to the land and their ancestors.

The children, their laughter echoing through the village, played games, mimicking the rhythms of nature. He watched them mimic the birds' flight and the wolves' hunt, their imagination weaving tales of the land. Their play was a form of education, a way of learning the skills and knowledge necessary for survival. The elders, their faces lined with the wisdom of a lifetime, would often observe from a distance, offering guidance and encouragement.

The men, tanned and muscular, spent their days crafting tools, fashioning weapons, and honing their skills as hunters. He witnessed the meticulous care they took in creating their implements, each piece a testament to their craftsmanship and intimate knowledge of the materials used. The tools weren't just utilitarian objects but extensions of themselves, imbued with their spirit and understanding of the natural world. They taught their sons the ancient ways of the hunt, sharing techniques and instilling in them a deep respect for the animals they pursued. It was a tradition that instilled in them a profound understanding of the delicate balance between predator and prey — a balance essential to their survival.

The village itself was a testament to their ingenuity and resilience.

The teepees, constructed from tanned hides and sturdy wooden frames, were arranged in a circle, creating a sense of unity and protection. Each teepee represented a family's life, offering a private sanctuary for intimate family moments. However, the shared spaces revealed the village's communal nature—the central fire pit where people shared stories and decided, and the common areas where they gathered for meals, ceremonies, and celebrations.

Witnessing the Lipan Indian people's spiritual practices, he observed their profound, rooted kinship to the land, reflected in their rituals and ceremonies. He followed the reverence with which they approached the natural world, their understanding that they were a part of it. He witnessed ceremonies that celebrated the changing seasons, honoring the sun, the moon, and the stars. The ceremonies were not religious observances; they were opportunities for the community to come together, reaffirm their shared identity, and celebrate their collective history. Those songs and dances held deeper meaning than mere entertainment. He found himself drawn to these ceremonies, finding solace in their simplicity.

Cole discovered that the Lipan Indian society was far more complex than he had imagined. The social structure wasn't a simple hierarchy, but a sophisticated one with defined roles and responsibilities. Yet, a fluidity and adaptability allowed for flexibility and individual expression. There was a deep respect for elders, whose wisdom and experience guided the community.

The community decided by consensus, incorporating the views of all parties involved. Although slow and deliberate, this process ensured that the community's best interests were served. He appreciated the importance of community in Lipan Indian culture, a value system that contrasted with the rugged individualism prevalent in his world.

His interactions with Tala deepened, their initial hesitant communication growing into a more fluent, though still imperfect, exchange of ideas. He learned more about her family, her role within the community, and her dreams for the future. She shared stories of her ancestors, their struggles and triumphs, and their unwavering rooted kinship to the land. He listened, captivated by her narrative, and recognized the strength and resilience that were the hallmarks of her people.

She learned about his life, background, and motivations. Dark eyes reflecting a mix of curiosity and understanding, she listened. She listened as he recounted his childhood, his experiences on the trail, and his dreams of establishing his ranch, his ambitions tempered by a new sense of humility and introspection.

Settlers' actions caused Lipan displacement and dispossession, a revelation that filled Tala with fear. He witnessed her quiet determination to preserve her culture and heritage. He grasped the depth of their struggle, their fight for survival, and the unrelenting outside pressure.

Through Tala, Cole gained insight into the complexities of the Lipan Indian worldview, their intricate relationship with the land, and their spiritual beliefs. He witnessed the respect they showed for the natural world and their understanding of the interconnectedness of all living things. He understood their reverence for the land, their deep-seated spiritual rooted kinship, and their dependence on it for survival. Increased knowledge fueled his admiration for their lifestyle, fostering a deep and lasting rooted kinship.

People often spent the evenings around the central fire, listening to the elders tell stories of their ancestors, tales of courage, resilience, and the enduring spirit of their people. He listened spellbound, his imagination soaring as they recounted the events that had shaped their history. The stories were filled with triumph and tragedy, but they always affirmed the enduring spirit of the Lipan Indian people and their profound, rooted kinship to the land.

Cole's interest in the Lipan Indian lifestyle deepened over several weeks. He found a sense of belonging and acceptance he had never experienced before. He appreciated their deep-rooted sense of community, respect for tradition, and profound, rooted kinship to the land.

He continued to learn their language, his progress slow but steady. His words were still clumsy and imperfect, but his efforts were met with patience and encouragement. Each new word and phrase represented a step closer to understanding, bridging the cultural chasm that had separated them. He discovered that language encompassed more than just words.

The nuances of their customs, traditions, and social structures became clear to him. Unspoken signals, subtle gestures, and quiet exchanges of glances, he learned, were just as meaningful as any spoken word. He grasped the complexities of their social structure, including the respect for elders and their cooperative way of life. He saw how their roles contributed to the community's overall well-being, a delicate balance that ensured their collective survival.

His admiration stemmed from their resourcefulness, ability to adapt, and resilience. Their strength, determination, and ability to face adversity with dignity and grace inspired him to re-evaluate his values and beliefs. He observed how they used every aspect of their environment, from plants to animals, demonstrating a remarkable understanding of the natural world and their place within it.

His interactions with Tala continued to deepen, as their shared experiences forged a thread of trust that transcended the cultural differences between them. The initial hesitancy had vanished, replaced by a growing trust and mutual respect. He deeply connected with her; their kinship felt intensely personal and thrilling. It was a rooted kinship forged by physical attraction and a shared respect for their cultures, histories, and struggles.

Time spent in the Lipan village held profound meaning for him. He gained a fresh perspective on life, himself, and his role in it. The vast Texas plains, the rhythmic pulse of the drum, and the warmth of the Lipan Indian community all shaped his future in unimaginably irrevocable ways, changing his life. The dance continued, with the music becoming richer and more complex. Continuing the journey, He discovered a profound sense of belonging, hinting at something extraordinary in the heart of the Lipan village.

Chapter 4: Tensions with the Rangers

The late afternoon sun cast long shadows across the Lipan Indian village as a young boy, breathless and wide-eyed, burst into the central gathering area. His words, delivered in rapid-fire Lipan Indian, sent a ripple of concern through the assembled villagers. Like the rustle of dry leaves, whispers spread, the air thickening with apprehension. Tala, her expression a mask of controlled worry, exchanged a brief, urgent glance with one of the village elders. The news, relayed in hushed tones, spoke of a Texas Ranger patrol sighted just beyond the creek, their numbers uncertain, their intentions ambiguous.

Cole, sitting beside Tala, felt a knot tighten in his stomach. The carefree ease of the past weeks vanished, replaced by a prickling sense of unease. He'd known, of course, that this tranquility was a fragile thing, a fleeting moment in the ongoing conflict between the settlers and the indigenous peoples. But the suddenness of the news, the palpable fear radiating from the villagers, brought the reality crashing down with brutal force.

The Rangers. The very name evoked fear and resentment among the Lipan Indians. They symbolized the encroaching white world and served a government that often ignored the rights and very existence of the Lipan Apache. The Lipan Indians wove stories of brutality, injustice, and forced displacement into the fabric of their collective memory. The Lipan Apache experienced casual violence and disrespect for life. Cole had heard whispers of such acts during his travels; now, the threat was real.

He watched Tala; her face a canvas of conflicting emotions. Fear was clear, but so was a fierce determination, a quiet strength born from generations of struggle and survival. There was also a flicker of something else–a subtle plea, a silent question hanging between them. He understood her unspoken question: "What will you do?"

The question resonated deep within him. His initial inclination was to flee, to melt back into the anonymity of the vast Texas landscape. He was an outsider, a stranger in this land, and his presence was a potential liability. He could easily disappear, leaving the Lipan Indians to face the Rangers alone. His survival instincts urged him to put distance between himself and the impending danger.

But something held him back. It was more than just the growing affection he felt for Tala. It was a deeper rooted kinship, a sense of responsibility from his weeks among the Lipan Indian people. He had shared their meals, their stories, and their laughter. He had even begun to understand and appreciate the rhythms of their lives and their spiritually rooted kinship to the world around them.

Departing felt like betrayal; cowardly desertion during peril. He knew the risk; the Rangers held little regard for the rights of the Lipan Indian, and his presence, as a white man, would complicate matters. He could become a pawn in a much larger game, a dangerous entanglement he couldn't expect.

The elders convened, their voices low but firm. They needed a strategy, a plan to avoid or mitigate the potential conflict. Some suggested a discreet retreat, seeking refuge in the plains' deeper canyons or in the land's vastness. Others, emboldened by a fierce pride and a deep-seated defiance, advocated a more confrontational approach, a show of force to deter the Rangers. The debate was intense, each option fraught with potential perils.

Cole listened, his understanding of the Lipan Indian language growing with each passing day. Subtle shifts in tone and expression revealed the depth of their fears and hopes, and he absorbed these along with the nuances of their discussion. He felt a responsibility to contribute, to offer his perspective, to share his knowledge of the ways of the white man, the tactics and strategies of the U.S. Cavalry and the Texas Rangers.

His calm voice measured his words amidst the rising tension. He offered his skills as a scout and his knowledge of the terrain. He could help them expect the Ranger movements, guide them to safer ground, or assist them in evading confrontation. He proposed a plan that combined tactical retreat and strategic observation. The plan was risky, but it offered a glimmer of hope, a chance to avert a violent confrontation.

The elders listened, their expressions unreadable. They weighed his words against their deep-seated wisdom, their understanding of the delicate balance of power. His offer, though unprecedented, held a certain appeal. A white man willing to side with them, a stranger offering his skills and his life for their safety–it was a gamble, but a gamble worth taking.

As the sun dipped below the horizon, casting the village in a twilight cloak, someone decided. Cole would assist the Lipan Indians, blending his knowledge of the outside world with their profound understanding of the land. The alliance was precarious, built on mutual respect and a shared sense of survival. He knew that his decision could have dire consequences. The Rangers' threat remained, a dark cloud looming over the village, disrupting their fragile peace once more.

The night brought a flurry of activity. A nervous energy, instead of the usual gentle rhythm of everyday life, filled the village. Preparations were made, plans completed, whispers exchanged. Cole, working alongside the Lipan Indian warriors, observed their meticulous preparations, their efficiency born from experience and a profound understanding of their environment. He helped them conceal their belongings, prepare defensive positions, and establish observation points.

He spent the night with Tala. Their silence crackled with unspoken anxieties and a growing sense of shared destiny. They spoke little, their words dwarfed by the enormity of the situation. Their hands met, their fingers intertwining, offering a silent reassurance. He felt her fear and apprehension, but he also sensed her strength.

A pale light washed over the village as dawn arrived. The air was heavy with anticipation, the tension palpable. The Rangers were nearby; that much was certain. Cole, equipped with his rifle and his knowledge of the terrain, stood alongside the Lipan Indian warriors, ready to face whatever the day might bring. His fate, and that of the Lipan Indian village, hung in the balance. The frenetic, unpredictable rhythm of the survival dance continued, its music a symphony of fear and defiance. Fate's brushstrokes would define the future.

Chapter 5: A Shared Meal

The aroma of roasting meat and simmering herbs hung heavy in the air, a comforting counterpoint to the tension that still clung to the village like a morning mist. Tala led Cole to a secluded area near the creek, where a fire crackled, casting dancing shadows on the faces of her family gathered around it. Her grandmother, her face etched with the wisdom of many years, smiled at him, offering a place beside her.

The meal offered a welcome pause, rich in flavor and culture, but beneath the warmth, tension still simmered.

Throughout the meal, a murmur of conversation filled the air, accompanied by the soft click of utensils and the satisfied sighs of contented diners. It was a scene of peaceful domesticity, a stark contrast to the Rangers' looming threat.

Cole, hesitant, relaxed into the warmth of the gathering. He watched Tala's deft hands as she portioned the food, her movements graceful and precise. Tala offered him a generous portion of the deer meat. He complimented the meal, his words halting at first but growing more fluent as he felt the barrier between them crumbling.

He learned the herbs were gathered from specific locations, each possessing unique medicinal properties. He listened as Tala's grandmother spoke of the intricate balance of nature and the symbiotic relationship between people and the land. This was a testament to their deep understanding of the environment and their reverence for the rhythms of life and death.

The conversation flowed, switching between Lipan Indian and English, with each word bridging the cultural and linguistic chasm. Tala's strong and silent father spoke little, but his approving glances toward Cole spoke volumes. He learned about the challenges—emotional, political, and generational faced by the Lipan Indians, their struggle to maintain their traditions in the face of relentless pressure from the encroaching white settlers. He heard tales of past conflicts, of resilience and survival, of the unwavering rooted kinship to their ancestral lands. He shared his own stories, including his upbringing in a faraway land, as well as his travels and adventures, omitting the less palatable details of his past. His painting depicted a different world, yet one that shared the same desire for survival and a brighter tomorrow.

As night fell, the firelight created long shadows that appeared to dance with the unspoken emotions in the air. Tala's eyes held a depth of understanding that went beyond the simple exchange of words. There was a shared understanding, a silent acknowledgment of the precariousness of their situation and the budding affection that threatened to blossom despite the imminent danger. The subtle touches of her hand as she offered him another portion of food, the lingering glances that spoke volumes, the quiet laughter that punctuated their conversations—these slight gestures were a silent language of their own, a testament to the growing thread of trust between them.

Cole watched Tala's family interact, their thread of trust as strong as the ancient oak trees surrounding their village. He saw their love and respect for each other, as well as their deep-rooted sense of community and shared purpose. He noticed how they helped each other, anticipating needs with no need for words. A deep longing for membership and acceptance consumed him, a yearning to be trusted by that community.

He discovered that sharing meals was a sacred ritual that strengthened their bonds and reaffirmed their deep connection to the land. Each ingredient and step in the preparation held deep meaning, reflecting their history, beliefs, and understanding of the natural world. He realized that the food itself was a metaphor for their lives—a blend of diverse ingredients that, when combined, created something extraordinary.

The conversation turned to the future; the uncertainties looming large. Tala spoke of her hopes and dreams, her quiet ambitions overshadowed by the ever-present threat of displacement and cultural erasure. She voiced her fears and anxieties, yet her voice held a quiet strength, an unwavering belief in the resilience of her people. Cole, moved by her vulnerability and steadfast spirit, was drawn deeper into her world. He wanted to shield her from the harsh realities of the encroaching frontier, to fight for her, her people, and their right to exist in the land that was their ancestral home.

Speaking of his dreams, he described a life defined by the harsh realities of survival, where love and happiness were rights, not luxuries. He sought escape from unending violence, aiming for peace to build his life, a future removed from Western turmoil. He understood that his desire went beyond his happiness.

As the moon ascended, casting its silvery glow, the meal came to a close. The fire embers died down, leaving a lingering warmth that mirrored the emotions stirred during their shared repast. They did not feel awkward in the silence. They were two souls drawn together by a shared experience, a shared sense of danger, a growing affection that felt as strong as the land they both called home. The night air carried unspoken promises, hinting at a hopeful love that surpassed the chaotic era they were in. The shared meal had served its purpose. It broke barriers, formed a thread of trust, and laid the groundwork for a romance that was ready to blossom in the rugged West.

Chapter 6: Journey to Fort Worth

The dawn broke, painting the eastern sky in hues of rose and gold as Cole and Tala prepared to leave the Lipan Indian village. A sense of bittersweet anticipation hung in the air. The previous evening's peace contrasted with the pre-journey anxiety. Tala's father, his weathered face etched with concern, presented Cole with a worn leather pouch containing dried meat, cornmeal, and a small flask of water—provisions for the journey ahead. Her mother, her eyes brimming with a mixture of pride and apprehension, embraced Tala, whispering words of encouragement and blessing. Though calm, Tala herself couldn't mask the tremor in her hand as she adjusted the saddlebags on her horse.

Their departure was quiet, a stark contrast to the vibrant life they were leaving behind in the village. As they rode out, the sun rose higher, casting long shadows that stretched behind them, like ghostly reminders of the life they were leaving behind. The path they followed wound through a landscape of breathtaking beauty. Towering mesas, their sides sculpted by the relentless wind and rain, loomed over them, their silhouettes sharp against the clear morning sky. Pine and damp earth perfumed the crisp, clean air, creating an invigorating yet calming fragrance.

Both horse and rider showed resilience throughout the journey. The terrain was unforgiving, a relentless succession of rocky trails, deep ravines, and seemingly endless stretches of prairie. The sun beat down, transforming the land into a shimmering expanse of heat haze. They encountered wildlife—a majestic pronghorn antelope that outpaced their horses, a family of wild turkeys foraging for food, their plumage a kaleidoscope of colors, and a lone coyote that watched them from a distant ridge, its eyes gleaming with cunning intelligence. Experienced as he was, Cole marveled at the beauty and ferocity of the untamed landscape.

One evening, a sudden storm erupted as they camped under a canopy of stars. The wind howled like a banshee, whipping up a furious sandstorm that threatened to engulf them. They huddled together for warmth and protection, their horses pawing the ground in response. The rain lashed down, turning the ground into a muddy quagmire. Sheltered alongside Tala, Cole felt a surge of protective instincts as he watched her face, her eyes wide with a mixture of fear and exhilaration. The storm raged for hours, testing their limits. They emerged from the storm battered but unbroken, their spirits strengthened by the shared ordeal. The shared fear and vulnerability had drawn them closer, strengthening the unspoken thread of trust that had bloomed between them.

Their journey wasn't without its close calls. On one occasion, they escaped a stampeding herd of wild mustangs, their horses rearing and snorting in fear. Cole's quick thinking and horsemanship prevented a disastrous collision. On another occasion, they encountered a group of unfriendly cowboys who suspected Tala's presence. Cole's smooth talking and the display of his Colt revolver convinced them that their intentions were honorable, dissuading them from further conflict. Each encounter underscored the inherent dangers of their journey, highlighting the wildness of the Texas frontier and the unpredictable nature of the people who inhabited it. These near misses were not mere incidents; they served as a constant reminder of the risks they were taking, fueling their determination to reach Fort Worth.

As they approached Fort Worth, the landscape underwent a change. The vast expanse of prairie gave way to a landscape dotted with scrub oak and mesquite trees. In the distance, they could make out the hazy silhouette of the town, a sign that their arduous journey was nearing its end. The change in the atmosphere mirrored the shift in the landscape. The sense of isolation and vulnerability that had accompanied them for so long dissipated, replaced by a growing sense of anticipation.

When they finally reached Fort Worth, it was a cacophony of sights, sounds, and smells. The air vibrated with a palpable energy, a mixture of excitement and tension. The town pulsed with life—a vibrant tapestry of cowboys, cattle breeders, merchants, and gamblers. Activity filled the bustling streets;

Having spent much time on the trails, Cole knew the bustling cattle town well. However, the scene overwhelmed Tala; her eyes widened with a mix of wonder and apprehension. The sheer scale of the operation was astounding. Herds of cattle, thousands strong, were driven through the streets, their low moans and bellows adding to the general din. The energy of commerce filled the air.

Sensing her unease, Cole took her hand, offering a reassuring smile. He guided her through the chaotic streets, pointing out the different establishments and explaining the dynamics of the cattle trade. Cole showed her the stockyards, where they sorted and sold cattle. Her quiet grace and presence impressed some of his cowboy and rancher acquaintances after he introduced her to them. He explained the harsh realities of their lives, including long hours, dangerous work, and the constant threat of injury or death.

He did not shy away from the darker aspects of Fort Worth. Showing her the less savory parts of town, he walked with her. Highlighting inequality, he showed her the stark contrast between the cattle barons' opulent wealth and the pervasive poverty of many working men. He also showed her the underbelly of the business, the shady deals, the corruption, and the exploitation of those less fortunate. He wanted her to understand the world she was entering.

As days turned into nights, Cole and Tala navigated the complexities of the cattle trade. They witnessed the thrilling spectacle of a cattle drive, the skillful work of the cowboys as they herded the massive herds. They witnessed cutthroat negotiations between buyers and sellers. The strong thread of thrusts of loyalty and friendship among cowboys developed from their observed camaraderie and shared experiences. However, they also witnessed the darker side of the trade—the brutality, exploitation, and relentless drive for profit at any cost.

Days held work; nights, a blend of festivity and stress. They attended a lively dance at a saloon, the music and laughter a welcome respite from the relentless energy of the daytime. Cole, reserved and surprised, Tala with his unexpected moves, showcasing the charm and grace that lay beneath his rugged exterior. The dance served as another opportunity for them to grow closer and solidify their unspoken thread of trust amid the chaotic backdrop of Fort Worth. Yet, even amid the revelry, the shadow of danger and uncertainty always seemed to lurk nearby. For all its vibrant energy, the town was a dangerous place, where survival depended on strength, cunning, and a healthy dose of luck. Their journey to Fort Worth had been more than just a trip; it had been a baptism of fire, a stark education in the realities of the Wild West, and a test of their love that was flourishing. The cattle deal itself, a complex and tense affair, was only one aspect of their growing journey.

Chapter 7: The Fort Worth Cattle Market

The air hung thick with the scent of dust, sweat, and cattle dung, a pungent perfume unique to Fort Worth. It clung to everything—the rough-hewn wooden buildings, the dusty streets, and even the cattle barons' fine clothes. The noise was overwhelming: the lowing of thousands of cattle, the shouts of cowboys, the clanging of metal as hooves struck the cobblestones, the raucous laughter spilling from saloons, and the rhythmic thud of hammers from the nearby blacksmith's shop. It was a sensory overload that left Tala breathless.

Cole, however, navigated the maelstrom with the practiced ease of a seasoned hand. Moving through throngs of people and cattle, his confidence bordered on arrogance, commanding respect from all. He knew this place, every back alley, every crooked deal, every whisper of rumor. He knew the players, their strengths, weaknesses, and hidden agendas. Fort Worth was his domain with its sprawling stockyards and chaotic market.

Clinging to his arm, Tala observed the scene with wide, assessing eyes. The sheer scale of the operation was astounding. Herds of cattle, thousands strong, were driven through the streets, their massive forms dwarfing the surrounding people. Cowboys, weathered and grizzled, guided the animals, their movements fluid and precise, a testament to the two years of experience and expertise they had gained. The air throbbed with the energy of commerce, a palpable sense of ambition and greed. Deals were struck with a casual swiftness that belied the significant sums of money. Fortunes appeared and disappeared rapidly, observed keenly by the town's most astute. The ruthlessness of it all, the cold efficiency of the capitalist machine, was a stark contrast to the communal spirit of her Lipan Indian people.

Cole led her through the stockyards—a vast expanse of pens and corrals—where they sorted and inspected the cattle. He explained the intricate process of animal grading and the negotiation between buyers and sellers. He pointed out the subtle cues — the perceptible shifts in posture and expression — that revealed a man's willingness to haggle, his determination to win. He spoke of the shrewd businessmen, the cattle barons who controlled vast tracts of land and immense fortunes, men who wielded power with a casual ruthlessness.

Tala listened, her face showing both fascination and apprehension. A stark contrast was apparent to her: her people's openness versus the settlers' calculated actions. She was unfamiliar with private ownership, profit and loss, and intense competition. She recognized the basic human instincts: the need for security, wealth, and survival. Although these drives surpassed cultural boundaries, their execution varied.

One afternoon, Cole took Tala to witness a cattle auction. The scene was pandemonium. Cowboys yelled out bids, their voices hoarse from shouting over the din. Men jostled and shoved, their determination palpable. The auctioneer, a whirlwind of energy, rattled off numbers and descriptions with lightning speed, his words audible above the cacophony. The price of cattle fluctuated, reflecting the market's unpredictable nature and the buyers' volatile personalities. With his keen eye and intimate knowledge of the cattle business, Cole navigated the chaos, securing a lucrative deal for a large herd. He conducted his negotiations with charm, firmness, and quiet authority, leaving his opponents impressed and bewildered. Tala watched, fascinated by his skill and the way he commanded respect.

Later, in the quiet of a less crowded street, Cole explained the finer points of the business to Tala. The cattle trail presented many difficulties. He discussed the politics, the rivalries between ranchers, and the power of influential individuals. He painted a picture of a system where the strong preyed on the weak, and where a slip could mean ruin.

Tala's understanding deepened. She witnessed the brutal efficiency of the system, as well as its manipulation and exploitation of individuals for profit. She saw the ruthless pursuit of wealth and the disregard for human dignity. It was a stark contrast to the values of her people. Yet, she also recognized the inherent human elements. She saw the pride in the cowboys' work, their loyalty to one another, and the camaraderie forged in the face of adversity.

She saw the determination of these men to carve a life out for themselves in a harsh, unforgiving land.

As the days turned into weeks, Tala's perspective shifted. The Fort Worth cattle market presented itself to her not only as a brutal business but also as a miniature depiction of wider American expansion, showcasing the clash of cultures and the intertwined nature of progress and exploitation. The city was a stark reflection of the broader societal issues of the era—wealth disparity, unchecked capitalism, and the clash between different cultural values.

She understood Cole's place within this system—a skilled negotiator, a shrewd businessman, yet a man with a strong moral compass. His past's untamed wilderness and his present's burgeoning city caught him between them, and he navigated their complexities with a resilience and adaptability that Tala found both admirable and intriguing. The contrasts of their worlds tested their already burgeoning relationship. She understood his ways, and he, hers. But there was a growing realization that their future together would require a delicate balance, a careful navigation between two different cultures and philosophies. More than commerce, the cattle market shaped their lives and love. The vibrant and chaotic life of Fort Worth served not only as a backdrop to their romance but also as a mirror, reflecting their unique challenges—emotional, political, and generational and the complex times in which they lived.

Chapter 8: Dangerous Liaisons

A cloying miasma of stale beer and inexpensive whiskey permeated the air, clinging stubbornly to the roughly hewn wooden beams that supported the ramshackle saloon. With his hand casually resting on the butt of his Colt Peacemaker, Cole surveyed the room, his eyes scanning the faces of those present. A palpable sense of impending violence hung heavy in the air. This event differed vastly from the refined and courteous atmosphere typically associated with cattle auctions, lacking the civility and decorum one would expect in such a setting.

On the opposite side of the room, Cole's eyes instantly fell upon Jebediah Stone, a familiar face from their shared history of competition and conflict on the Chisholm Trail. With eyes like cold, hard flint, Jebediah silently spoke with three disreputable individuals, his words measured. The shadows were deep enough to obscure their features, yet Cole's sharp gaze caught the glint of malice in their eyes. A dangerous and ominous situation was developing, with a potential for serious and harmful consequences.

Standing beside him, Tala couldn't shake the feeling of a growing, unsettling apprehension that sent shivers down her spine. From where he stood, the previously vibrant sounds of boisterous singing and raucous laughter from the saloon were now distant and muted, a stark contrast to the rising tension. Having observed Cole's impressive skill in navigating the often chaotic world of cattle auctions, and his remarkable ability to maintain composure even amidst the frenzy, she recognized this situation was profoundly different. This matter was of a deeply personal and sensitive nature.

With a reassuring squeeze of Tala's hand, Cole excused himself, offering a silent promise of his support and care. With a slow and steady gait, he moved through the room. Approaching Stone's table, he carried with him an air of such quiet dignity and authority that those present fell silent out of respect.

Cole's voice, sharp and clear, sliced through the low hum of conversation as he spoke the single word, "Stone," his quiet authority instantly silencing the room. "Your presence here, in this unusual and delightful place, surprised and pleased me." Stone's smile, a predatory expression lacking any warmth or trace of humor, sent a chill down the spines of those who witnessed it. "Cole," he said, the name stretched out in a slow, affected drawl, his voice coated in a layer of feigned cordiality that felt anything but genuine. It has been far too long since our last encounter, hasn't it? The message was clearly implied. Stone subtly suggested that Cole was profiting from transactions of questionable legality, hinting at unethical business practices that benefited Cole. In a calm and resolute tone, Cole responded he favored earning his own way in life.

A palpable tension filled the air, crackling with anticipation as Stone's companions subtly shifted their weight, their hands hovering nervously just above their weapons, poised for action. Given the circumstances and the escalating animosity, a fight was about to break out. What began as a seemingly innocuous conversation rapidly deteriorated into an exchange of veiled threats and insinuations, ultimately escalating into a far more serious situation. As accusations flew back and forth, old grudges resurfaced, and every carefully chosen word felt like a poisoned dart thrown into the heart of the conflict. A palpable tension filled the saloon; every person held their breath, the silence heavy with the unspoken anticipation of a violent eruption that felt unavoidable. With quiet confidence, Cole calmly and effectively met the challenge that Stone had presented. His mastery of intimidation was legendary; he used his imposing presence, his established reputation, and his incredibly sharp wit as weapons, each as effective as any firearm.

Concealed beneath Stone's smug grin was a deep-seated and long-simmering sense of entitlement that had festered for quite some time. In Stone's opinion, Fort Worth was obligated to him for reasons he felt were significant and undeniable. For him, possessing power wasn't a sufficient goal; he craved something greater, a more significant and far-reaching dominance. Cole, a man of significant alliances, considerable influence, and quiet defiance, stood as the singular opponent Stone had never overcome in any of their past encounters.

Amid this confrontation, a brawl erupted elsewhere in the saloon. Two drunken cowboys, spurred by a misplaced glance or a spilled drink, engaged in a furious exchange of fists and insults. The chaos created a diversion, a smokescreen for Cole and Stone's escalating standoff. However, Cole seized the opportunity.

Using the distraction of the bar fight, Cole subtly shifted his position, creating a space between himself and Stone. He spoke low, his words cutting through the brawl's noise, a subtle shift that gave the illusion of backing down. Stone, momentarily thrown off by Cole's retreat, missed the change in tactics.

With incredible speed and precision, Cole flawlessly performed an amazing maneuver that completely shocked Stone's companions, leaving them speechless with astonishment. Before Stone could react, Cole swiftly disarmed a man, then using this man as a shield against the attack of a second man, and finally repositioned himself to use the wall as cover. Taking advantage of the chaotic circumstances, he carefully and strategically positioned himself for success. The unexpected change in circumstances dramatically altered the power dynamic, leaving Stone and his team exposed to an imminent attack.

With a grace that flowed like water, Cole moved, his strength hidden beneath an almost deceptive fluidity. He acted to neutralize the threat, carefully avoiding any action that might unnecessarily escalate the situation. His dance, a carefully choreographed display of controlled violence, showcased his years of experience on the trail and deep understanding of human nature. He went to great lengths to circumvent any potential disagreements or confrontations, always seeking peaceful resolutions.

In a flash, a cacophony of crashing chairs, shattering bottles, and flying fists filled the room. As the fight escalated, it spilled out into the street, rapidly devolving into a chaotic melee characterized by flailing limbs, desperate shouts, and a general air of uncontrolled violence. Having finally found a safe way out of the dangerous situation he was in, Cole skillfully used the surrounding chaos and confusion to his advantage, making a clean escape without being seen, leaving Stone and his men enraged and frustrated by their failure to capture him.

Outside, Tala waited anxiously, her heart pounding with anticipation for his arrival. Forgoing a detailed explanation, he embraced her, finding solace in her comforting presence. Aware of the very real and present danger that they were both in, he leaned in close and whispered reassurances to comfort her. With cunning and precision, Cole navigated the complex and treacherous world of shady deals and clandestine meetings, skillfully evading his pursuers and maintaining a precarious lead over those who sought to undermine him. In order to outsmart his pursuers, he skillfully used his sharp intellect, deep understanding of human nature, and intimate knowledge of the town's complex network of streets and alleyways to elude Stone's relentless men.

He moved like a ghost through the city's underbelly, his actions a tapestry of calculated moves and weighed risks. He used his knowledge of the city's undercurrents, its secret passages, and hidden alleys to evade Stone's pursuit. Each encounter sharpened his awareness and honed his instincts. Reading the subtle cues, the unspoken street language, and the subtle shifts in body language that betrayed a man's intentions, he learned. He wasn't simply surviving, but he was flourishing and exceeding expectations in all that he did.

Lost in her own world, Tala simultaneously immersed herself in the social whirl of Fort Worth's elite, deftly maneuvering the complexities of their interconnected networks and relationships. Among the women she met were those from all walks of life, ranging from the wives of wealthy cattle barons to working-class barmaids and prostitutes, offering a comprehensive cross-section of the city's female population. While Tala examined the lives of the city's inhabitants, her understanding of the intricate social dynamics and complexities of urban life steadily deepened, shaping her perspective. Because of her sharp and perceptive nature, she could swiftly understand the implicit regulations and subtle details that governed social interactions.

Through her keen observations in Fort Worth, she developed a heightened awareness of the social inequalities and the myriad struggles that women endured within the rigid system of social stratification. As she observed the opulent lifestyles enjoyed by the wives of wealthy cattle barons juxtaposed against the stark hardships endured by women in the less fortunate segments of society, a stark contrast became strikingly clear. In the unforgiving environment of Fort Worth, she learned of the remarkable hidden strength and resilience showed by the women who survived there. In observing these women, she recognized and appreciated the profound strength of their friendships, how shared experiences enriched their lives, and the remarkable support system they provided for each other.

The remarkable strength and impressive resourcefulness displayed by these women as they navigated the perilous and challenging environment of a frontier town garnered them a significant amount of well-deserved appreciation. Because she understood this, she gained a new perspective that allowed her to appreciate the strength and resilience of the women who lived in Fort Worth. In a surprising turn of events, the alliances she painstakingly forged turned out to be unexpectedly beneficial.

With evening, Cole and Tala, using their cleverness and wit, evaded the persistent pursuit of Stone, ultimately finding refuge in a hidden spot nestled unexpectedly within the vibrant and bustling city. In hushed, fearful tones, their voices barely above a whisper, they recounted their experiences, each word laden with the unspoken anxieties and precariousness of their circumstances. Through an in-depth and engaging conversation, they meticulously examined their observations of the city and its people, including a detailed exploration of the intricate dynamics of power structures and subtle shifts in political alliances, leading to a deeper understanding of the urban landscape.

As their love blossomed, their romance unfolded against the unforgiving backdrop of the Texas frontier, a landscape as harsh and unforgiving as it was beautiful.

Chapter 9: A Night on the Town

The air hung thick with the scent of sweat, whiskey, and anticipation. Fort Worth at night was a kaleidoscope of sights and sounds, a vibrant tapestry woven from the threads of ambition, desperation, and fleeting pleasure. Cole led Tala down Exchange Avenue, the cobblestones slick beneath their boots. The street throbbed with a raw energy, a symphony of clinking glasses, raucous laughter, and the mournful wail of a lone fiddle from a nearby saloon.

Her dark eyes were wide, and she had a mixture of wonder and apprehension. Tala took in the scene. She'd seen the bustling marketplace during the day and the cattle auctions' organized chaos, but this nocturnal transformation was something else. Lanterns cast a flickering light on the faces of the crowd, revealing a spectrum of emotions–excitement, greed, weariness, and the ever-present shadow of danger.

They passed a string of establishments, each with its distinct character. In contrast to the Cattleman's Rest, a boisterous establishment where cowboys celebrated or commiserated with cheap whiskey, the Golden Spur saloon offered refined elegance with its polished mahogany and crystal chandeliers. Music filled the air: the rhythmic thud of boots on the wooden floors, the clinking of spurs, the boisterous singing of drunken patrons, and the lilting melodies of saloon pianists all melded together to form the unforgettable soundtrack of Fort Worth's nightlife.

Cole, ever watchful, kept a hand near the butt of his Colt Peacemaker. Even amidst the revelry, the undercurrent of tension remained, a constant reminder of the town's volatile nature and the ever-present threat of violence. He moved through the crowd with a calm confidence. He knew this city, its hidden alleys and secret corners, shadowy figures, and agendas as if they were his extensions. This was his domain, and he navigated it with the skill of a seasoned hunter tracking prey.

They entered the Blue Bonnet Saloon, known for its lively music and even livelier clientele. The air inside was thick with cigar smoke and the scent of perfume, a heady mix that stung Tala's nostrils. An energetic band played a rollicking tune, driving the crowd to a frenzy of dancing and shouting. Cole selected a peaceful table.

Tala, hesitant, found herself drawn into the rhythm of the music, her usual reticence dissolving into the intoxicating atmosphere. The music resonated within her, connecting her to the town's energy and spirit. She allowed herself a slow, deliberate sway to the music, her movements graceful and fluid, starkly contrasting the rough energy around her.

As the night wore on, Cole and Tala's conversation deepened, moving beyond the polite pleasantries of their previous encounters. They shared stories of their lives, their voices low against the backdrop of the boisterous music. Cole spoke of his life on the trail, the hardships, the camaraderie, and the constant threat of danger. His family, his hoped-for ranch, and future ambitions were all subjects he spoke of. He spoke of his past, the mistakes and the regrets, the paths not taken, and the lessons learned. He discussed a vulnerability that surprised Tala, revealing a deep emotion she hadn't expected.

Tala shared her experiences growing up within the Lipan Indian Apache community, speaking of her traditions, beliefs, and the challenges—emotional, political, and generational of adapting to a changing world. She spoke of her family, her concerns about their future, and her dreams for her people. She said it with quiet strength, which filled Cole with admiration.

Tala observed the other patrons between sips of her drink: the cowboys with their broad shoulders and weathered faces, the gamblers with their nervous eyes and restless hands, and the women, whose laughter often masked a more profound vulnerability. She noted the unspoken hierarchy, the subtle power dynamics, and the constant undercurrent of danger threaded through every interaction.

Cole, noticing her keen observations, admired her astute awareness. He saw the way she absorbed her surroundings, the way she interpreted the city's unspoken language, and the insights she gleaned from observing human interactions. He knew the dangers lurking in Fort Worth extended beyond the streets and saloons.

The music swelled, the laughter intensified, and the city's energy enveloped them. Cole reached for Tala's hand, their fingers intertwining as they acknowledged their burgeoning love.

But amidst the joy and intimacy, the threat lingered. A fleeting glimpse of Jebediah Stone across the room sent a shiver down Cole's spine. Stone, his face grim and unforgiving, was watching them. The subtle shift in his gaze and the imperceptible tightening of his jaw spoke volumes. The tension, though momentarily subdued, was far from gone. It was a silent threat, a reminder of the precarious balance they were attempting to maintain, the dangerous game they were playing.

Cole subtly adjusted his position, shielding Tala with his body, his hand always close to his weapon. The night's revelry provided a convenient cover, but the danger remained palpable, a specter lurking in the shadows of their burgeoning romance.

With daybreak, Cole and Tala exited the saloon together. The streets were quieter now, the raucous energy of the night replaced by a calm stillness that held its own brand of tension. They walked, their unspoken thoughts and anxieties hanging heavily in the air. The night's exhilarating and terrifying adventures deepened their thread of trust, but the dangers that threatened them remained. Their love, however, was growing stronger, a resilient flower blooming amidst a storm. Fort Worth offered a journey showcasing their burgeoning love, yet highlighted a challenging future. Their love story unfolded against the vibrant and dangerous backdrop of the city, a stage where their romance was both celebrated and challenged.

Chapter 10: Whispers of Conspiracy

The next morning, the sun beat down on Fort Worth with a ferocity that mirrored the simmering tension Cole felt. He'd slept; the image of Jebediah Stone's malevolent gaze burned into his mind. The jovial atmosphere of the Blue Bonnet Saloon felt like a distant memory, replaced by a chilling awareness of the lurking danger. He found Tala already awake, her expression thoughtful, her gaze distant. She'd sensed the shift in the atmosphere, the unspoken weight of the previous night's events.

"Stone... I saw him," Cole began, breaking the silence. "He's watching us."

Tala nodded slowly, her dark eyes betraying a quiet understanding. "I sensed it too," she replied, her voice low. Cole, something besides cattle rustling, is happening. Something... bigger."

Her words struck a chord with Cole. He'd noticed inconsistencies in the cattle trade for months–shipments going missing, brands altered, and rumors of bribery amongst local officials. He'd dismissed them as isolated incidents, the usual underbelly of a booming frontier town, but Tala's intuition suggested something far more sinister. The whispers he'd overheard in saloons and along the trails, dismissed as drunken ramblings, now seemed to coalesce into a disturbing pattern.

That day, they began their investigation. Cole, using his rooted kinships in the cattle trade, gathered information. He spoke to ranchers, cowboys, and even some less reputable characters who frequented the saloons and gambling dens. He learned about missing herds, falsified paperwork, and shipments disappearing from the rail yards. The trail led him to several corrupt officials, men who held positions of power and influence, their pockets lined with ill-gotten gains.

Meanwhile, Tala used her network, her rooted kinships within the Lipan Indian Apache community, and her uncanny ability to read people to gather intelligence. She spoke to the Native American traders and other individuals who frequented the fringes of Fort Worth, those who operated outside the law and possessed knowledge otherwise unavailable. Her insights often proved more accurate and insightful than any Cole could gain through conventional means. She was aware of unspoken tensions and hidden agendas, a skill honed by years of survival in a harsh and unforgiving world.

Their investigations revealed a complex web of conspiracy. It wasn't just cattle theft; it was a sophisticated operation involving forged documents, manipulated land titles, and the systematic exploitation of both ranchers and Native American tribes. The stolen cattle were being funneled through a network of clandestine buyers, their trail leading far beyond the borders of Texas, disappearing into the vast expanse of the American West.

While Cole met with a reluctant rancher who possessed crucial evidence one evening, Tala uncovered a hidden message concealed within a seemingly innocuous piece of trade goods. It was a coded message, detailing the location of a secret rendezvous where the conspirators planned to transfer a large shipment of stolen cattle. This discovery sped up their investigation, providing them with concrete evidence and crucial information.

The rendezvous took place outside Fort Worth, in a secluded area known as Kickapoo Creek. They chose the location because its name commemorates its historical significance as a Lipan Indian refuge, offering seclusion and a rapid escape route.

They confronted the criminals, but Cole knew they were against a formidable foe. Jebediah Stone wasn't just a ruthless cattle thief but a shrewd operator with powerful rooted kinships within the city. He had the means and the willingness to use violence to protect his operation.

Tension filled the rendezvous night. Under the cover of darkness, Cole and Tala approached the designated location, their hearts pounding in their chests. They found a group of men, their faces obscured by shadows, surrounding a large herd of cattle. Jebediah Stone stood at their center, a grim smile on his lips.

Before they could make their move, a gunshot shattered the silence.

Chaos erupted. Cole and Tala fought their way through a hail of bullets, using their combined skills and knowledge to survive. Cole's marksmanship and Tala's agility, coupled with her deep understanding of the terrain, proved deadly.

The ensuing battle was fierce. Cole's quick draw and precision shots, combined with Tala's deft use of her knife and exceptional understanding of the area, proved critical in outmaneuvering the criminals. The clash of steel and the roar of gunfire echoed through the night, illuminating the dark underbelly of Fort Worth's prosperity.

Amid the mayhem, Cole captured Stone, but the victory was short-lived. As they attempted to secure their prisoner, the sound of approaching cavalry shattered the night. The U.S. Cavalry was a shocking twist, leaving them wondering if they were facing a conspiracy far greater than they'd imagined. The cavalrymen surrounded them, their rifles pointed, under the command of a figure they hadn't expected–a man who had been friendly but involved in the scheme.

Tala's sharp eyes caught a detail Cole missed: someone subtly altered the insignia on the cavalryman's uniform. It wasn't the official symbol of the U.S. Army; it was a counterfeit. This discovery revealed sophistication and organization far beyond the reach of simple cattle thieves. It showed a deep-seated conspiracy that extended far beyond Fort Worth, implicating high-ranking officials in a web of corruption and deceit.

Tala's desperate gamble created a diversion as they were about to be taken prisoner. Exploiting a gap in the cavalry's formation, she freed Cole, creating a path for escape. Their escape into darkness, pursued relentlessly, offered no respite; the struggle persisted. They had uncovered a conspiracy of immense proportions — a web of deceit involving corrupt officials, cattle thieves, and even elements within the U.S. military. Their love story had become entangled in a far greater struggle that threatened their lives and the very fabric of the burgeoning West.

A chilling certainty of facing a more formidable and well-connected enemy than one could have imagined marked an uncertain and dangerous future. The fate of Fort Worth, and perhaps more, rested on their shoulders as they disappeared into the vast, starlit expanse beyond Kickapoo Creek, the sounds of the pursuing cavalry a relentless reminder that their fight had just begun. The cliffhanger left them breathless, unsure what awaited them in the Texan wilderness's shadowy depths.

Chapter 11: The Cavalry Arrives

What initially appeared to be a mirage in the shimmering Texas heat, a dust cloud on the horizon, soon resolved into a squadron of U.S. Cavalry; their blue uniforms were a stark contrast to the ochre landscape, presenting a grim reality. With a determined purpose, they rode on, the rhythmic drumming of their hooves against the dry, cracked earth creating a relentless beat that mirrored the frantic pounding of Cole's heart. He felt a cold dread wash over him; it was a feeling far sharper and more intense than the biting dry wind that cut through the air.

Tala, with her posture as stiff as a board, rode the horse beside him. As if drawn by an unseen force, her hand sought his, the touch unexpectedly cool and steady. No words came from her lips; she did not speak. It wasn't necessary for her to do that. In a single, fleeting glance of their eyes, a silent yet profound understanding passed between them, conveying every unspoken warning and shared concern without a single word being exchanged.

In a tightly controlled and compact formation, the cavalry presented a formidable, unified front. This garment fits poorly; it's too small. It wasn't a routine patrol; rather, it was a carefully planned operation with a specific aim in mind. It was a message that was sent.

With the practiced ease of a seasoned performer, the officer in charge carefully and gracefully dismounted, devoting a meticulous amount of time to brushing the dust from his gloves, as if time itself were completely at his command and disposal. The polished saber that hung at his side stressed his height and broad shoulders. However, despite his words, the cold, deliberate glint in his eyes hinted at a hidden agenda, a deeper, more sinister intention that belied the surface meaning of his carefully chosen words. At this moment, I'm engaged in carrying out many calculations. We call a statement a performative utterance when its very speaking causes the action it describes.

A subtle, barely perceptible smile touched the man's lips as he uttered the name, "Cole Travis," a name that seemed to hang suspended in the air. "Do you have any recollection of ever having encountered me before, possibly at a location we both used to visit regularly?" A dryness in his mouth, a complete lack of moisture that left Cole feeling parched and uncomfortable, made him acutely aware of his dehydration.

"Prior to our meeting, I had received various accounts detailing both your remarkable achievements and the significant reputation you have diligently cultivated throughout your time here." With painstaking slowness and meticulous care, Harrison removed his gloves, each movement deliberate and hinting at a deeply considered process. It's quite fascinating to consider the unique blend of responsibilities held by this individual, encompassing the diverse roles of broker, rider, and peacekeeper.

Although the speaker's words were not explicitly critical, their lack of finesse in conveying the intended message resulted in misinterpretations by the audience. This action felt like a thinly veiled, deliberate provocation disguised with false politeness, rather than a kind, appreciated gesture. Directing everyone's attention to their considerable distance from San Saba, Cole emphasized the remarkable length of the journey that lay ahead. "We inquisitive people strongly desire to understand why the cavalry surprisingly and unsettlingly invaded the cattle territory."

For those who had the pleasure of witnessing it, Harrison's smile conveyed a sense of geniality and approachability, leaving a lasting impression of warmth and friendliness. "Because of unexpected problems, we temporarily reassigned the task to another colleague for management." When Harrison extended his hand in a gesture of greeting, Cole hesitated for a moment, appearing unsure whether to accept this friendly overture, a moment of uncertainty hanging in the air between the two. The moment of hesitation wasn't too short or too long. The handshake, while firm, had a strange quality to it, as if the man were attempting to determine the precise skeletal structure of his hand through the intensity of his grip, a disconcerting display of strength and perhaps something more. With precise and measured movements, the cavalry spread out behind him, forming a subtle yet deliberate arc that was carefully planned and executed with precision. Despite their state of rest, the rifles were fully prepared and poised, ready for deployment at a moment's notice.

A primal scream, a visceral warning from deep within, caused Cole to feel a sudden surge of instinct. It was an event that was far from ordinary. What had felt like a triumphant victory over Jebediah Stone now seemed distant and insignificant, a pale and faded prelude to a more sinister overture to come. This was not a random occurrence; it was a carefully orchestrated event. With the cavalry's arrival, it became clear to Cole that he was still very much a part of the game, a game he hadn't known he was still playing. "I'm sorry," Harrison said, his gaze briefly diverting to the bundle of documents in his hands, "but we cannot socialize; we're here strictly for work. Cole Travis, you're under arrest." The words affected the listener with the force and speed of a bullet. Cole remained outwardly calm, his expression betraying no sign of fear, yet a subtle unease manifested itself in the ground's sensation, feeling less solid beneath his feet. With a steady voice, he politely questioned his captain about the purpose behind whatever was happening.

"Engaging in the illegal activity of stealing cattle." He gestured with a slight nod of his head toward the man, Jebediah Stone, who sat silently in the dust next to them, his face bruised and bearing an expression that was impossible to interpret, bound as he was. Harrison, looking over at Tala, further commented that, besides the speaker, it seemed her associate was also similarly involved in the entanglement. Tala remained silent, offering no response or comment whatsoever. She remained completely still and motionless, not making the slightest movement. Cole, however, noticed a palpable tension accumulating on her shoulders, coupled with a sharp, almost imperceptible glint in her eyes that belied her outwardly calm demeanor.

Maintaining a calm tone, though internally struggling, Cole stated the situation was a misunderstanding. Captain, I must inform you that the documents in your possession appear to be counterfeit. We have completed a thorough review of the material. He extended his arm and presented Cole with a rather thick folder, careful to maintain a neutral expression as he did so. Financial accounts showing transactions. A map provides a visual representation of a specific area or region. Every detail was present, creating a scene that was excessively tidy and flawless to the point of artificiality. Every single piece of that information is completely and utterly false. The artistry and skill displayed in the craftsmanship were absolutely stunning, exceeding all expectations. The individual who had falsified these documents possessed a comprehensive understanding of the cattle industry, the local geography, and the complexities of government procurement. Their access was not merely theoretical; it was substantial and provided by established institutions.

Fear gripped Cole, his blood running cold as a horrifying realization washed over him. This matter had nothing to do with the cattle themselves; rather, it was a question of who held the power and control. In a hushed tone barely audible to Tala, he accused them, his words heavy with implication, "They're trying to set us up." Her gaze remained steadfast, fixed on whatever was before her. "I possess certain knowledge regarding this matter." Recalling the silent day when his trust in Elias irrevocably broke, Cole's mind wandered to Elias. "We continue to unveil more, lifting another mask and revealing a deeper understanding. Yet another individual, deceptively similar in appearance to a genuine friend, but clad in a uniform, betrayed my trust." With a decisive and swift move, the cavalry units drew closer together, creating a more compact and secure perimeter. Although they weren't overtly aggressive in their position, they communicated their intentions and opinions with unmistakable clarity. They confidently expected that they would not encounter any opposition whatsoever. Cole realized, with a sudden rush of clarity, that they had made a significant error in their approach.

Driven not by a show of courage but by the sheer pressure of the situation, a plan took shape. It was a calculation made with desperation, a precarious decision on the very edge of a knife. They required a significant amount of time to pass, a considerable distance to separate them, and a substantial doubt as to settle in their minds. Tala's hand gave a single, almost imperceptible twitch. The subtle differences in the collars of some cavalrymen suggested these soldiers were new recruits transferred from other divisions, and thus unfamiliar with the local landscape. Their success stemmed from that characteristic, which proved to be their definitive advantage. Harrison ordered their detainment.

Tala cleverly employed a strategy of misdirection to deceive her opponent. In a gesture that seemed to suggest surrender, she fell to one knee and pointed towards a spot behind the group. She gasped out a warning, a sharp, breathless, "Behind you!" One by one, every head turned towards the source of the commotion. For Cole, that was the pivotal moment, the one he'd been expecting and desperately requiring. Seizing Tala's wrist with a firm grip, he swiftly swung himself up into the saddle before powerfully kicking his heels into the horse's flanks. As the horse bolted, a sudden and chaotic volley of gunfire erupted, the sharp reports scattered and echoing through the air. Riding hard, they ducked low as they urged their horses into the dense brush, the thunder of hooves pounding the cracked earth while branches tore at their sides and whipped past them.

A resounding and tumultuous noise accompanied the instantly beginning chase. A multitude of men shouted boisterously, their voices echoing through the air. The dogs in the neighborhood barked incessantly throughout the night, disturbing the peace of the residents. However, Cole possessed an unparalleled familiarity with this terrain, surpassing the knowledge of any other individual. Guiding them through arid gullies, he led them between the narrow crests of the hills and down into the arroyos where the sounds became distorted and the environment obscured their vision. The vast and untamed Texas wilderness provided them with the protection and concealment they desperately needed. By the time midnight arrived, they had successfully traversed the arid riverbeds situated to the west of Mesilla, a treacherous region that proved too challenging for wagons and navigable only by the surefooted Lipan scouts. A fine layer of glistening dust seemed to cover the shimmering landscape under the silvery moonlight. As they fled, the wind swallowed each shout, and with every powerful beat of their hooves, they carried not only the hope of freedom but also a resounding defiance against their pursuers.

"We aren't simply running," Cole said, his breath coming in short, ragged gasps. We are actively and resolutely showing our resistance. With his eyes fixed, Tala gave a penetrating look. In that case, let's make sure that this endeavor has a significant and lasting impact. Unwavering in their resolve, they continued their advance, pushing forward relentlessly. As dawn broke, the troopers' pursuit of the trail, which split across the stony ridges, began to weaken and slow. With their supplies dwindling to dangerously low levels, the weary horses began staggering under the strain of their burdens, showing clear signs of exhaustion. They pressed on with determination and perseverance. With each inhale and exhale, Cole was acutely aware of the gravity of the situation, the memory of Harrison's chilling smile and Elias's unnerving quietude resonating with every thud of his heart. The struggle was no longer merely about staying alive; it had developed into something more profound and significant.

Chapter 12: A Standoff at Kickapoo Creek

The cavalry's pursuit pushed them toward Kickapoo Creek. Swollen by recent rains, the creek roared with the fury of a trapped beast, no longer a serene ribbon of water. The towering canyon walls, slick with moisture and shadowed by overhanging trees, provided a natural, albeit dangerous, refuge.

Cole, his breath ragged, assessed their situation. The cavalry was closing in, their shouts echoing off the canyon walls, a chilling symphony of impending doom. Tala, her face grim but resolute, pointed towards a narrow path that wound its way along the edge of the creek. It was risky; one wrong step could send them tumbling into the churning water below. But it was their only option. The open plains offered no cover, and a confrontation would be suicidal.

They plunged into the labyrinthine path, the narrow passage wide enough for their horses. The air hung heavy with the scent of damp earth and the acrid smell of gunpowder. The sound of the pursuing cavalry grew louder, closer, their horses' hooves pounding against the rocky terrain.

As they rounded a sharp bend in the creek, they found themselves face-to-face with a group of Lipan Indian warriors, their faces painted in war paint, their eyes blazing with defiance. The air crackled with tension, the unspoken question hanging between them: friend or foe?

Ever the diplomat, Cole raised his hands in a gesture of peace. "We are not your enemies," he shouted, his voice audible above the roar of the creek. "The cavalry is pursuing us."

The Lipan Indian warriors remained wary, their hands hovering near their weapons. Their chief, a grizzled older man with piercing eyes, stepped forward. He spoke in Lipan Indian, his words tumbling from his lips like a torrent of water. Tala translated, her voice calm and measured.

"They say you are cattle rustlers, working with Stone," she relayed. "They say you betrayed the trust of the white man."

Cole knew he had to act quickly. His credibility hung in the balance. Emphasizing his efforts to shield Tala and the Lipan people from Jebediah Stone's ruthlessness, he recounted their encounter with the notorious figure. He laid bare the forged documents, highlighting the inconsistencies and showcasing his innocence. He appealed to their shared understanding, their common struggle against oppression.

The Lipan Indian chief listened, his gaze unwavering. The other warriors remained watchful, their spears poised, ready to react to sudden movements. This was a delicate negotiation on the brink of war. One wrong step could shatter the fragile truce and unleash a bloodbath.

The situation was fraught with peril. A conflict between their traditions and the encroaching influence of white settlers trapped the Lipan Indians. Siding with Cole and Tala would risk the wrath of the U.S. Cavalry; remaining neutral would betray their kinship and the principles of their tribe.

Cole's reputation amongst the Lipan Indians was strong, built on trust and mutual respect. Yet, the forged evidence posed a formidable challenge to their belief in his innocence. He needed to bridge the gap between their mutual suspicion and their shared desire for survival.

The ensuing discussions were tense, a delicate ballet of words and gestures, punctuated by the occasional nervous cough or the rustle of weaponry. The Lipan Indians acted. Cole appealed to their sense of justice, as well as their ingrained respect for bravery and honor. He laid out his case, detailing the conspiracy against him and Tala while highlighting the danger it posed to the entire community. He spoke of their shared plight and mutual vulnerability in the face of a greater threat.

Slowly, the Lipan Indian chief saw the truth in Cole's words.

Unraveling occurred with the meticulously crafted deception. The forged documents, intended to tarnish Cole's reputation, revealed a more profound corruption that affected everyone, not just Cole and Tala.

The cavalry at Kickapoo Creek marked a turning point in the standoff. The narrow, treacherous terrain presented a strategic advantage. The Lipan Indian warriors, skilled in guerrilla warfare, set up ambushes, using the natural cover provided by the canyon walls. With his knowledge of firearms and tactical awareness, Cole coordinated the defense. He and the Lipan Indian fought, their actions fluid and efficient.

The battle was fierce, a chaotic clash of steel and gunfire that echoed through the gorge. Cole, displaying his exceptional marksmanship and tactical skills, took down several cavalrymen before they could get a clear shot. The Lipan Indian warriors, using their knowledge of the terrain to their advantage, inflicted heavy casualties.

Weapons clashed, wounded cried, creek roared; chaos reigned. Cole found himself amid the maelstrom, fighting not only for his life, but for the lives of the Lipan Indian warriors fighting beside him. He was a part of the Lipan Indian people, and his heart aligned with their cause.

However, the cavalry's numbers were overwhelming. Cole knew he couldn't win a prolonged fight. He needed to create an opening, a chance to break the deadlock and escape the canyon. Combining his understanding of warfare and diplomacy, he decided on a constructed diversion.

As the cavalry focused its firepower on one particular section of the gorge, a planned maneuver by the Lipan Indians created a temporary lull in the fighting. It allowed Cole to orchestrate a calculated retreat, guiding the Lipan Indians and Tala through a hidden passage known only to the locals. This path wound through the labyrinthine creek bed.

The escape was a treacherous journey through the narrow, winding passageways. Every footstep was a gamble, every sound could reveal their location to the pursuing cavalry. Yet, with Cole's guidance and Tala's intimate knowledge of the terrain, they evaded their pursuers, emerging from the gorge hours later, exhausted, but alive.

Kickapoo Creek witnessed more than a battle; it represented a defining moment, a turning point. It confirmed Cole's commitment to Tala and the Lipan Indian people, solidifying his place within their community. But it also served as a harsh reminder of the complexities of the West, the constant struggles for survival, and the ever-present threat of violence and betrayal. The fight for justice appeared unfinished.

Chapter 13: Betrayal and Redemption

Someone enacted the betrayal not with a dramatic gunshot or a swift knife thrust, but through a campaign of insidious, soft, and calculated whispers. Subtle whispers, like worms burrowing into the ears of the powerful, gradually eroded the thread of trust, much like rust consumes iron. Elias, who was once Cole's closest friend and companion, had shockingly abandoned his loyalty to Cole, exchanging it for monetary gain and forsaking the noble cause they once shared for a life of ease and comfort. The events hadn't unfolded in a single moment; instead, they had occurred gradually over a period. The process was agonizingly slow, marked by frustrating delays and a general lack of progress. The accumulation of a hundred small choices, each seemingly insignificant on its own, can shape a life's trajectory. A thousand lies remained unspoken, hidden beneath a veneer of polite conversation and carefully constructed facades.

Now, the repercussions of his actions weighed heavily on Cole. It was Chayton, a scout with quiet eyes, who finally provided irrefutable evidence. The boy, eavesdropping on a hushed conversation between Elias and another man—a man who was easily identifiable as Jebediah Stone's associate because of his ever-present pipe smoke aroma and the suspiciously large amount of gold coins bulging from his pockets—had picked up on their cautious words. Following Chayton's revelation, Cole remained silent for an extended period, perhaps lost in thought considering what he had just been told. He remained motionless, his shoulders tense and rigid, his gaze fixed on the ground as if it held an alternate explanation, a different narrative, a truth hidden from plain sight.

The Elias before them was not the courageous Elias who had previously, during a Comanche attack, pulled a bleeding Cole to safety from under a collapsing wagon. It was not Elias, surprisingly, who openly wept at his brother's burial beneath the soil of Kickapoo Creek, a fact that surprised many who knew him. A considerable amount of time had passed since that man's departure; he was nowhere to be found. The bitter thought struck Cole: maybe, just maybe, he had never truly existed.

Trust, despite often being lost amidst acts of violence, did not always disappear. Sometimes its death was quiet, a slow, agonizing process akin to the creeping numbness of frostbite. Even before he mentioned it, Tala had already observed a subtle shift in his demeanor, a change that was perceptible even before he himself acknowledged it. Observing him, she noticed the way he'd over-tighten the leather straps on his possessions, or continue chopping wood long past the point of necessity, and it was these minor details that revealed a truth she hadn't expected to see. Lost in his own thoughts, his mind had retreated inward, becoming distant and detached from the world around him. His eyes showed the burden of meticulously assessing the destruction.

She chose not to ask questions at all. It will not be workable right now. Although she remained close by, she was patient and waited without interfering. He finally spoke only after a long silence, his voice low and barely audible as he sat by the warm glow of the fire. With a sigh, he confessed he had placed his complete and unwavering trust in that person, entrusting them with all aspects of his life. And thus, for a paltry sum of silver, he betrayed us into slavery, a transaction that forever stained his name. Tala's response was devoid of both judgment and sympathy, offering neither condemnation nor compassion. In a simple, unassuming gesture, she laid her hand atop his. Your trust in him stemmed from your optimistic and trusting nature, a belief in the inherent goodness of people.

In the weeks following that event, Cole adopted a methodical approach to everything he did, carefully planning each step and action. Instead of using traditional methods like bloodhounds or bounty posters, he meticulously tracked Elias's trail by examining various financial ledgers, tracing rerouted herds of livestock across the land, and piecing together clues from misplaced and incomplete maps. While intercepting couriers and copying their letters, he remained tight-lipped and spoke very little, if at all. Each newly discovered piece of evidence stung him with its familiarity—foreign bribes bearing his handwriting, meticulous reports detailing grazing routes, and shipment manifests deceitfully stamped with Stone's official seal.

He toiled in solitude, his efforts relentless, until his strength finally gave way. Subsequently, in a hushed tone, he discreetly sought help, not only from two respected Lipan tribal elders but also from a cavalry officer serving as a liaison, an individual who, during a prior patrol, had almost mistakenly shot him because of a regrettable misunderstanding. They did not assume trust. Slowly, he extended it, inch by agonizing inch, as if the process itself held some profound significance or demanded the utmost care.

Finally, he called a council under the ancient sycamore. Lipan, settlers, ex-soldiers. They gathered, shoulder to shoulder—some out of duty, some out of curiosity, a few out of disbelief. Cole stood before them without flair. He laid out what he'd found—documents, maps, bribes, and, most damning, a confession from one of Stone's couriers. Elias had undermined grazing negotiations, rerouted supplies meant for winter, and leaked defensive plans. "He didn't break faith with me," Cole said. "He broke it with all of us." There was no uproar. Just an indistinct murmur, like a hive disturbed.

At that point in the proceedings, Elder Nantan assumed a standing position, signifying the commencement of a new phase. In his statement, he clarified that the matter was significantly broader in scope than just one person's actions or influence. There was no vote. Only silence. Agreement shaped not by hands raised, but by a room that did not walk away. That night, Tala found Cole staring at the sycamore long after the others had left. "I keep looking for a reason," he said. "Some way this could make sense. He wasn't always like this."

"Maybe he was," Tala said. "Or maybe the world wore him down. But that's not your burden to carry." Still, Cole felt the echo. He carried it into every decision that followed.

When the moment arrived to counteract the considerable sway Stone held, Cole proceeded with meticulous care and precision in his actions. Avoid making any presumptions without sufficient evidence or information. With careful attention to detail, they reviewed every plan and examined each hand to guarantee everything was correct. He meticulously reviewed and verified the accuracy of all the established trade routes to ensure their continued viability and efficiency. They checked the messengers three times to ensure accurate message delivery. On one occasion, when a young settler boy selflessly volunteered his wagon to serve as a decoy for a shipment of goods, Cole initially hesitated before making a quick decision to assign two guards for protection and to change the planned route at the very last minute. Is it you harbor some doubt regarding his trustworthiness, or is there another reason behind your skepticism? Tala inquired with a questioning tone. "I have faith in humanity," Cole said, expressing his belief in the inherent goodness of people. I harbor a deep-seated distrust of absolute certainty, finding it unreliable and potentially misleading.

The dismantling of Stone's operations proceeded gradually, beginning with the disruption of their supply lines and subsequently encompassing a thorough examination and seizure of their financial records. Once federal marshals became involved, the situation became surprisingly simple. Once exposed to the light of truth, the vast and seemingly impenetrable empire that Stone had painstakingly constructed, much like all falsehoods, crumbled rapidly and completely. However, despite the fall, Cole did not experience any sense of contentment or fulfillment. The outcome did not result in a victory. The lingering ache of Elias's betrayal was all that remained, a constant reminder of the losses suffered not only by Elias himself but by everyone who had strived to build something honest, a deep wound that refused to heal.

Time passed, but the ache remained, refusing to fade. The underlying tension between the Lipan people and the settlers became apparent in fleeting moments, such as when a Lipan child would involuntarily recoil at the sound of approaching boots, or when a settler would pause, uncertain, before offering a handshake. The lingering sense of doubt and uncertainty, a caution that had taken root even in friendships, settled heavily in the cracks of their trust. However, the realignment of alliances took place once again. "It is imperative that we move forward, not haphazardly, but with a keen awareness and a well-defined vision of our goals." Rather than making assumptions, Cole listened carefully and thoughtfully to what was being said.

When the trading council erupted once more, this time into a heated debate about the unfair pricing of Lipan beadwork in the town's marketplaces, Cole made a conscious decision to not immediately intervene and attempt to settle the dispute. He permitted both sides to address him, deliberately letting the ensuing silence linger and amplify the tension.

Instead of jumping to conclusions about whether the other person's intentions were good or bad, he withheld judgment. It was only Tala, and no one else, whose actions completely calmed the very tense atmosphere that had been present that day. "Remember," she stated emphatically, "that unity doesn't require a complete lack of tension or disagreement. It's the choice to keep speaking through it." Cole remained standing beside her, his silence a testament to his unwavering support and steadfast presence. In her words, he heard a reflection of his own steadfast resolve: a commitment to diligently shield and preserve the progress they had achieved, and to avoid seeking an impossible ideal of perfection.

Later that week, while they stood together at the riverbank, observing the smoke rising gracefully from the cooking fires in the distance, Cole leaned in and whispered a heartfelt confession, "If I ever lose myself again..." Tala's tone was firm as she replied with a decisive, "You won't."

"But if I do," he continued, "don't wait to call me back." Turning towards him, her face was beautifully lit by the warm glow of the firelight. "You have already returned to your previous location." He gave a nod in agreement. The events of the past had indelibly etched themselves into the fabric of the present, leaving an undeniable mark on everything that followed.

Chapter 14: Reconciliation with the Rangers

The air hung heavy with the scent of sagebrush and anticipation as Cole rode towards the designated meeting place–a neutral point on the vast Texas plains, equidistant from the Lipan Indian encampment and the nearest Texas Ranger outpost. He carried the weight of two worlds on his shoulders, the fate of the Lipan Indian people and the uneasy peace with the Rangers hanging in the balance. He knew the stakes were high; a misstep could ignite a conflict that would consume the fragile harmony they had built.

His heart pounded a rhythm of apprehension against his ribs. He wasn't a mediator; he was a bridge, a fragile structure connecting two different cultures, each with its own rooted suspicions and prejudices. The Rangers, hardened by years of skirmishes with various Native American tribes, viewed the Lipan Indians with a mixture of suspicion and disdain, fueled by ingrained stereotypes and a history of violent clashes. The Lipan Indian held a justified distrust of the Rangers, a distrust born of broken treaties, land grabs, and unwarranted aggression.

Cole, however, held a unique position. His upbringing among cowboys and his deep respect and love for Tala and her people had given him an intimate understanding of both sides. In both senses of the word, he spoke both languages. He knew the nuances of their cultures, motivations, fears, and aspirations. He understood the ingrained mistrust, the historical grievances, and the simmering resentments that fueled the conflict.

As he approached the designated spot, he spotted Captain Brody, a grizzled veteran of countless campaigns, his face etched with the lines of a life lived on the harsh frontier. Brody's unyielding resolve and iron fist commanded respect and fear among the Rangers. His presence signified the importance the Rangers placed on this negotiation. Cole noticed the tension radiating off Brody's shoulders, starkly contrasting the usual swagger of the Texas law enforcement officers.

Unease filled the meeting's opening moments; only wind rustling in the grass broke the silence. Brody, unwavering, started with a formal address, his words chosen, betraying a cautious optimism. He acknowledged the Lipan Indian's right to their land and the need to foster a relationship built on mutual respect and understanding. Cole listened, interpreting Brody's words for the benefit of the Lipan Indian delegation. He saw a glimmer of something beyond the hardened exterior, a hint of recognition of the Lipan Indian's humanity.

The Lipan Indian chiefs, cautious, responded with measured tones.

Their words were firm yet laced with a cautious willingness to engage in dialogue. They outlined their grievances, concerns about the Rangers' encroachment on their traditional lands, and fears about the potential for future conflicts. Cole translated their words, preserving the nuances of their language and tone.

The ensuing hours were a delicate dance of diplomacy and negotiation. Cole shuttled back and forth, acting as a conduit to convey messages, clarify misunderstandings, and bridge the vast cultural gap that separated the two sides. He worked, leveraging his intimate knowledge of both sides to ease tensions, to build trust, and to foster a sense of mutual understanding.

The discussion often became heated. Participants reopened old, long-buried wounds during the debate. Accusations flew, tempers flared, and the threat of violence hung in the air like a storm cloud. Yet, through it all, Cole persevered. Their shared humanity, mutual desire for peace, and common interest in protecting their way of life were what he appealed to.

He described shared hardships, bravery, resilience, and moments of unexpected camaraderie between Rangers and Lipan Indian warriors, who fought against a common enemy. He recalled their shared history, highlighting cooperative successes versus the losses and bloodshed of conflict.

Slowly, a shift occurred. The air, thick with suspicion just moments earlier, cleared. The rigid postures softened, and the complex expressions yielded to thoughtful consideration. Brody, surprisingly, showed a willingness to listen and acknowledge the legitimacy of the Lipan Indian's concerns. He dropped his guard and displayed a surprising level of empathy. Despite his reputation for strength and unwavering resolve, he actively sought a compromise.

The breakthrough came when Cole suggested a joint effort to combat a common enemy: a band of ruthless outlaws who had been terrorizing both the Rangers' patrol area and the Lipan Indian hunting grounds. This shared enemy provided a common cause that allowed both sides to focus on the threat rather than on their differences. Both sides approved the proposal. The Lipan Indian's intimate knowledge of the terrain and their exceptional tracking skills would be invaluable to the Rangers. The Rangers' superior weaponry and training would provide support to the Lipan Indians.

This unexpected collaboration opened up a new avenue of communication. By working side by side, sharing resources and strategies, Rangers and Lipan Indian warriors developed a newfound respect for one another, dispelling long-held prejudices.

The meeting concluded as the sun began to set, casting long shadows across the plains. It wasn't a perfect solution or a complete reconciliation, but it was a significant step forward. They reached a tentative agreement, establishing a fragile peace. A joint effort against the outlaws would facilitate continued interaction and trust. Cole felt a sense of hope, a rare feeling, despite the upcoming difficulties. The bridge was still fragile, yet it stood, connecting two disparate worlds — a testament to the power of reconciliation and the enduring strength of the human spirit.

Chapter 15: The Price of Peace

Under the vast expanse of the Texas sky, a fragile peace, brokered with difficulty between the Texas Rangers and the Lipan Apache, felt less like a hard-won victory and more like a precarious truce, tenuously maintained by sheer willpower and a desperate clinging to hope. The agreement, while necessary, was also incredibly complex and risky, demanding that Cole lead a combined force of Rangers and Lipan warriors deep into dangerous outlaw territory. All the official documents showed a united front, at least on paper. In all honesty, the decision was a gamble with potentially devastating consequences.

Leaving meant giving up protecting the Lipan camp, the tranquil and dignified existence they shared, and the reliable comfort of having Tala at his side. It meant resuming the precarious balancing act of bridging the divide between two cultures whose recent conflict had left deep scars and a living memory of mutual distrust, requiring a delicate approach to heal the rift.

Despite the gravity of what he was telling her, Tala's eyes remained steadfast, betraying none of the fear that must have been churning within her. With a gentle nod, she leaned down, kissed his forehead softly, and then, placing a small, cold, smooth river stone marked with a single, vibrant red stripe into his waiting hand, she offered a silent gesture of comfort. "To ensure everything is in equilibrium," she stated, emphasizing the importance of balance in the situation. The feeling of instability is present when the ground beneath your feet feels unsteady and unreliable.

However, she maintained her grasp for an excessively prolonged duration. In her eyes, dark as the earth drenched in a relentless storm, he perceived emotions and unspoken truths that she could not bring herself to articulate. Do not give your life to individuals who will not lament your death; it would be a sacrifice in vain.

The forces, though combined, were ultimately an uneasy union, marked by mistrust and internal conflict. With an air of pride and precision, the Rangers rode in straight lines, their uniforms stiff, and their rifles gleaming in the sunlight. With the silence and deliberate pace of water, the Lipan moved, their eyes constantly scanning the surrounding brush for any sign of danger or opportunity. One group viewed themselves as the upholders of the law, believing themselves to be above reproach and accountable only to their own self-defined sense of justice. The others, meanwhile, stood as resolute defenders of the ancestral lands they had inherited from their forefathers. In the dim light, they both perceived spectral figures lurking within the shadows cast by their respective forms. Aware his voice would be barely audible once the shooting started, Cole rode between them.

The first few days were tense. A Lipan scout suggested a route, but a Ranger captain ignored him. When the scout's path turned out to be safer and faster, the captain muttered something about "lucky guesses." On another day, a Ranger cleaned his rifle in full view of Lipan warriors who were in mourning. When someone asked him to be more discreet, he bristled and snapped, "We're not here to follow rituals."

The Lipan men said nothing, but Cole noticed their body language—they drifted farther from the shared fire that night. The air between both camps grew thick with unease. Old wounds reopened quickly. That night, Cole stood between two fires. On one side, Rangers murmured about loyalty. Lipan warriors questioned whether this alliance was worth the insults. A Ranger accused a Lipan scout of withholding information. The scout, his face heavy with loss, didn't respond—he simply walked away.

Cole called for calm. "This isn't a treaty on parchment. It's forged in action. Either we fight together, or we die alone." After that, no one spoke. But the silence felt different. The next morning, they discovered outlaw tracks leading into a narrow canyon carved into the earth like a scar. "They'll use the cliffs," warned one Lipan elder. "They'll strike from above." A young Ranger laughed. "Ain't the first canyon I've seen." It was the last thing he ever said.

The ambush came hard and fast. Bullets rained down from prominent ridges. The outlaws—men with nothing to lose—fought like cornered animals. Cole shouted orders, riding alongside Kaelen, Tala's brother, who moved like a spirit through dust and fire. The Rangers adjusted their formation with disciplined precision, while the Lipan scattered and then converged like hawks. It wasn't seamless, but it worked. Still, the cost was high: three Rangers and two Lipan warriors died, one warrior barely sixteen years old.

Once the fight concluded, and as the blood dried upon the ground and the cries of the injured slowly subsided into silence, the old mistrust, like a serpent, once again insinuated itself into the hearts and minds of those present. Whispers of postponement and scheduling delays circulated amongst the park rangers. The Lipan warriors, their faces grim, spoke in hushed tones of the arrogance they had witnessed. As Cole approached the perimeter of the camp, his eyes fell upon a gruesome scene: two men, one from each opposing faction, stood over a lifeless body, locked in a furious argument regarding their respective failures to protect him.

Stepping between them, Cole declared solemnly, "That boy, though deceased, died with great honor." "Don't make his death smaller with blame."

Despite their retreat, a palpable sense of resentment remained. As the night deepened, the two fires, which had been close together earlier, burned independently, once again separated by a considerable distance. Exhausted from their exertions, Cole and Kaelen sat together in silence, lacking the energy even for conversation. Lost in thought, Kaelen stared into the flickering flames, his mind adrift in a sea of memories and emotions. Our continued fear and distrust, symbolized by keeping weapons close at hand while we sleep, prevents us from achieving true peace.

In a quiet voice, Cole offered a single, definitive word of refusal, "No. But it's still better than war."

The next morning, after a restless night, Cole called a meeting of his team to discuss pressing issues. There will be no speeches at the event. Please refrain from any posturing or attempts to appear more important than you actually are. The list only comprises names. Without exception, he compiled a comprehensive list of every fallen man, ensuring each man was remembered. Following that, he deliberately and individually looked each survivor directly in their eyes, giving each of them his full attention. You have the choice of viewing their loss as a heavy burden, a crushing weight, or you can instead choose to carry it as a badge of honor, a testament to their memory.

After a brief pause, he raised the stone, a gift from Tala, for everyone to see, turning it over in his hands. She explained that the reason for this was to maintain equilibrium.

Having finished what he needed to do, he then walked away from the area. It wasn't defiance that caused this, but an overwhelming sense of exhaustion that led to this outcome.

No one touched the fires that night. However, individuals from each of the opposing sides sat closer to the central area of the room. One ranger, extending an arm and offered a flask of liquid to a brave Lipan warrior. The gesture, while seemingly insignificant, held a deeper meaning. However, that it happened held significant importance and weight.

As the week concluded, the outlaws found themselves scattered far and wide, fleeing from authorities. Flames consumed their heavily defended stronghold, reducing it to smoldering rubble. Authorities killed or imprisoned the gang's leaders, effectively neutralizing the group. The mission, despite its inherent challenges, ultimately concluded successfully.

Although they had won, the victory felt oddly muted, like a quiet whisper lost among the many reverberating echoes of the vast valley.

Silence reigned during the return journey, a stark contrast to the lively atmosphere of the outward trip. Although the tension remained, it had undergone a noticeable shift in character. People were less inclined to steal furtive glances to the side; the sideways glances had become noticeably less frequent. As the fire crackled merrily, a few people gathered close to share stories. A single laugh escaped Kaelen's lips, a solitary chuckle in response to a remark made by one of the Rangers.

Feelings of triumph and victory eluded Cole; he did not feel triumphant at all. Overcome by a profound sense of emptiness, he felt like a shell of his former self, hollowed out and devoid of emotion. The cost of peace was far greater than simply lives lost; it encompassed profound sacrifices, enduring hardships, and deep-seated societal trauma. The blood analysis revealed a disturbing truth: the precarious and ever-present proximity of alliance to bitter hatred.

As he reached the Lipan encampment, he found Tala waiting patiently for his arrival. Running towards him, her fingers pressed against his cheeks, as if to confirm that he was actually real and not some figment of her imagination. Although their kiss lingered for a long time, it lacked any genuine joy or happiness, leaving a sense of emptiness. The emotions were a knot of relief and sorrow, so deeply tangled that it was difficult to tell one from the other.

As the night progressed, he recounted the events of the day, detailing Kaelen's courageous actions, the tragic fall of the young boy, and that their once warm campfire had remained cold for days. Without a word, she listened carefully to everything that was being said. In a hushed tone, barely audible, she breathed the words, "You brought them back, completely unharmed and in one piece." Her voice filled with wonder and relief.

He shook his head, a gesture of disbelief washing over his features. "Not whole. Just... together."

As the morning light broke over the camp, Cole's walk revealed a palpable change in the atmosphere. A few of the older people in attendance gave a quiet nod, signifying their approval or perhaps simply their attention to the proceedings. Some people in the crowd averted their gazes, unwilling or unable to meet the eyes of those around them. Despite his efforts, several people remained unconvinced and continued to harbor distrust towards him. He didn't hold them accountable for what happened.

He did not possess the characteristics typically associated with heroism. The man was someone who attempted to keep hold of two halves of a story, never letting go of one for the other, a difficult feat indeed.

Later that same afternoon, a group of young Lipan Apache men, curious and eager to learn, approached him with a request: to show a specific rifle maneuver they had observed the Rangers expertly execute earlier. Despite the tragic loss of a cousin in the canyon, which had deeply affected one of them, he still attempted to come. Though the sign was tiny, its impact was profoundly influential.

The delicate unity, although precarious, remained intact for the moment. Despite the repairs, however, thin lines in the stone remained, showing that the damage was still present. It dawned on Cole that peace wasn't merely a boundary to be traversed, but a continuous state of being that required consistent effort.

Chapter 16: A New Beginning

As the sun, resembling a molten orb, sank below the horizon, its descent casting long shadows across the Lipan Indian encampment, Cole carefully dismounted from his weary horse. Taking a deep breath, the familiar scents of woodsmoke and roasting meat, a soothing balm to his senses that calmed both his mind and body, instantly comforted him. Unlike a conquering hero's triumphant return, profound grief, exhaustion, and an emotional emptiness born from his arduous experiences marked his homecoming.

As he was securing the reins to the bridle, completely without warning, Tala appeared before him. Driven by a fierce urgency and a desperate, almost primal need for closeness, she wrapped her arms tightly around him, pulling him in towards her as if he were her only lifeline, the only thing tethering her to safety and sanity in a chaotic world. It was quite some time—a substantial, noticeable stretch of time—before either person in the room broke the silence with even a single word. Their embrace spoke volumes, a silent exchange conveying the unspoken sentiment, "I missed you," a powerful message that transcended the limitations of spoken language and held a deeper, more profound meaning than any words could express. Cole was significantly worried and concerned about the present circumstances, and he realized that his continued presence was necessary at the camp.

The initial days passed by in a tranquil and peaceful manner, undisturbed by any significant events or happenings. In companionable silence, they shared a meal, their gazes intently fixed on each other's faces, searching for any subtle clues that might reveal the effects of their time apart. Cole found solace and comfort in the predictable structure of his daily routines, which he carefully organized around familiar activities. Although he was initially uncertain, he could sense a palpable shift in the atmosphere surrounding him, showing a significant alteration of the environment. The summer camp, once a place of cherished memories, had irrevocably changed, losing the charm and familiarity it once held dear.

Cole's movements had become noticeably slower and more deliberate than before, and he smiled less frequently. Haunted by memories of the canyon, his sleep was shallow and restless. Tala perceived the subtle shift in the atmosphere, registering the change. Though she remained silent, her unwavering support was evident in her small, tender gestures—a warm blanket for the night, a comforting touch on his shoulder, and a silently placed bowl of soup beside him.

Cole poured himself into helping with the rebuilding efforts marked by hardship and renewal. He joined the younger men in reinforcing fences and helped butcher a deer brought in by hunters. His hands, once calloused from riding, became rougher still with labor. As partners, he and Tala began clearing a section of land next to the riverbank. Together, they would construct a modest yet sturdy cabin, blending stone and wood, where time-honored traditions met the practical demands of the day. Every morning, they worked in unison, their efforts intertwined as they labored side by side. In the evenings, they would sit beneath the starlit sky, their shared exhaustion comforting them like a warm blanket.

As the night progressed, Cole gently traced the long scar etched into Tala's arm, his fingers lingering on the raised, pale skin. "Was that from the raid?" he inquired gently, his voice barely above a whisper. Tala gave a slight nod of her head in acknowledgment. The injury had healed long ago. He responded, "Mine too," although he was referring to an internal, rather than an external, problem.

In the process of constructing their house, they also reconstructed and strengthened their relationship with one another. The walls of the cabin rose slowly and majestically into the sky above. They carefully constructed and shaped a hearth using fieldstone. A simple, woven mat served as a clear and easily identifiable marker for the entrance. That thing belonged to them. It's not merely a house; rather, it's a home built upon a foundation of compromise, mutual respect, and the unspoken promises that bind a family together.

Still, some people in the camp viewed Cole's presence with narrowed eyes. Others questioned Tala's choice. There were whispers—about allegiances, about loyalty. Once, someone left a piece of broken pottery outside their door, a silent message about what didn't belong. Tala held her head high. "Let them look," she said. "We've weathered worse than stares." Cole nodded, but in the quiet moments, it stung. He had fought beside her people. Risked his life. But he hadn't earned their full trust. Not yet. And perhaps never entirely.

They didn't give up. Tala began teaching the local child's words in English—"not to forget who we are," she explained, "but to know how to speak back." Cole carved toys from cedar, handing them out with a shy smile. Beyond the superficial aspects, he immersed himself in a study of the deeper, more subtle cultural customs. As the seasons changed, he became a regular participant alongside the elders in their performance of the time-honored rituals. With a curious mind, he asked several questions, delving deeper into the subject with each inquiry. With rapt attention, he listened to every word that was spoken.

Upon hearing the unsettling rumors of a cattle dispute that threatened to rekindle the conflict between their village and a neighboring ranch, Cole and Tala stepped forward with an offer to mediate the disagreement. Gathered around the comforting glow of the fire, they could articulate their deepest fears and frustrations, transforming intangible anxieties into understandable words and fostering a sense of shared experience and healing—like mending broken pottery with gold, every scar a story. An elder leveled accusations of greed against the ranchers, while a Ranger scout simultaneously responded by accusing them of theft. Angry voices filled the air, rising in a crescendo of frustration and rage. With a gentle raising of his hand, Cole softly revealed the heartbreaking truth about the boy who lost his life in the canyon; he was just sixteen years old. A hush fell over the room as his words resonated, silencing the previous chatter and leaving everyone captivated.

While general dissatisfaction permeated the atmosphere, a sense of relief washed over everyone as the situation concluded peacefully, with no escalation to violence or the unlawful use of firearms. The central lesson learned from that experience was that achieving peace was anything but simple, demanding complex negotiations and compromises to reconcile the conflicting desires and objectives of the various parties involved.

As time passed, their cabin, once perhaps ordinary, gradually became a tranquil and isolated haven — a peaceful retreat where they could quietly spend time with those they held most dear: friends and family alike. The elders, sharing their wisdom and life experiences through storytelling and conversation, were present while the children played games and interacted, thoroughly enjoying themselves. With passing time, the initial suspicion slowly dissipated, giving way to a growing feeling of comfortable familiarity.

One day, Tala went to the storage area and brought back her grandmother's much-loved blanket, a truly exceptional example of textile artistry. Using a graceful and deliberate movement, she carefully positioned the item so that it would hang attractively over the recently installed doorway. She explained the item served a dual purpose, offering protection while simultaneously preserving a cherished memory, emphasizing both aspects with a deliberate intonation.

As the seasons changed and summer finally arrived, it brought with it a kaleidoscope of festivals, and the joyous, vibrant echoes of music resonated throughout the canyons, filling the air with lively sounds and festive cheer. Cole, watching from the shade of a nearby tree, a genuine smile finally softening his features, observed Tala's unrestrained and fluid dance in the warm dust as she moved barefoot. During the frigid winter months, they huddled close together, seeking warmth from the fire's comforting glow as they quietly read.

As spring arrived, Cole and Tala embarked on their first gardening project, diligently coaxing a crop of beans and squash from the initially dry and challenging soil. By harking to the Lipan elders, Cole gained valuable knowledge about irrigation, including how to align rows with prevailing winds and interpret mountain shadows to predict rainfall.

Although they encountered countless difficulties and hardships during their lifetimes, they created a unique and inspiring life story, a testament to their resilience and compassion, painstakingly built with diligent effort and unwavering determination. As each month passed, the cabin's walls, once perceived as protective barriers, subtly shifted from barriers to an inviting embrace, gently urging them toward the mystery ahead. Among their guests were mixed-race couples, older adults traveling together, and a woman from another community who was particularly interested in learning more about the local schools, highlighting the diverse backgrounds represented.

Despite the war's conclusion, the land remained marred by the conflict's lasting wounds, and the memories of those who experienced it lingered in their minds, serving as a constant reminder of the devastation. Instead of dodging the difficulties they encountered, Tala and Cole bravely confronted them directly. As the evening deepened, the sky blazed with such brilliance that it was almost painful to look at, and under this dazzling expanse, Cole and Tala sat side by side, quietly watching as a group of children gleefully captured fireflies in their small, cupped hands.

He stated that time would heal all wounds, and that the most troublesome parts would be forgotten, conveying hope and reassurance. She replied with a single, definitive "no," her lack of further explanation revealing her complete agreement. Despite the challenges—emotional, political, and generational we face, we remain steadfast in our commitment to completing this project and are determined to achieve success. With a gentle, graceful movement, Cole reached out his hand to take hers, a tender gesture that spoke volumes. With a hint of apprehension, he inquired whether their unwavering faith in his abilities and the team's capabilities persisted.

Tala kept her gaze fixed on the distant horizon, her attention completely absorbed by the far-off expanse, especially given the current, rather unusual circumstances.

Chapter 17: Building Bridges

The following spring brought the vibrant green of recent growth and a tentative thaw in the icy relations between the Lipan Indians and the surrounding settlements. Cole, having earned the respect of both communities through his actions, became an unlikely bridge between the two worlds. He organized a series of informal gatherings, small and cautious, where Lipan Indian artisans could showcase their crafts—the beaded moccasins, the woven baskets, and the stunning silver jewelry. These events, held on neutral ground outside the Lipan Indian encampment and the nearest Texas town, were a calculated risk. Still, Cole's reputation and Tala's quiet diplomacy eased the initial anxieties.

Hesitant curiosity outweighed ingrained prejudices, resulting in sparse attendance at the gatherings. Whispers and sidelong glances were familiar, a testament to the lingering mistrust that had once been a part of their lives. But Cole, with his simple charm and unwavering sincerity, chipped away at the barriers. He would introduce Tala's father, a respected elder known for quiet wisdom, to ranchers and townsfolk, emphasizing the Lipan Indian's deep land knowledge and inherent respect for its resources. To avoid misunderstandings, he patiently translated conversations, bridging understanding gaps and explaining cultural nuances. He also helped several Lipan Indian families get a small loan for new tools, thereby proving cooperation's economic advantages.

Gradually, a community spirit formed. Starting with apprehension, I became cautiously curious, then genuinely interested, and finally, grudgingly respectful. Despite Lipan artisans' reluctance to show their work, outsiders still valued their skills and artistry. Achieving economic self-sufficiency, a long-sought goal, Lipan artisans built a market for their goods. The ranchers, skeptical of trading with the Lipan Indians, discovered the value of their knowledge of the land, their understanding of weather patterns, and their innate ability to navigate the treacherous terrain. The mutual exchange of expertise and resources fostered a sense of collaboration rather than conflict.

Cole's efforts extended beyond the economic sphere. He helped establish a small school, teaching basic literacy and arithmetic to Lipan Indian children while also sharing stories and legends from both cultures. This fostered a sense of shared history and a common understanding of their respective heritages. The school, a small wooden structure nestled near the Lipan Indian encampment, became a beacon of hope, a testament to the potential of cross-cultural collaboration. The children, free from the prejudice of the adult world, embraced each other with an easy camaraderie, proving that friendship and understanding could blossom even amidst the lingering tensions of the past.

Tala played a pivotal role in these efforts; her grace and diplomacy bridged cultural gaps, surpassing Cole's attempts. She could navigate the complexities of both cultures with an understanding born from a lifetime spent balancing two different worlds. She organized community events, fostering a sense of shared purpose and a common understanding of their collective heritage. Her quiet dignity, coupled with her inherent strength, helped to overcome the lingering skepticism and resentment.

The transformations weren't immediate, nor were they embraced. Some individuals, both within the Lipan Indian community and the surrounding settlements, remained resistant to change, clinging to old prejudices and fears. However, the slow, steady progress, fueled by Cole and Tala's efforts, was positive. Whispers of hostility faded, giving way to conversations, bartering, and shared laughter. The once-tense atmosphere between the two communities eased, replaced by a tentative but hopeful sense of co-existence. The success of the gatherings fostered a growing sense of economic interdependence, enabling the Lipan Indians to take part more fully in the broader economy and thereby improve their quality of life.

Nestled on the edge of the encampment, their cabin became a symbol of this changing landscape. It was more than a home; it was a testament to their love, a sanctuary from the lingering tensions, and a meeting place for friends from both communities. Evenings often found the cabin filled with laughter, the aroma of roasting meat and baked bread filling the air. Friends from both worlds gathered, sharing stories, learning from each other, and forging thread of thrusts of friendship that transcended cultural differences. Cole and Tala's home became a microcosm of the larger change sweeping across the Lipan Indian community and the surrounding settlements, a living testament to the power of understanding, mutual respect, and the enduring power of love.

The burgeoning cattle trade in Fort Worth, once a source of conflict, has now become a source of opportunity. Using his extensive knowledge of the cattle industry, Cole helped the Lipan Indians negotiate fair prices for their livestock, improving their economic standing and ensuring unscrupulous traders didn't exploit them. He established a trust network between the Lipan Indians and the ranchers, leveraging his reputation to foster fair trade and provide the Community's economic independence. This further Strengthened the growing sense of mutual respect and collaboration.

One sweltering summer afternoon, as Cole and Tala sat on their porch, watching the children play in the meadow, they realized the enormity of the changes they had helped to bring about. The years of conflict, the bitterness, the distrust—it all seemed distant, a fading memory. They had not erased the differences between the Lipan Indians and the surrounding communities. Still, they had bridged the gap, foster understanding, and build a future based on mutual respect and collaboration.

Their journey was far from over. Challenges remained, subtle prejudices lingered, and the threat of external conflict always loomed. But Cole and Tala, together, felt ready to face these challenges—emotional, political, and generational. Their love story, once a forbidden romance, had blossomed into a beacon of hope, a symbol of the transformative power of cross-cultural understanding, and a testament to the human spirit's resilience. Their future was no longer a question of survival, but a promise of a shared life built on mutual respect, understanding, and a love that defied the boundaries of culture and tradition.

The quiet hum of progress was a sweet sound to their ears, a sign of a future where peace and cooperation reigned, a future they had fought for and had built. They built their success not on physical assets but on strong relationships and cooperation, creating a lasting impact. The future was still uncertain, but now it held the promise of a harmonious coexistence—a testament to their love—and a future built on the bedrock of their shared hope and determination. The sun dipped below the horizon, painting the sky in fiery orange and soft pink shades, mirroring the warm glow of hope blooming in their hearts.

Chapter 18: Challenges of Assimilation

The initial euphoria of their burgeoning relationship and the tentative steps towards inter-community harmony faded as Tala confronted the harsh realities of assimilation. The warmth of Cole's embrace couldn't entirely shield her from the subtle, sometimes not-so-subtle, prejudices permeating the Texan society. While Cole had brokered a fragile peace between the Lipan Indians and the settlers, the underlying cultural chasm remained, a silent, ever-present barrier.

The most immediate challenge was the language. Although Cole was fluent in Spanish and had attempted to learn some Lipan Indian, he missed the nuances of everyday Texan life in translation. Simple interactions—such as shopping in town, visiting the doctor, or ordering food at a local saloon—became unexpectedly complex, frustrating, and sometimes humiliating. Tala constantly relied on Cole, a dependency that gnawed at her ingrained independence. She missed the effortless flow of communication within her community, the shared understanding, the unspoken language of glances and gestures that bound them together. The Texan dialect, clipped tones, and unfamiliar idioms felt like a foreign tongue, a constant reminder of her outsider status.

Beyond language, the cultural differences proved far more significant. The Lipan Indian way of life clashed starkly with the individualistic, materialistic values of the settlers. Settlers often met Tala's deep-rooted kinship to nature, her understanding of the land's rhythms, and its spiritual significance with bewilderment, even ridicule. The settlers saw the Lipan Indian's communal lifestyle as primitive, their spiritual beliefs as superstitious. Simple acts, like gathering herbs for medicinal purposes or performing traditional rituals, drew curious stares and hushed whispers.

Initially hesitant, the women of the town had grown more receptive. However, the acceptance was conditional, tinged with a paternalistic attitude that grated on Tala's sensibilities. They admired her skills in weaving and beadwork. Still, their praise was often condescending, reducing her artistry to mere curiosities, exotic items to be showcased and consumed by the dominant culture. Clearly, their world defined Tala's worth by her ability to fit in and adapt; this was their underlying sentiment. The constant pressure to assimilate, to abandon aspects of her culture, eroded her identity, leaving her feeling lost and uncertain of herself.

Hope, however, glimmered in the children. Educated in the new school Cole had helped establish, the settlers' children were less constrained by adult prejudices. They quickly saw past the cultural differences, drawn to Tala's gentle nature and ability to share stories from her people. They admired her intricate beadwork and her knowledge of native plants, treating her as an outsider and a friend. Through these children, Tala found a sense of belonging, a validation of her identity that was missing in the adult world. The shared games and laughter in the schoolyard provided a much-needed escape from the constant pressures of assimilation.

Even Cole, her unwavering support, couldn't entirely protect her from the insidious nature of prejudice. Sometimes, the casual remarks, the unintentional slights, the blatant disregard for Lipan Indian customs pierced through their shared happiness. He tried his best to explain these societal complexities and educate his friends and neighbors, but his sincere efforts often met with resistance or incomprehension. He would hold Tala close, offering words of comfort and reassurance, but he couldn't entirely erase the pain she felt. Their love became a haven, a sanctuary from the storms of prejudice and misunderstanding, but the emotional toll was undeniable.

One evening, after a disheartening encounter at the town market, Tala sat by the fire, her face etched with a quiet sadness. Sensing her distress, Cole sat beside her, his arm around her shoulders. He didn't minimize her pain, nor offer empty platitudes. He listened, his presence a silent affirmation of his love and support. She explained the constant pressure to conform, the subtle dismissal of her culture, and the painful feeling of being an outsider, always on the periphery.

Cole, touched by her vulnerability, spoke of his struggles with prejudice as a child of pioneer parents. He described how others viewed his family as outsiders, judging and misunderstanding their lives. His journey of self-discovery, his acceptance of his heritage, and his determination to understand the culture of his loved ones were all shared by him. He discussed the complexities of prejudice, its underlying fears and misunderstandings. He emphasized it was not about erasing differences but celebrating diversity, acknowledging the strengths and beauty of both cultures, and finding common ground in their shared humanity.

Their conversation stretched long into the night. It wasn't about assimilation, but about the layered nuances of cultural understanding, the necessity of empathy and respect, and the enduring power of love to overcome even the deepest-rooted prejudice. That conversation renewed their shared purpose and determination to fight for a future celebrating their love's transformative power, unbound by cultural boundaries.

The dawn broke, painting the eastern sky in hues of gold and rose, a silent promise of a brighter future. This future would require resilience, perseverance, and an unwavering commitment to a shared vision of harmony and mutual respect. They would face these trials together, their love a shield against the storms.

Chapter 19: Economic Independence

The fragile peace they had established didn't solve their economic anxieties. The reality of life for Lipan Indians in Texas was harsh.

While Cole's cattle drives brought in a steady income, it was a precarious livelihood, dependent on the market's whims and the unpredictable nature of Texas weather. Tala, accustomed to the self-sufficiency of her Lipan Indian community, felt a growing unease at their dependence on Cole's trade. She yearned for economic independence, a way to contribute to their shared future, and to prove her worth beyond the confines of their nascent romance. This desire wasn't about financial security, but about establishing her identity and agency within this new world.

Her inherent skills, honed over years of living close to the land, sparked an idea. The Lipan Indian women were renowned for their intricate beadwork and weaving, their artistry reflecting a deep-rooted kinship to their cultural heritage. Tala saw an opportunity to combine her tradition with the burgeoning market demands of Fort Worth. The intricate designs imbued with the Lipan Indian's rich symbolism were appealing. She envisioned creating exquisite pieces—including necklaces, bracelets, belts, and blankets—that would serve as both mere ornaments and wearable art, telling stories of their history and heritage.

Cole, ever supportive of Tala's ambition, embraced her plan. He saw in her entrepreneurial spirit a reflection of his own, a shared desire for self-reliance and a future not dictated by the limitations imposed by prejudice. He used his rooted kinships within the burgeoning cattle trade to promote Tala's artistry, showcasing her work among his fellow ranchers and traders. The initial response was cautious, but Tala's creations' sheer beauty and unique nature turned heads. Word of her exquisite beadwork and woven blankets spread like wildfire, sparking curiosity and a surge in demand.

They established a small workshop near their home, a cozy space where Tala's artistry flourished. The aroma of natural dyes and the rhythmic click of her loom filled the air, a testament to their collaborative endeavor. While unskilled in the crafts, Cole became her invaluable business partner, managing marketing and distribution logistics. He learned to appreciate the nuances of her work, the cultural significance imbued in each stitch and bead. He took charge of the business aspects, negotiating prices, handling payments, and establishing rooted kinships with potential buyers in Fort Worth's bustling market.

The initial sales were tentative, small orders from curious customers eager to own a piece of Lipan Indian artistry. However, as the word of Tala's skill spread, the demand escalated. Soon, affluent women in Fort Worth were clamoring for her unique pieces. They weren't buying crafts, but investing in a piece of living history — a testament to the skill and spirit of a culture too often overlooked. The success of their venture transcended mere economics; it was a powerful statement, a subtle defiance against the prevailing societal biases.

Their small workshop became a hub of activity, a bridge between two cultures. Tala employed other Lipan Indian women, providing them with economic independence and a sense of purpose.

The workshop, a collaborative space, symbolized female empowerment; it preserved, celebrated, and shared cultural traditions with the broader community. The shared work, the exchange of skills and knowledge, fostered a sense of community within their shared endeavor. It allowed the Lipan Indian women to interact with the broader Texan community and showcase their heritage on their terms. This sense of community served as a powerful antidote against the isolating effects of prejudice.

However, their business didn't escape the scrutiny of those who opposed their relationship and shared ambition. Some settlers, clinging to their prejudices, attempted to undermine their success by spreading rumors and boycotting their goods. They faced moments of fierce resistance, encountering individuals who found their intercultural collaboration threatening to their established norms. The very success of their enterprise sparked resentment among some who feared the changing social dynamics of Lipan Indians and the potential erosion of their traditional power structures.

Cole and Tala used their success to challenge the prejudices that sought to stifle them. Their profits enabled them to invest back into their community, supporting the Lipan Indian people and contributing to the stability of their shared home. They built a school, had better facilities for their community, and assisted those in need, demonstrating their commitment to fostering a harmonious and fair society. Their actions spoke louder than words, dismantling prejudice one successful transaction at a time.

The success of their business extended beyond mere financial gain.

It gave them a sense of identity and purpose, strengthening their thread of trust and deepening their understanding of each other's cultures. Their shared enterprise became a testament to the power of collaboration, resilience, and the unifying force of love in overcoming adversity.

They learned to navigate the market's complexities, adapting their strategy to meet changing demands. They established a system for distributing their goods, expanding their network of buyers, and ensuring consistent revenue streams. Their reputation for quality and creativity ensured a steady flow of orders, allowing them to reinvest their profits and expand their operations. They explored new markets, diversifying their products to cater to the ever-develop tastes of their customers.

Their success also allowed them to invest in their relationship, securing a stable home for themselves and planning for a future family. The financial independence they gained gave them the power to make choices, free from the limitations of dependence. Their business venture secured their economic stability and strengthened their thread of trust, providing a platform for shared dreams and goals.

Tala's artistic talents, perceived by some as mere curiosities, had become a powerful symbol of cultural pride and economic empowerment. She had transformed a personal expression of her heritage into a successful business venture, demonstrating the power of resilience, creativity, and the collaborative spirit. With his business acumen, Cole had transformed from a cattle rancher into a supportive business partner, navigating the complexities of the marketplace to ensure her success. The success of their enterprise not only secured their future, but it also redefined their identities within the context of a wider community and the broader narrative of westward expansion. Their story, interwoven with threads of love, resilience, and economic empowerment, continued to inspire and uplift. Their business, love, and shared future were a testament to the strength of the human spirit and the power of shared dreams to overcome prejudice and build a better world.

Chapter 20: A Lasting Legacy

The years that followed saw their small workshop blossom into a thriving enterprise. The rhythmic click of Tala's loom, once a solitary sound in their humble home, now echoed through a larger space, filled with the laughter and chatter of Lipan Indian women crafting their unique designs. Ever the pragmatist, Cole had overseen the expansion, securing a larger building in Fort Worth's burgeoning artisan district. The location, a gamble, proved a stroke of genius. The proximity to the town's affluent clientele ensured a steady stream of customers drawn to Tala's creations, which offered unique beauty and cultural significance.

Their success wasn't just about profits; it was about empowerment. Tala employed not only other Lipan Indian women but also women from neighboring communities, forging rooted kinships that transcended tribal boundaries. Cultures melded with the vibrant workshop as shared skills and stories fostered mutual understanding. The women learned from each other, sharing techniques and exchanging stories, enriching their crafts, and fostering a sense of shared accomplishment. The once-isolated Lipan Indian women found themselves independent and engaged, taking part in a larger community while maintaining their cultural identity.

Reflecting the collaborative workshop spirit, the designs themselves developed. While Tala initially based her creations on traditional Lipan Indian symbolism, the women added their own interpretations, blending elements of their diverse heritage into the designs. The resulting pieces were a testament to the power of cultural exchange, showcasing a vibrant tapestry of traditions and woven together. The designs developed into a powerful narrative, reflecting the changing identity of the Lipan Indian community within the broader context of Texan society.

There were still whispers and murmurings, attempts to discredit their work and undermine their success. Cole had to navigate complex political and economic landscapes, using his sharp business acumen to overcome the obstacles created by those who opposed their intercultural partnership. He used his influence within the ranching community to safeguard their interests and advocate for the Lipan Indian people, challenging prevailing prejudices, and fighting for their rights.

However, with every challenge, they found new ways to overcome the obstacles. Cole's ability to navigate the complexities of the cattle trade and the broader Texan economy proved invaluable. He leveraged his rooted kinships and influence to establish a system that ensured fair prices for Lipan Indian artisans, enabling them to benefit from the hard work that went into their exquisite creations. His business expertise ensured recognition and reward for Tala's artistry, protecting her and her artisans from exploitation.

Their response to opposition was not confrontational but a demonstration of their enduring commitment to their vision. They invested a significant portion of their profits back into the Lipan Indian community, funding improvements in education, healthcare, and infrastructure. The community thrived, its resilience and spirit strengthened by its success. Their actions spoke volumes, silencing the critics with tangible evidence of the positive impact of their intercultural enterprise. They showed to doubters that the success of the Lipan Indian community was not a threat to the broader society but an asset. Their shared enterprise proved to be a powerful force for good, improving the lives of their community and fostering stronger rooted kinships between their community and the wider Texan society.

The school they built symbolized their commitment to education and social progress. It offered traditional Lipan Indian education and modern schooling, preparing the younger generation for the future while preserving their rich cultural heritage. The improved healthcare facilities enhanced the well-being of the Lipan Indian community, providing better access to medical care and promoting overall health and wellness. These investments weren't charitable acts, but strategic moves that strengthened the community's foundation and promoted its self-sufficiency.

The impact of their enterprise extended far beyond the Lipan Indian community. Initially sold in Fort Worth, their creations soon found their way to larger markets, showcasing the beauty of Lipan Indian artistry to a national audience. The unique designs, imbued with cultural significance and crafted with exceptional skill, captivated collectors and art enthusiasts, cementing the Lipan Indian's place in the tapestry of American art history. Their success brought recognition and respect to the Lipan Indian culture, challenging stereotypes and fostering a greater understanding of their traditions.

In their later years, Cole and Tala watched with pride as their living memory took root. The workshop, now a renowned artisan center, continued to thrive, providing employment and empowerment to generations of Lipan Indian women. Serving as a model for other indigenous communities, their business inspired them to embrace their heritage and achieve economic independence using their skills. Their remarkable success powerfully exemplifies cultural understanding, reconciliation, and the indomitable spirit that defies the odds.

Their inspiring love story powerfully showed the strength of intercultural relationships and love's resilience against adversity. Raised with a deep understanding of their cultural backgrounds, their children became bridges between communities, fostering peace and understanding. Their living memory went beyond material success; it was a living memory of love, empowerment, and reconciliation that continues to inspire and shape the future of the Lipan Indian people and the broader Texan community. Once a humble dwelling, their home became a symbol of hope.

Their story became a testament to the power of perseverance in the face of societal prejudice and adversity. The enduring living memory of Cole and Tala was not just about economic success, but about bridging cultural divides, fostering understanding, and building a future where different cultures could coexist and thrive. Future generations continued to find inspiration in their living memory, proving that love, determination, and collective effort could overcome insurmountable obstacles. Their story serves as a potent reminder that progress is possible and essential. It is a story of the triumph of the human spirit and a testament to the power of love to transcend prejudice and inspire a better future for all. The echo of their actions and the living memory of their love resonates through the years, shaping the lives of countless individuals and leaving an imprint on the very fabric of the community. They helped build the community. The vibrant tapestry they wove together, threads of love, resilience, and community, continues to inspire hope and celebrate the power of unity and collaboration.

Chapter 21: Haunted by Memories

The rhythmic clang of the blacksmith's hammer, a sound that once soothed him, now grated on Cole's nerves. The scent of hot iron, a comforting aroma, felt suffocating tonight. He sat on the porch of their Fort Worth home, the bustling city noises a distant hum compared to the insistent echoes in his mind. He'd been quiet these past few weeks, starkly contrasting with the jovial, outgoing man Tala knew. The vibrant energy that had propelled him through the challenges of building their business seemed to have dimmed, replaced by a pensive stillness that worried her.

He traced the outline of a worn leather-bound journal resting on his knee, its pages filled with the faded script of his past. It was a past that refused to stay buried. The memories, sharp and vivid as if etched into his very soul, clawed their way to the surface, disrupting the peaceful rhythm of his present life. He hadn't meant for Tala to discover it, but she had found it nestled amongst his belongings during one of her cleaning sprees. She had asked, without judgment, her large, expressive eyes filled with an unspoken concern, "What troubles you, Cole?"

The question had disarmed him. He had always been open with Tala about his life. But this... this was different. This was the dark underbelly, the shadowed corners of his soul he'd kept hidden, even from himself. The journal was a chronicle of his younger years, a testament to youthful recklessness and the mistakes that still haunted him.

He had been a different man then, fueled by a restless spirit and a thirst for freedom that bordered on rebellion. Eager to escape the life laid out for him, he'd run away from the stifling expectations of his wealthy ranching family in eastern Texas. He craved the West's untamed wildness, the open range's freedom. The journal recounted the thrill of his first cattle drive, the camaraderie of fellow cowboys, the beauty of the vast landscapes, and the harsh realities of frontier life. But within these vibrant.

descriptions lay a darker thread, a self-destructive streak that had cost him everything.

He'd been impetuous, quick to anger, prone to reckless decisions fueled by alcohol and a desperate need to prove himself. He'd gotten into brawls, lost his life in a confrontation with a band of outlaws, and made choices he regretted. One entry recounted a harrowing experience, a night of heavy drinking that led to a disastrous confrontation with some local ranchers who held prejudiced views against his family. The details were fuzzy now, lost in the mists of time and alcohol, but the shame and the lingering self-reproach were ever-present. He'd almost killed a man that night, a man who'd been nothing but belligerent and hateful, fueled by racism and blind hatred towards those who didn't fit his narrow view of the world. His stomach clenched at the memory;

Documented in the journal was his gradual awakening, a slow but steady process of self-reflection. Recognizing the flaws in his behavior, he saw the destructive path he was following. He questioned his prejudices, noticing the similarities between his past actions and the attitudes of those he had despised. He realized his actions had consequences for both himself and others. It was a painful journey, a struggle against the ingrained attitudes and behaviors he had learned in his youth.

The most significant catalyst for change, he realized, was his encounter with a band of Lipan Indian Apache. He'd stumbled upon their camp while lost and injured during a fierce storm. They'd taken him in, nursed him back to health, and treated him with kindness and respect he'd never experienced before. Their generosity and strength humbled him, starkly contrasting the prejudices and hatred he'd encountered in his earlier years. The experience had been transformative, shattering his preconceived notions and forcing him to confront his biases.

This encounter was a turning point, the beginning of his journey towards understanding and respect for other cultures. His journal entries detailing this experience expressed a sense of wonder, a gradual realization of his ignorance, and the richness of the Lipan Indian culture. He learned their language, customs, and history, seeing humanity beneath the stereotypes and misconceptions that often clouded his understanding of them. He'd documented their resilience in the face of adversity, their deep-rooted kinship to the land, and their rich traditions, recognizing their value.

Never had he told Tala about this experience, fearing it revealed the depth of his past transgressions. He'd feared judgment, a fear rooted in his self-doubt and guilt. He'd worried that the darker aspects of his past would overshadow the man he was now, the man he'd become through his relationship with her and his interactions with the Lipan Indian community.

But seeing Tala's gentle concern and unwavering support, he felt the weight of his unspoken burden ease. He knew she wouldn't judge him like the others had. She had seen his vulnerability, his capacity for both good and bad, and his transformation from a restless youth to a responsible man.

Closing the journal, he felt the worn leather cool against his fingertips.

He needed to tell her, to share the truth of his past, not just the sanitized version he'd presented. Perhaps by sharing, he could lay the ghosts of his past to rest and embrace the future he had built with Tala. The city lights twinkled in the distance, a beacon of hope in the gathering darkness. He would tell her everything. The truth, however painful, would set him free. He would face his past, not with shame, but with acceptance. With the unwavering support of the woman who had shown him the true meaning of love and redemption, he would confront the shadow of his past and embrace the light of his future.

Chapter 22: Talas Family History

The fire crackled, casting dancing shadows on the faces gathered in Tala's family's kiva. The air hung thick with the scent of woodsmoke and roasting venison, a familiar comfort in the cool night air. Cole sat beside Tala, his hand resting on hers, the warmth a grounding presence amidst the unfolding narrative. He had confessed his past, the turbulent journey from reckless youth to a man striving for redemption, and the weight on his chest had lessened. Now, Tala's turn promised to unravel yet another layer of the intricate tapestry of her life.

Tala's voice, vibrant and melodious, held a quiet reverence as she began her story. She spoke of her grandmother, Nana Chavela, a woman whose strength and wisdom had shaped Tala's understanding of their Lipan Indian heritage. Nana Chavela, Tala explained, had lived through the tumultuous changes that swept through their people, including the forced removals, broken treaties, and the constant struggle for survival in the face of encroaching white settlement. She had witnessed firsthand the devastating impact of westward expansion, as well as the relentless pressure to assimilate and abandon their traditions to embrace a foreign way of life.

"She told stories," Tala said, her eyes distant, remembering. "Stories of our ancestors, fierce warriors and healers, who roamed these lands long before the first white men arrived. Stories of cunning strategists who outsmarted their enemies, brave women who protected their families, and the deep spiritual rooted kinship our people held with this land. This rooted kinship ran deeper than blood itself."

Cole listened, captivated by the cadence of her words, the passion simmering beneath her calm exterior. He saw a strength in her, a resilience forged in the fires of her ancestors' struggles, a strength that mirrored the indomitable spirit of the Lipan Indian people. He had witnessed this resilience firsthand in the community, in how they had preserved their culture and traditions despite facing immense adversity.

Nana Chavela's stories, Tala continued, were not just tales of the

Past, but lessons for the future. They were a testament to the importance of preserving their cultural identity, honoring their heritage, and remembering the sacrifices made by previous generations. These stories had instilled in Tala a profound sense of responsibility, a deep commitment to her people and their traditions. They were the foundation upon which her identity rested, the source of her strength and determination.

Tala recounted her family's struggles, not only with external forces but also the internal conflicts that arose as the Lipan Indian people navigated the changing landscape. Some sought to assimilate, believing that embracing the ways of the white man was the only path to survival. Some clung fiercely to their traditions, determined to preserve their heritage at all costs. These internal tensions, Tala explained, were as challenging as the external pressures they faced, testing the strength and unity of their community.

She spoke of her father, a man torn between two worlds who struggled to reconcile his Lipan Indian heritage with the demands of a transforming society. He had witnessed the slow erosion of their way of life, losing their ancestral lands, and the dwindling numbers of their people. He had striven to provide for his family while trying to hold on to the traditions that defined them, an almost impossible task in the face of relentless pressure.

Tala explained that her father's struggle had affected her own life. She had seen firsthand the pain and frustration he experienced and the internal conflict that ravaged him. Yet, she had also witnessed his unwavering love for his family and his fierce determination to protect his children from the harsh realities of their circumstances. He had instilled in her a deep respect for their history, a deep understanding of their culture, and a fierce pride in her Lipan Indian heritage.

The narrative shifted, transitioning from the broader sweep of her family history to more personal recollections. She spoke of her childhood, the games she played with her siblings, and the stories her mother would tell her as she tucked her into bed at night. These were stories of bravery, resilience, and the deep spiritual rooted kinship with the Lipan Indian people held with the land. They were stories that filled her with a sense of belonging, a sense of pride, a sense of her place within the larger narrative of her people's history. These stories had provided her with a strong sense of identity, a foundation upon which she had built her life.

She shared her experiences growing up in a world that often lacked acceptance and understanding. She encountered prejudice, misunderstanding, and the painful realization that those outside her did not always value her culture community. Despite these challenges—emotional, political, and generational — she remained steadfast in her commitment to her heritage and her people. The stories she had listened to since childhood had only strengthened her resolve.

Cole listened, mesmerized by the unfolding narrative. Her strength of character, commitment to her heritage, and unwavering cultural pride were all clear to him. He understood now the roots of her quiet dignity, the fierce independence that characterized her spirit. He saw the echoes of her ancestors in her eyes, the echoes of their resilience and strength.

Tala's story also illuminated the intricate web of relationships within her family. The deep thread of trusts of loyalty and love amongst her siblings, and the unwavering support they showed each other during adversity, were subjects she discussed. She spoke of the complex dynamics between different generations, of the challenges—emotional, political, and generational that arose as older traditions clashed with the changing realities of their lives. She said of the unspoken tensions, the occasional disagreements, the quiet acts of love and support that held their community together. There were moments of laughter, lightheartedness, and joy peppered within the seriousness, providing a fuller picture of family life within the context of their culture.

Her story was a testament to the enduring strength of the human spirit, a powerful narrative of perseverance and pride. It resonated with Cole, who had also undergone his journey of self-discovery and redemption. He saw in Tala's story a reflection of his struggles and his journey toward self-acceptance.

As Tala's story concluded, a silence fell over the kiva, filled with the weight of history, the echoes of past struggles, and the quiet determination to keep the flame of their culture alive. As the fire crackled warmly on their faces, Cole held her hand. The shadows of their pasts, once daunting specters, now seemed less formidable, illuminated by the shared light of their love and understanding.

Chapter 23: Resurfacing Conflicts

The embers glowed, casting a warm, orange light on the faces of Cole and Tala as they sat in comfortable silence, the aftermath of her story settling around them like a fine dust. The quietude, however, was deceptive. Once thick with the aroma of woodsmoke and venison, the air now carried a subtle undercurrent of tension, a silent tremor beneath the surface of their newfound peace. Earlier hints of the past cast a long shadow over their present, threatening the fragile harmony they had built.

Harsh realities of their shared existence arrived with the next morning. The usual jovial greetings from Tala's family felt strained, replaced by a hesitant politeness. Whispers followed them like shadows, fragments of hushed conversations drifting on the morning breeze, audible yet unsettling. Ever attuned to the nuances of body language and unspoken communication, Cole sensed a shift in the atmosphere, detecting a deep unease beneath the surface of their daily routines. The uninhibited laughter and camaraderie that had filled the kiva had faded, replaced by a palpable tension.

It was old Man Chacon, Tala's uncle, a man weathered by years of hardship and etched with the wisdom—and bitterness—of generations past, who broke the silence. He approached Cole, his gaze unwavering, his expression a mixture of suspicion and resentment. He spoke in heavily accented Spanish, his words slow and deliberate, each syllable carrying the weight of a long-held grievance.

"I haven't forgotten your kindness, Cole," he began, his voice raspy with age, "But kindness cannot erase the past. The scars remain, deep and painful."

Cole listened, his hands resting at his sides, understanding dawning in his eyes. Chacon's words weren't a personal attack, but a reflection of the deeper, long-simmering conflicts within the Lipan Indian community, conflicts that Cole's presence had stirred. These were not personal disagreements, but generational wounds — old hurts that had festered and grown over time, fueled by historical injustices and the lingering bitterness of betrayal.

Chacon spoke of broken treaties, of stolen lands, of the forced assimilation that had ripped apart the fabric of their culture and heritage. He spoke of the injustices suffered at the hands of the white man, a broad stroke that painted Cole, despite his good intentions, with the same brush. He spoke of the rangers, the cavalry, and the countless acts of violence and oppression that had decimated their people. His words were a torrent of suppressed anger and grief, a raw outpouring of years of pain and frustration.

Cole listened without interruption, offering no excuses, no justifications. He understood the weight of history and the immense suffering endured by the Lipan Indian people. He had witnessed firsthand their resilience and tenacity in the face of overwhelming odds. But understanding did not erase the hurt and deep-seated resentment passed down through generations.

"My family... we have suffered," Chacon continued, his voice cracking. "And some...they still believe that peace with the whites is impossible. They see only betrayal."

Chacon's words revealed a rift within the Lipan Indian community, a division simmering beneath the surface, waiting for the right spark to ignite. Cole's presence, his unexpected thread of trust with Tala, had become that spark. His arrival had stirred up long-buried resentments, dredging up painful memories and forcing the Lipan Indian people to confront uncomfortable truths about their past and their future.

Cole spent the next few days trying to understand the complexities of the situation. Reaching out to others in the community, he engaged them in conversations to bridge the gap between differing perspectives. He listened to their stories, their fears, and their hopes. He learned about the different factions within the community, the differing views on the best way to navigate their future, and the tension between those who sought accommodation and those who remained fiercely resistant to assimilation.

Chacon found others shared his concerns. Many within the community harbored deep distrust towards outsiders, those associated with the U.S. Cavalry and the Texas Rangers. The scars of past conflicts ran deep, leaving behind a living memory of suspicion and fear. The presence of Cole, despite his declared intentions, brought a resurgence of these old anxieties, casting a shadow over his budding relationship with Tala.

As days passed, Cole realized the conflict ran deep, rooted not in land or resources but in history and culture. Every encounter, every word, revealed how far the divide between his world and Tala's truly reached.

Adding to the already difficult situation, U.S. Cavalry soldiers arrived, their presence a stark reminder of the ever-present threat of conflict and the uneasy truce between the Lipan Apache and the American government. The soldiers were there to protect the settlers and enforce the law, but their presence heightened tensions within the community. The whispers intensified, the unease deepened, and the shadows of the past loomed larger than ever.

Cole found himself caught in the middle, his love for Tala pitted against the deep-seated distrust of his people in her community. He was an outsider, a trespasser in a world he was only beginning to understand, a world with its history of pain, violence, and betrayal. His initial naïve optimism waned as he faced the stark reality of the situation, the weight of history bearing down on him.

He spent hours talking with Tala, explaining his position and seeking her understanding and counsel. Tala, with her deep knowledge of her people and their history, helped him navigate the treacherous terrain of these ancient wounds. She explained the generational trauma that had shaped the perspectives of her people and the distrust that ran deep into their hearts.

She admitted that even within her family, disagreements existed.

Some favored cautious integration into the broader American society, while others, like her uncle Chacon, held to their traditional ways. This internal struggle mirrored the broader conflict between assimilation and cultural preservation.

Tala hoped for a future where both cultures could coexist, acknowledging the past but refusing to let it control the present. She believed in the potential for a unique relationship, one built on mutual respect and understanding rather than domination and conquest. This belief offered Cole a fragile yet powerful beacon of hope in the increasingly turbulent waters of their shared situation.

The conflict deepened as rumors of renewed land disputes and threats from neighboring communities circulated. Both external forces and internal divisions threatened the precarious peace, creating a climate of uncertainty and fear.

Chapter 24: Confronting Ghosts

The following days were a blur of hushed conversations, furtive glances, and the ever-present weight of unspoken anxieties. Cole, seeking to understand the depth of the resentment, spent hours listening to the stories of the Lipan Indian elders. He heard tales of forced removals, broken promises, and the systematic dismantling of their way of life. He discovered their vibrant culture, a culture rich in tradition, spirituality, and a profound, rooted kinship to the land that forces had suppressed. Each story was a testament to their resilience, their unwavering spirit in the face of unimaginable hardship. Yet, each story also served as a stark reminder of the deep wounds that still festered, wounds that his presence, however unintentional, had reopened.

One evening, under the vast expanse of the Texas sky, speckled with a million stars, Cole and Tala sat by a crackling fire. The flames danced, their light reflecting in Tala's dark eyes, mirroring the turmoil within her heart. She spoke of her grandmother, a woman who had witnessed firsthand the brutal displacement of her people, the forced march from their ancestral lands, losing loved ones, and the slow, agonizing erosion of their culture. The pain in Tala's voice was palpable, raw, and unfiltered. It was a pain that transcended generations, a living memory of sorrow passed down through whispered stories and shared memories.

Cole listened, his heart aching with empathy. He understood the weight of her words, the deep-seated trauma that shaped her worldview. He had witnessed the scars of history etched onto the faces of the Lipan Indian people, a silent testimony to their enduring struggle for survival. But hearing it from Tala, seeing the pain etched in her own eyes, broke through the veil of his relative ignorance. He wasn't just dealing with abstract historical events; he was confronting the very real and present consequences of a brutal past.

"There's more to it than just the land," Tala said emotionally. We're losing our identity, our traditions are fading, and our spirit is being crushed.

Cole reached out, taking her hand. His touch was gentle, reassuring. He had come to Texas seeking adventure, seeking fortune. Still, he had found something far more profound–a love that transcended cultural differences and demanded understanding, empathy, and a willingness to confront the darkest chapters of history. Their love story was not a fairytale; it was a gritty, complex narrative woven into the very fabric of the land — a narrative that demanded both courage and compassion.

Cole gained a new understanding thanks to Tala's words. He engaged their relationship with innocent optimism, oblivious to the community's underlying mistrust and resentment. Despite his pure intentions, he understood they weren't enough. Mere good intentions and simple acts of kindness weren't enough for him. Active engagement with their history, acknowledgment of past injustices, and genuine remorse for ancestral wrongs were necessary for him.

He admitted his inner turmoil, the guilt over his role in a culture that caused immense suffering. He understood his family had also been involved in the historical injustices. This wasn't a confession of blame or self-reproach, but a recognition of mutual accountability and the necessity for communal recovery.

In sharing their vulnerability, Cole and Tala found a deeper rooted kinship — a thread of trust forged not just in romance, but in mutual understanding and a shared commitment to facing the harsh realities of their past. They spent the next few nights poring over old documents, maps, and chronicles, piecing together the fragmented history of the Lipan Indian people, their struggles, and their resilience. The more they learned, the more Cole understood the complexities of the situation, the intricate web of grievances, betrayals, and broken promises. He understood why mistrust ran so deep, why the shadows of the past held such a powerful grip on the present.

Their journey of understanding wasn't solely an intellectual exercise. It became a journey of self-discovery, an exploration of their identities and their relationship with the land, its history, and its people. Cole, a man who had always cherished the freedom of the open range, found himself drawn to the Lipan Indians' deep-rooted kinship to their ancestral lands. He found kinship with their reverence for the earth, respect for nature's rhythms, and a profound spiritual rooted kinship to the land.

The relationship deepened, but not without its share of conflict. There were moments of frustration and doubt, times when the weight of history overwhelmed them. But each time, they found their way back to each other, their love serving as a beacon of hope, guiding them through the treacherous terrain of their past traumas.

Cole worked to bridge the gap between the Lipan Indian community and the wider world. He became a mediator, seeking common ground between the Lipan Indian elders, the U.S. government representatives, and the Texas Rangers. It was a hard task, fraught with peril, demanding immense patience and diplomatic skills. He had to navigate a web of conflicting interests, competing loyalties, and deep-seated prejudices. He sought to explain the Lipan Indian perspective, translating their needs and desires to those who remained deaf to their pleas.

The process was slow, fraught with setbacks, and often frustrating. But Cole remained steadfast in his commitment, fueled by his love for Tala and his growing appreciation for the Lipan Indian people's rich culture and heritage. Tala guided and translated for him, interpreting the complexities of Lipan Indian customs and traditions, and explaining nuances that would otherwise have been missed.

A glimmer of hope emerged. Cole's efforts and Tala's persistent diplomacy bore fruit. The initial distrust faded slowly, giving way to cautious optimism. Although the deep-seated wounds of the past remained, they built a tentative bridge, creating space for dialogue and mutual respect to grow.

Cole and Tala had found a strength in each other, a shared resilience born from facing their individual and collective traumas. Their love story, set against the backdrop of the untamed Texas frontier, was becoming a testament to the power of compassion, understanding, and the human spirit's enduring strength. The path ahead remained uncertain, but they were walking it together, hand in hand, facing the ghosts of the past with newfound courage and hope for a future built on mutual respect and understanding.

Chapter 25: Forging a Stronger Union

The following weeks were a crucible, testing the strength of their burgeoning love. The whispers of disapproval within the Lipan Indian community, though quieter, still lingered like the scent of wood smoke on a still morning. Ever the pragmatist, Cole understood the need for tangible progress, not just heartfelt gestures. He began actively taking part in the daily life of the Lipan Indian people, learning their customs, sharing in their work, and offering his skills where possible. He helped repair fences, assisted with herding, and even learned to craft some of their traditional tools; his clumsy attempts met with amused tolerance and quiet encouragement from Tala's family.

This immersion wasn't a romantic gesture, but a deliberate act of integration. Instead of merely stating his respect, he sought to show it, securing his place within the community. He came to admire their horsemanship's intricate details, their graceful movement through the landscape, and their deep rooted kinship to nature. He came to respect their traditions, spirituality, and profound rooted kinship to the land deeply.

However, some people resisted his efforts. There were those among the Lipan Indians who remained suspicious, their mistrust rooted in centuries of betrayal and broken promises. These individuals viewed Cole's actions with a cynical eye, seeing them as a calculated move, a tactic to gain their favor rather than a genuine expression of respect. Tala withstood this resistance, caught between her love for Cole and her loyalty towards her people. The conflict weighed heavily upon her, creating a chasm between her heart and her community.

One evening, under the mournful gaze of a blood-red sunset, Tala confronted Cole. Pain and frustration laced her words. "They don't trust you, Cole," she said, her voice low and strained. "They see you as another outsider, another representative of the world that has tried to destroy us." Cole listened intently, his heart heavy with understanding. He knew he couldn't force their acceptance; he could only earn it through persistent effort and unwavering respect.

His voice was calm but resolute, he stated, "I understand." "I know I haven't earned their trust, but I will work for it. I won't give up on them, and I won't give up on us." He didn't just offer empty platitudes;

Their relationship became a beacon of hope amidst the lingering shadows of the past. They navigated the complexities of their love with remarkable grace, their commitment deepening with each challenge they faced. Their story, woven into the harsh Texas landscape, was a testament to the resilience of the human spirit and the enduring power of love. Yet, even as their thread of trust strengthened, the external pressures intensified. The tension between the Lipan Indians and the encroaching forces of westward expansion continued to simmer, threatening to boil over at any moment.

One day, news arrived of a planned land grab by a powerful cattle baron, a ruthless business owner who cared little for the rights or the traditions of the Lipan Indians. He sought to claim a significant portion of their ancestral lands, driving them further from their homes and erasing their culture. The threat hung heavy over the community, a palpable fear spreading like wildfire.

Cole witnessed Tala's despair and her community's fear. He leveraged his influence, network, and expertise to address the situation. His understanding of both cultures and the legal system helped him win over sympathetic ranchers and government officials, allowing successful maneuvering of the complex political landscape. Using evidence, testimonials, and historical documents, he argued in defense of the Lipan Indians' ancestral land claim. Powerful forces opposed him, resorting to threats and intimidation, making his endeavors perilous.

This fight relied heavily on Tala and the Lipan Indian elders. Acting as a bridge between Cole and her community, she translated, interpreted, and guided his work. With fierce dignity and unwavering resolve, she powerfully voiced her people's concerns and demands. Her help allowed Cole to better grasp Lipan Indian law and custom, resulting in a more interesting and sensitive case presentation.

The fight was long and arduous, filled with setbacks and disappointments. There were moments of profound despair when Cole and Tala questioned whether they could achieve anything positive. But their love, shared commitment, and unwavering faith in justice sustained them. They worked side by side, their thread of trust deepening with each challenge they faced.

The climax arrived during a tense hearing before a federal judge. Cole, speaking with a mixture of passion and legal precision, presented the Lipan Indian's case. His words resonated with the truth of their history, the injustice of their dispossession, and the strength of their spirit. Tala, testifying in her native tongue with Cole providing a simultaneous translation, recounted stories of generations past, tales of resilience, resistance, and an unwavering rooted kinship to the land. Her testimony was a powerful testament to the Lipan Indian's enduring culture and their right to self-determination.

The evidence presented moved the judge, known for his impartiality,. His decision was a landmark victory for the Lipan Indians, granting them legal protection of their ancestral lands and recognition of their sovereignty. The victory wasn't complete; the fight for justice would continue. However, it was a significant turning point, a testament to the power of collaboration, perseverance, and the strength of love that transcends cultural differences.

After the victory, Cole and Tala's love deepened into a profound and enduring thread of trust. They had faced the shadows of the past, battled powerful forces, and emerged stronger, their union forged in the fires of adversity. Their love story, set against the backdrop of the untamed Texas frontier, became a legend, a tale of courage, compassion, and the enduring power of the human spirit to overcome even the darkest chapters of history. Their victory was not only a legal triumph but also a personal one, a testament to the transformative power of love, understanding, and unwavering commitment to justice.

The future remained uncertain, but they faced it together, hand in hand, ready to embrace whatever challenges lay ahead. Their story became a symbol of hope, not just for the Lipan Indian people but for all those who sought a future built on mutual respect, understanding, and the enduring power of the human spirit. The healing was far from over, but they had forged a path towards a brighter future, together.

Chapter 26: Ominous Signs

The late-summer sun beat down on the parched earth, baking the land and mirroring the rising tensions within the Lipan Indian community. Even the vibrant landscape seemed to wilt under the oppressive atmosphere, the vibrant green of the mesquite bushes fading to a dusty brown. The air, thick with the scent of dry grass and impending rain, crackled with an unspoken anxiety. Whispers, once hushed and confined to the shadows of the wickiups, now carried on the wind, spreading a sense of foreboding throughout the settlement.

Old Man Coyote, the Lipan Indian shaman, his face etched with the wisdom and weariness of many years, seemed to sense the shift in the balance of nature, the subtle tremor that foretold the coming storm. He dedicated unusual time to observing the stars, birds, and clouds, seeking meaning in their movements. His pronouncements, cryptic and open to interpretation, became increasingly dire, hinting at a coming darkness that would test the very heart of the Lipan Indian nation.

One evening, as the sun dipped below the horizon, painting the sky in hues of blood orange and bruised purple, a raven landed on the branch of a withered mesquite tree outside Coyote's wickiup. The bird, a symbol of ill omen in Lipan Indian lore, remained perched there for a long time, its harsh caw echoing through the darkening landscape.

The villagers exchanged uneasy glances, their faces reflecting the unease that settled upon them like a shroud. Stoic and resolute, Tala felt a chill run down her spine.

The rumors, once faint whispers, now grew louder and more menacing. Stories of escalating violence between settlers and other tribes circulated, fueled by exaggerated accounts and simmering prejudice. Tales of cattle rustling, land disputes, and retaliatory raids painted a grim picture of a region teetering on the brink of all-out war. The news spread like wildfire, reaching even the most remote corners of the Lipan Indian territory, stoking fear and resentment.

Cole, ever vigilant, noticed the change in the mood of the Lipan Indian people. Gone was the cheerful noise; tense silence, only occasionally broken by nervous whispers, reigned instead. He noticed Tala's worry; dark circles shadowed her eyes. He knew that their victory in protecting their ancestral lands had postponed the inevitable conflict, that the fragile peace was a reprieve.

The weather, too, seemed to reflect the growing tension. Unseasonal storms raged across the plains, unleashing torrential downpours that transformed the arid landscape into a muddy wasteland. Flash floods swept through the canyons, washing away trails and damaging crops. Dark, brooding clouds, their ominous presence a constant reminder of the impending storm obscured the sky, often clear and bright.

Placid and accustomed to the harsh landscape, the animals seemed agitated. The horses whinnied, their coats bristling with apprehension. The cattle stampeded at the slightest provocation, their panicked bellows adding to the unsettling symphony of the changing times. Coyotes howled at the moon with a ferocity that sent shivers down the spines of the bravest warriors, their cries echoing the rising tensions within the community.

Something disrupted the Lipan Indian camp's once peaceful routine. For hours, the elders debated strategies, analyzed ominous signs, and prepared for the worst in hushed council. The warriors sharpened their spears and honed their tomahawks, their movements sharp and precise, fueled by a grim determination. The women gathered supplies, storing food and water, readying themselves for whatever challenges—emotional, political, and generational lay ahead.

Though apprehensive, Cole tried to stay calm and reassuring. Working with the Lipan Indians, he helped them carry their loads and offered his expertise. Displaying fear, he realized, would exacerbate the community's pre-existing anxieties. He reinforced the settlement's protective palisade against attack. He instructed the Lipan Apache warriors to use modern weaponry, sharing his expertise in firearms and tactics.

Despite their efforts, a deep sense of unease lingered in the air. The ominous signs were undeniable, the whispers of war too loud to ignore. The approaching conflict was not a clash of cultures or a land dispute; it was a fight for survival, a struggle for the soul of the Lipan Indian nation. The future remained uncertain, shrouded in the shadows of an approaching storm. Cole, alongside Tala and the rest of the Lipan Indian people, braced themselves, preparing to face the tempest that threatened to engulf them.

One night, a lone scout returned to the camp, pale and drawn. He bore news that sent a wave of icy dread through the hearts of the Lipan Indian people. A large contingent of Texas Rangers, augmented by a detachment of U.S. Cavalry, was marching towards their settlement. Land-grab rumors weren't mere whispers;

The news destroyed the already delicate peace. A palpable tension electrified the camp's atmosphere. War's quiet whispers escalated into a thunderous roar, replacing quiet dread with grim determination. An emergency council convened, bringing together Cole, Tala, and other Lipan Indian leaders. With an attack about to happen, they didn't have enough time to prepare;

The options were stark: surrender and face the consequences of displacement and cultural annihilation, or fight back and risk a devastating conflict. The decision weighed heavily upon their shoulders, a burden that threatened to crush them under its weight. Yet, despite the overwhelming odds, a fierce spirit of resistance ignited within them. The tough times molded the Lipan Indians, who resolved to resist without giving up.

As the first rays of dawn illuminated the eastern horizon, the Lipan Indian prepared for war. The ominous signs, whispers, rumors, and impending storm had all coalesced into a single, terrifying reality. The fight for their survival, culture, and very existence had begun. A resolute clang, drumbeat, and collective resolve shattered the morning's quiet, a people fighting for survival. The once vibrant and alive land now seemed to hold its breath, waiting to witness the clash that would determine the fate of the Lipan Indian nation and the future of their ancestral lands. The whispers of war had become a deafening roar, and the Lipan Indians were ready to answer the call.

Chapter 27: Political Intrigue

Colonel Beaumont's arrival — a stern-faced man with eyes that missed nothing — shifted the dynamics of the conflict beyond a simple land dispute. His arrival with a contingent of U.S. Cavalry, to "maintain order," was a veiled threat. Beaumont, a man whispered to be embroiled in land speculation schemes involving influential figures in Austin and Fort Worth, wasn't interested in peaceful resolutions. He sought to gain the Lipan Indian lands, a vast expanse rich in grazing land and rumored to hold valuable mineral deposits.

His arrival brought with him Captain Sterling, a younger, more ambitious officer whose loyalty seemed less to Beaumont and more to his burgeoning political ambitions. Sterling saw in the situation an opportunity to advance his career by showcasing his ruthlessness in subduing the "hostile" Lipan Indian. His charm, a deceptive veneer masking his ambition, allowed him to infiltrate the social circles of the burgeoning cattle barons in Fort Worth, gathering support for Beaumont's land grab under the guise of "civilizing" the frontier.

Meanwhile, whispers of a different kind circulated within the Texas Rangers, a force charged with maintaining law and order, but often used as a tool for furthering the interests of wealthy landowners. Ranger Captain Silas Gage, a grizzled veteran known for his integrity and fairness, suspected Beaumont's true intentions. Gage, conflicted by the brutal realities of westward expansion, understood the Lipan Indian's right to their land, and felt a growing unease about the machinations surrounding Beaumont's "peacekeeping" mission. He was at odds with his superiors, who were in Beaumont's pocket.

The political intrigue extended beyond the immediate players. In Fort Worth, powerful cattle barons, eager to expand their ranches, funded

Beaumont's operations, offering logistical support and turning a blind eye to the unethical methods he employed. They viewed the Lipan Indian lands as a barrier to their financial ambitions and were willing to ignore the moral consequences of displacing the native population.

During his time with the Lipan, Cole observed delicate changes in power. The subtle nods, exchanged glances, veiled threats, and crafted lies didn't escape his notice. Beaumont's representatives met with and manipulated more compliant Lipan Indians, using gifts and promises of safety to exploit divisions within the tribe, all witnessed by him. The approaching conflict, he knew, extended beyond the battlefield, encompassing a clandestine war waged through rhetoric and manipulation.

Tala, wise beyond her years, recognized the threat of Beaumont's sophisticated political maneuvering. She saw the Colonel wasn't just interested in land; he aimed to erase the Lipan Indian culture, to replace their rich history with a narrative of progress and 'civilization' that erased the Lipan Indian's rightful claim to the land. She understood the subtle art of political negotiation, inherited from generations of Lipan Indian leaders who had navigated the treacherous landscape of power dynamics.

Tala, along with the Lipan Indian elders, used their understanding of politics to counter Beaumont's strategy. Tala and the Lipan elders identified potential allies, such as Captain Gage, among the Texas Rangers who had not succumbed entirely to the greed and ambition of the dominant power structure. They relied on their established network of informants, using their intimate knowledge of the land and its people to gather information and uncover the truth behind Beaumont's façade.

The information they gathered was crucial. They discovered evidence of Beaumont's land speculation dealings, his rooted kinships with corrupt officials in Austin, and the financial backing he received from the cattle barons. They discovered that someone had fabricated the official documentation proving Lipan Indian land ownership, forging it to exploit a legal loophole.

Armed with this knowledge, the Lipan Indians and their newfound allies within the Rangers devised a strategy. Their plan was to expose Beaumont's scheme to the public and influential government figures susceptible to evidence of corruption. They planned to use the media—the fledgling newspapers of Fort Worth and beyond—to expose Beaumont's misdeeds, hoping to ignite public outrage and mobilize support for the Lipan Indians' cause.

Aware that revealing Beaumont's deceptions might prove insufficient, the Lipan Indians made ready for war. Demonstrating their commitment and capacity to protect their ancestral lands was necessary for them. They bolstered their defenses, gathered supplies, and honed their skills. Political maneuvering, strategic alliances, and military preparedness were all crucial to their survival.

The ensuing weeks were a whirlwind of clandestine meetings, whispered conversations, and orchestrated events. Cole and Tala played a critical role in this intricate political chess game, using their skills and knowledge to navigate the treacherous terrain of power struggles. They were no longer fighting for their land; they were fighting for their very existence, against a well-funded and connected enemy who aimed to erase them from history.

Their shared hardship strengthened their thread of trust, making it unbreakable. Their romance, set against political machinations, represented defiance, showcasing humanity's strength and resilience despite impossible challenges—emotional, political, and generational. What began as subtle threats of war had escalated into a multifaceted political struggle, a conflict fought on many fronts, and the Lipan Indian nation's future was uncertain. Though the future was unclear, their resolve shone like a beacon of hope amidst the growing darkness.

The political battle reached its peak. The conflict was multifaceted and complex; weapons included not just spears and rifles, but also words, influence, and strategically placed information meant to reveal the hypocrisy and greed of their opponents.

The fight for survival, culture, and identity extended beyond the physical realm into the tangled web of political power and influence. And in the heart of this struggle, Cole and Tala stood, ready to face whatever came next.

Chapter 28: Preparing for Conflict

The air crackled with anticipation, a palpable tension hanging heavy over the Lipan Indian village. A once faint murmuring of war became a deafening roar, echoing universally. Cole, his usual effortless charm tempered by a grim determination, moved among the people, his presence a reassuring anchor in the storm gathering on the horizon. He wasn't just a trail boss anymore; he was a leader and protector, his every action scrutinized, and his every word weighed with significance.

Tala worked tirelessly alongside him, her bright eyes shadowed with concern but resolute in their purpose. She moved with a quiet grace, a natural leader who inspired unwavering loyalty. She spoke with the elders, her voice carrying the weight of generations of Lipan Indian wisdom and resilience, outlining strategies and assigning tasks to them. The preparations were not solely military; they were a testament to the Lipan Indians' deep-rooted community spirit and their capacity for unity in the face of adversity.

Feverish activity and purposeful movement filled the days. Warriors honed their skills, their movements precise and deadly, each blow carrying the weight of generations of ancestral knowledge. The rhythmic thud of tomahawks against sharpened stakes filled the air, punctuated by the occasional sharp cry of practiced combat. Women gathered supplies, their hands moving as they stored dried meats, berries, and other essential provisions. Instructors taught children too young to fight for survival skills, including identifying edible plants, building fires, and remaining silent when facing danger. Even older adults, frail but unwavering in their support, played their part, sharing stories of past battles, weaving tales of resilience and strength to inspire the younger generation.

Understanding the importance of strategic defense, Cole oversaw the strengthening of the village's fortifications. Cole reinforced the existing palisades and brought fresh logs from the surrounding forest to raise the walls. Hidden trenches were dug, camouflaged with brush and earth, creating a network of defenses that allowed for ambush and retreat. He collaborated with the Lipan Indian warriors, integrating their knowledge of the terrain and their unique fighting style into the defense strategy. The goal: not repelling attack, but making invasion prohibitively expensive, forcing Beaumont's reconsideration.

Tala, meanwhile, focused on the political front. She held clandestine meetings with Captain Gage and his trusted lieutenants, sharing the information they had gathered—the forged documents, the evidence of Beaumont's corrupt dealings, the names of the complicit cattle barons. She relied on her network of informants, a web of trusted individuals who provided critical insights into the enemy's movements and plans. Her communications with Gage weren't just about conveying intelligence; they were about building trust and forging a relationship based on mutual respect and shared goals.

It was delicate work, exposing Beaumont's manipulations. It was essential to collect conclusive proof. The fraudulent land deeds represented only one aspect of the puzzle. Tala and Gage worked together to uncover additional evidence—letters, financial records, and testimonies from those intimidated or bribed into silence. The meticulous documentation and preservation of each piece of information stands as proof of the dedication and determination of those striving for justice.

Their success depended on the media's involvement in their strategy. Via trusted contacts, they leaked information in Fort Worth's newspapers. Early reports hinted at unease, focusing on the Cavalry's unsettling presence, land disputes, and the worries of concerned citizens. The aim was to craft a story showing a growing conflict, thus undermining public confidence in Beaumont's peacekeeping assertions.

It was a slow, painstaking process that demanded patience and careful planning. Every article and statement was part of a long-term plan. Lipan Apache warriors aimed to protect their honor and living memory. Their goal was to prevent Beaumont's false narrative from overshadowing their own.

Beyond the fortifications and the political maneuvering, a different preparation was underway. The Lipan Indian community came together, sharing stories, songs, and prayers. These weren't religious rituals but collective remembrance, reaffirmations of identity, and expressions of unwavering hope. Elders passed down ancestral knowledge, ensuring the continuity of their cultural heritage, for they knew that even if they lost their land, their spirit would endure.

The women, the heart of the community, prepared for the long haul. They ensured that there was sufficient food, medicine, and clothing to last through a prolonged conflict. Their hands were busy with tasks that reinforced the community's resilience. Their contributions were not only practical, but also essential to maintaining morale. It was a demonstration of their strength, their commitment to unity, and their unwavering belief in the righteousness of their cause.

As the days turned into weeks, a tangible sense of readiness permeated the Lipan Indian community. This wasn't a matter of military readiness, but a reflection of the community's profound spiritual and cultural strength. Their determination, fueled by a deep love for their land and a shared history, was a formidable weapon, a force that would be impossible to underestimate. Cole and Tala, standing side by side, watched over their people, their hearts heavy with the weight of the impending battle, but their spirits unbroken. Their love story, born amidst the chaos of westward expansion, became a beacon of hope, a symbol of resistance against the forces that threatened to extinguish their culture and existence.

Chapter 29: Gathering Support

The rhythmic thud of tomahawks against sharpened stakes, the women's hushed conversations as they prepared supplies, and the elders' indistinct murmurs of ancient stories faded into the background as Cole sought those who might offer aid beyond the Lipan Indian village. His first stop was the dusty, sunbaked town of Fort Worth. He needed to tread carefully; overt displays of support for the Lipan Indians could be perilous, even dangerous, in a city where Beaumont's influence stretched like a poisonous vine.

His first contact was a gruff, weathered rancher named Silas Blackwood, known for his independence and shrewd business sense. Blackwood, though not sympathetic to the Lipan Indian cause, was distrustful of Beaumont's land-grabbing tactics. He recognized the potential for chaos and instability that Beaumont's actions created, which threatened his livelihood. Over a bottle of whiskey in a lit saloon, Cole laid out the facts—the forged documents, the intimidation tactics, Beaumont's disregard for the law. Blackwood listened intently, his gaze unwavering. He didn't express overt support, but the glint in his eye suggested a simmering resentment towards Beaumont's high-handed methods.

"Beaumont's a snake, Cole," Blackwood conceded, swirling the amber liquid in his glass. "But a powerful one. You will contend with someone highly influential. Confronting him requires more than righteous anger. He paused, his gaze shifting to the dusty window.,"But I wouldn't mind seeing him lose some cattle. Minor range incidents occurred. He offered a grim smile. "Let me say 'Cole,' and my men will be there to 'help' things along."

Cole thanked him, his heart buoyed by this unexpected alliance. Blackwood's support wasn't a public declaration of war, but a substantial first step. He would provide a much-needed distraction, drawing Beaumont's resources and attention away from the Lipan Indian village, creating a crucial window of opportunity.

Next, Cole sought the aid of a different kind–Reverend Elias Thorne, a man of faith known for his quiet courage and unwavering compassion. Thorne, unlike Blackwood, supported the rights of the Lipan Indian, believing that God's grace extended to all people, regardless of their race or tribal affiliation. His church, on the edge of town, offered a space for diverse individuals to meet, a meeting that could help rally support for the Lipan Indian cause.

Ranchers, merchants, and a few sympathetic cavalry members comprised this small but consequential meeting. Cole, speaking with passion and sincerity, articulated the injustice of Beaumont's actions, painting a vivid picture of the looming threat to the Lipan Indian people. He didn't appeal to their greed or self-interest; instead, he spoke of fairness, justice, and the moral obligation to protect the innocent.

Reverend Thorne, his voice resonating with conviction, offered a prayer for the Lipan Indian people and for the strength to prevail against oppression. His words, carried by the quiet reverence of the assembled people, created a powerful sense of solidarity. The meeting yielded pledges of financial aid and material support—food, medicine, clothing, even horses—a testament to the growing awareness and concern regarding Beaumont's actions.

But Cole didn't limit his quest for the support of Fort Worth. He made a secret journey north to a secluded ranch owned by a former cavalry scout named Jedediah Stone. Stone, a veteran of the Indian Wars, was renowned for his expertise in tracking, survival, and unconventional warfare. He was a man of few words, his weathered face a mask of hardened experience, but his reputation preceded him. He was the master of guerrilla tactics, the one who could teach the Lipan Indian warriors how to fight a larger, more heavily armed enemy.

The training was arduous and brutal. Stone didn't coddle the warriors; he pushed them to their limits, honing their stealth, camouflage, and hand-to-hand combat skills. He taught them to use the terrain to their advantage, to exploit the enemy's weaknesses, and to fight with cunning and resilience. Though skeptical of Stone's unorthodox methods, the Lipan Indian warriors quickly recognized his skill and commitment to their cause.

Tala, meanwhile, continued her work on the political front. She had established a network of informants throughout Fort Worth and the surrounding countryside—saloon keepers, stable hands, and even some disgruntled members of Beaumont's crew. These informants provided valuable intelligence, uncovering crucial details about Beaumont's movements, alliances, and plans. She communicated with Captain Gage, providing him with information that helped solidify the case against Beaumont and build public support for the prosecution.

Through Tala's efforts, several anonymous articles began appearing in various newspapers across Texas. These articles detailed Beaumont's land-grabbing tactics, his use of intimidation, and his complicity in corrupt dealings. While never mentioning the Lipan Indians, the articles painted a disturbing picture of the abuse of power, turning public opinion against Beaumont. The subtle allusions to land disputes and the vulnerability of Native American communities evoked sympathy and concern among readers.

The momentum was shifting. Blackwood's covert actions created diversions, Reverend Thorne's support rallied public opinion, and Jedediah Stone's training hardened the Lipan Indian warriors. Tala's political maneuvering and media campaign sowed seeds of doubt about Beaumont, weakening his position and undermining his authority. Cole stood on the precipice of war, armed with courage, skill, and a network of unexpected allies, ready to fight for their shared future. War's murmurs intensified, becoming an undeniable force. And, this time, they would not standalone.

Chapter 30: A Gathering Storm

The wind, a gentle caress across the plains, now carried a sharper edge, whispering secrets of impending conflict. Dust devils, swirling like miniature tornadoes, danced across the parched earth, mirroring the unrest that simmered beneath the surface of Lipan Indian life. Even the sun, a benevolent presence, seemed to cast a harsher, more menacing glow, its rays baking the land in a suffocating heat that mirrored the rising tension.

Cole felt it most acutely. A grim determination had replaced the lightness of his earlier optimism, a resolve that hardened his features and tightened the lines around his eyes. The quiet strength he'd always possessed now shone with a fierce intensity, a reflection of the gravity of the situation. He spent his days overseeing the final preparations, his every move precise, his every order crisp and clear. He trained alongside the Lipan Indian warriors, his skill honed alongside theirs under Jedediah Stone's watchful eye, the metallic tang of sweat and blood mingling with the scent of pine and earth.

The training was relentless. Days bled into nights, punctuated only by brief periods of rest. The warriors, weary from the grueling exercises, found a rhythm, a harmony in their movement, mirroring the unified purpose that had solidified among them. The drills served a purpose beyond practice. Stone, taciturn, spoke volumes through deeds; He taught them combat techniques and the crucial art of strategic thinking, exploiting their environment and the enemy's weaknesses.

Tala, meanwhile, continued her tireless efforts on the political front. Her network of informants grew, her reach extending farther than even Cole had expected. She gathered intelligence with the precision of a seasoned operative, and her insights provided critical information to Captain Gage, working tirelessly within the confines of the law to build a strong case against

Beaumont. Their collaboration was a delicate dance, each aware of the inherent risks yet resolute in their shared purpose.

The information Tala gathered painted a horrifying picture of Beaumont's escalating actions. He was not only seizing land through fraudulent means but also actively suppressing any opposition, resorting to threats, intimidation, and even violence to silence dissent. He was merging power and accumulating resources, leaving no doubt of his intention to claim absolute control over the region. His arrogance was a dangerous cloak, masking a daily cruelty that grew increasingly palpable.

The emotional impact on the Lipan Indian people was profound. Fear was a constant companion, but it was not the dominant emotion. A fierce defiance and burning anger laced their resistance. The elders, steeped in the traditions and wisdom of their ancestors, provided a grounding force, their unwavering faith in their heritage bolstering the spirits of their people. Their stories, passed down through generations, spoke of resilience and survival against insurmountable odds, reinforcing their belief in their ability to weather the storm.

The women, the keepers of the home, the nurturers of their community, became vital players in this impending war. Their roles expanded beyond the traditional; they were now involved in logistical preparations, gathering supplies, tending to the wounded, and serving as communicators, keeping lines of communication open between the various factions fighting for Lipan Indian Creek. Their quiet strength and unwavering support formed a crucial backbone of the resistance. The children, bewildered by the atmosphere of tension, understood the severity of the situation, their innocence tinged with newfound maturity. Once sparkling with carefree joy, their eyes now held a mixture of apprehension and determined resolve, an early display of the strength and resilience that would soon define their generation.

A shift had occurred in the atmosphere of Fort Worth. Instead of its typical lively buzz, the town felt strained and quiet. Usually boisterous, the saloons were unusually quiet, their patrons subdued. An unspoken threat of violence cast a shadow of uncertainty over the future. Distinguishing allies from enemies was difficult; trust was rare, and conversations felt ominous.

Cole's support was becoming genuinely useful. Posing as ranchers, Blackwood's operatives were sabotaging Beaumont's business, creating delays, losses, and widespread disruption. Reverend Thorne's church remained a refuge, giving spiritual comfort and practical aid, a secure place for planning and strategizing. Anonymous newspaper articles, which Tala worked hard to create, damaged Beaumont's carefully constructed image, causing public doubt.

The tension reached its peak. Bright stars offered little comfort against the approaching storm's cold light. On the edge, Cole surveyed the quiet Lipan village, burdened by duty, his eyes mirroring his inner fire.

The once subtle threat of war exploded into a deafening roar, forever altering Lipan Indian Creek and its inhabitants. The battle was imminent.

Chapter 31: The First Shots

The first shot shattered the pre-dawn stillness, a sharp crack that ripped through the deceptive quiet like thunderbolts. It wasn't a warning shot but a declaration of war, a brutal punctuation mark to the mounting tension that had choked the breath from Lipan Indian Creek for weeks. The sound echoed across the valley, bouncing off the mesas and canyons, a stark summons that roused the sleeping village from its uneasy slumber.

Chaos erupted. The tidal wave of gunfire and screams swept away the laid plans, the meticulous preparations, and the hushed whispers of strategy. Cole, jolted awake by the explosion of violence, sprang from his bed, his hand reaching for his Colt Peacemaker. The familiar weight of the weapon offered a small measure of comfort in the swirling maelstrom of terror. He scrambled for his boots; the leather creaking a discordant symphony against the cacophony of the attack.

From his vantage point, he could see the initial assault. Beaumont's men, a ragged band of hired guns and land-grabbers, were pouring into the valley from the north. Their advance was a jagged line of fire, their movements fueled by a brutal efficiency born of malice and greed. They were not fighting fair; this was an ambush, a calculated strike designed to overwhelm the defenders before they could organize.

The Lipan Indian warriors, roused from their sleep, responded with a ferocity that belied their initial surprise. Their arrows, honed to deadly sharpness, rained down upon the attackers, finding their marks with astonishing accuracy. Whistling projectiles, affecting thuds, and guttural battle cries filled the air. Cole could see Tala, a whirlwind of motion, her rifle spitting deadly fire, her movements as fluid and lethal as a striking serpent. Jedediah Stone, a grim figure of unwavering resolve, stood at the forefront of the defense, his weathered face a mask of icy determination, his rifle an extension of his will, relentless in its purpose.

Under the unforgiving gaze of the rising sun, a brutal ballet of death unfolded. The ground quickly became a gruesome tapestry woven from blood and shattered hopes. The scent of gunpowder hung heavy in the air, mingling with the coppery tang of blood and the acrid smell of burning wood as the attackers attempted to set fire to Lipan Indian dwellings.

Cole, amidst the pandemonium, moved with a chilling efficiency. Years spent on the trail sharpened his practiced movements. He directed his men with barked commands, his voice clear and strong above the din, his presence a beacon of calm in the storm's eye. He observed the enemy's tactics, recognizing the calculated cruelty behind their assault. This wasn't a simple land grab; it was a deliberate attempt to annihilate the Lipan Indian people, to erase their culture, their history, their very existence.

Blackwood's men, concealed, now emerged from the shadows, adding a potent element of surprise to the Lipan Indian defense. Their presence disrupted the enemy's lines, creating confusion and diverting their attention. The coordinated strikes of Blackwood's sharpshooters picked off key figures in Beaumont's ranks, disrupting the flow of their attack. The flanking maneuver, executed with precision and timing, was a crucial turning point in the early stages of the fight, pushing back the initial wave of attackers and allowing the Lipan Indian warriors to regroup and solidify their defenses.

Far from passive onlookers, the women of the Lipan Indians played a pivotal role in the conflict. They ferried water and ammunition to the fighters, tended to the wounded, and offered unwavering support. Their courage and dedication were a testament to their strength and resilience, proving their invaluable contribution to the battle. The children, shielded as much as possible, observed the violence with wide, frightened eyes, their innocence tainted by the harsh realities of war.

Combat continued intensely throughout the morning; survival was a constant struggle under Texas' relentless sun. Blood soaked the ground beneath their feet. Seeing the savagery of the attack, Cole felt a surge of righteous fury that fueled his fighting spirit. He moved with a deadly grace, his every shot true, his every move calculated, his determination unshakeable. He battled for Lipan land, Tala, and their future together.

The battle raged; however, the initial advance was beaten back by the Lipan Indians. Beaumont's men, surprised by the strength and tenacity of the Lipan Indian resistance, faltered. Their organized advance had disintegrated into a desperate scramble, their numbers dwindling under the hail of arrows and gunfire. Recognizing the shift in momentum, Cole ordered a counterattack, a coordinated strike aimed at pushing Beaumont's forces back and gaining the upper hand. The Lipan Indian warriors responded with renewed vigor, their fury unleashed, their determination etched upon their faces.

As the sun climbed higher in the sky, casting long shadows across the battlefield, the intensity of the fighting waned.

Beaumont's men, disheartened and depleted, began a disorganized retreat, their initial confidence replaced by a palpable sense of defeat. The victory was hard won, purchased with the blood and sacrifice of many. Despite everything, their courage and unity secured victory for the Lipan people.

Chapter 32: Fighting for Survival

The counterattack, a whirlwind of coordinated fury, pushed Beaumont's remaining forces back towards the northern mesas. Cole, his Colt Peacemaker spitting fire, led the charge, a relentless figure cutting through the chaos. Tala, her movements a blur of grace and deadly precision, fought alongside him, her rifle a constant extension of her fierce spirit. She moved with an almost supernatural agility, weaving through the fray, her keen eyes spotting and neutralizing threats before they could materialize.

All shot was a testament to her skill, each movement a demonstration of her unwavering resolve. Jedediah, a granite wall of steadfast determination, anchored the Lipan Indian defense, his booming voice directing the warriors with an authority that inspired respect and courage. Blackwood's sharpshooters, perched on vantage points, continued their relentless harassment, picking off straggling enemies and disrupting any attempts at regrouping.

The battle raged for hours under the merciless Texas sun. A cacophony of gunfire and screams filled the air, heavy with the smell of gunpowder and sweat. The ground, once fertile and vibrant, was now a gruesome tapestry of blood and shattered dreams. Cole witnessed acts of both unspeakable cruelty and unwavering heroism. He saw Lipan Indian warriors fall, their spirit unyielding even in death, and he felt the chilling pang of loss with each fallen comrade. He saw Beaumont's men, their initial arrogance replaced by a desperate fear, driven by a primal instinct to survive. Endurance tested severely; life's fragility, survival's brutality stark.

Cole's worry for Tala grew amid the chaos. A hail of bullets flew past her, narrowly missing her as she expertly dodged them, even a musket ball that grazed her head. He watched her skillfully care for an injured warrior, her touch both gentle and quick as she stopped the bleeding. Her eyes showed a fierce determination, an unwavering resolve burning within her.

His certainty, surpassing even his fear, told him she was fighting for them, for their survival and future. Initially fragile, their love blossomed into resilience after facing intense challenges—emotional, political, and generational.

The battle reached a fever pitch around midday. Beaumont, witnessing the collapse of his assault and the increasing effectiveness of the Lipan Indian defense, attempted to break through the lines. He led a charge, a desperate gambit fueled by desperation and the knowledge that his failure meant certain death or capture. The ensuing melee was a brutal collision of raw force and desperate courage. Cole found himself in a hand-to-hand struggle with one of Beaumont's lieutenants, a hulking brute his savagery matched whose rage only. The fight was fierce, each blow a testament to their desperation. Cole's years of experience in close-quarters combat served him well, but the lieutenant proved a formidable opponent. With a desperate lunge, Cole disarmed the man, leaving him vulnerable—the defeated lieutenant crumpled to the ground, his struggle for survival over.

Several of Beaumont's men surrounded Tala; meanwhile, her ammunition dwindled. She fought with the ferocity of a cornered animal, her rifle spitting fire, her knife flashing in the sunlight as she repelled their advances. Just as she tired, Jedediah Stone, sensing her predicament, arrived, his rifle barking in support. His timely intervention allowed Tala to break free and regroup, her spirit unbroken.

Long shadows stretched across the battlefield as the sun set, marking a turning point in the battle. A disorderly retreat began as Beaumont's soldiers were exhausted, wounded, and demoralized. As their confidence crumbled and the ranks thinned, their advance halted. Their surprise attack, intended to destroy the Lipan completely, their first plan, had failed. Their retreat, though, continued;

As the enemy lines crumbled, Cole launched a last attack. Encouraged by the approaching... the Lipan Indian warriors... With renewed energy, the team responded to their victory. Arrows pursued the retreating men relentlessly, and rifle fire transformed their retreat into a rout. The critical initial battle of Kickapoo Creek resulted in a decisive victory; however, the larger conflict persisted.

Utterly devastated, the scene lay after the battle. The valley, strewn with the dead and injured, gave a stark impression of the battle's ferocity. Though battered, the Lipan people persevered, tending to the injured and performing burial rites for the fallen. The air was thick with the smell of blood, gunpowder, and death.

Amidst the chaos, Cole and Tala, their bodies aching and clothes torn, found a moment of quiet. They embraced, trembling from exhaustion and the relief of having survived the day. Their victory was bittersweet, hard won, and purchased at a heavy price, but it was still a victory. It reaffirmed their love, shared purpose, and unwavering commitment to each other and the survival of their people.

While they'd initially succeeded at Kickapoo Creek, the battle raged on. Their struggle for survival went on, but as the sun fell, they recovered and plan for what was coming. The persistent sounds of distant gunfire were a constant reminder of their desperate fight for survival, love, and their community's future.

Chapter 33: Unexpected Alliances

The fighting ebbed and flowed, a relentless tide of violence punctuated by moments of terrifying calm. Cole, amidst the chaos, witnessed something unexpected. A small contingent of Texas Rangers, led by a man he recognized from Fort Worth saloons — a grizzled veteran named Silas — appeared on the periphery of the battlefield, their arrival unnoticed amid the din of battle. They didn't join the fray; instead, they observed, their rifles held ready, their eyes scanning the battlefield with a practiced intensity. Cole, momentarily surprised, watched Silas's men. They weren't firing on either side. Their presence, their studied neutrality, was a riddle wrapped in a mystery.

Then, with a sudden, almost imperceptible shift in the tactical landscape, Silas's Rangers picked off straggling soldiers from Beaumont's retreating force. Silas's Rangers aimed their precise and deadly shots solely at the fleeing men. It wasn't a full-scale assault, but a calculated harassment—a strategic hindrance to the enemy's escape. It was a silent, deadly ballet of sharpshooting that prevented Beaumont's men from reforming their lines or mounting any meaningful counterattack. Their actions were subtle yet impactful, creating confusion and further demoralizing the already shattered ranks of Beaumont's forces.

The momentum shift was astonishing. Unexpectedly aided by Silas's Rangers, the Lipan warriors, engaged in a fierce defensive battle, found their lines strengthened. The Lipan Indians' deep understanding of the land and their exceptional shooting skills aided the Rangers' success. This surprising alliance shows war's unpredictable nature and fate's twists. It showed that survival sometimes demanded alliances that transcended personal grudges or societal divisions.

The sight of the Rangers' actions drew Cole's attention away from the immediate conflict. He was trying to make sense of it all. Why were these men–Texas Rangers, sworn to uphold the law and subdue native populations–fighting alongside the Lipan Indians? The answer, he suspected, lay far deeper than the immediate clash of arms. The whispers in Fort Worth had spoken of dissent within the ranks of the Texas Rangers, whispers of corruption and conflicting loyalties within the force itself. Silas's actions seemed to confirm these whispers, painting a picture of a man operating outside the constraints of official orders, driven by a personal code of ethics that transcended the rigid military hierarchy.

The next significant shift in the battle came from an entirely different direction. A small contingent of U.S. Cavalry, considered part of Beaumont's reinforcements, unexpectedly broke away from the primary force. They weren't part of Beaumont's organized assault; instead, they engaged in flanking maneuvers that dislodged enemy soldiers from their positions, creating openings for the combined Lipan Indian and Ranger forces to exploit. The Cavalry's actions, like those of Silas's Rangers, were precise and calculated, a testament to their tactical understanding and ability to operate effectively.

The Cavalry's involvement presented a further enigma. Beaumont's men, dressed in similar uniforms, were not easily distinguishable from their adversaries at first glance, amid the chaotic and frenzied battle. The cavalry's actions, however, were unmistakable. They were fighting for the Lipan Indians, adding to the growing intrigue surrounding the battle's shifting alliances.

The unexpected intervention of these two forces, seemingly out of nowhere, turned the tide. Beaumont's forces, already reeling from the Lipan Indian's unexpectedly fierce defense, were now caught in a pincer movement. Their retreat, once a disorganized scramble, quickly devolved into a full-blown rout. The battle, which had begun as a desperate defense, had transformed into a resounding victory, secured not only by the Lipan Indian warriors' courage but also by these surprising and mysterious allies.

As the sun dipped below the horizon, casting long shadows across the blood-soaked battlefield, Cole stood alongside Silas, an uneasy truce forged in the crucible of shared victory. Silas, his face etched with weariness and a hint of grim satisfaction, offered a curt nod of acknowledgement. "Didn't expect to fight alongside the Apaches," Silas remarked, his voice rough but laced with a grudging respect. "Beaumont's a snake, a rotten one at that. He's hedged his bets far too long."

Cole offered a cautious acknowledgement. He was still wary of this man, a Texas Ranger, yet Silas's actions spoke louder than words. "We have a shared enemy, at least for today," Cole replied, his words chosen, his gaze scanning the landscape for any sign of renewed hostility.

Silas grunted in agreement. "It's more than just Beaumont, though, "he added, his gaze turning towards the setting sun. "It's about what happens after this. The question involves Texas land, cattle, and future control. His words hinted at the larger political battles brewing beneath the surface of this isolated conflict, hinting at a broader struggle for power and control. The temporary alliance, born out of necessity, had provided an unexpected glimpse into the intricate web of alliances and rivalries that governed this turbulent region.

Unexpected wartime alliances changed the balance of power. The hard-won, costly victory at Kickapoo Creek provided a brutal yet clear demonstration of how unreliable loyalty can be and how unpredictable alliances can form, even amidst violence. Their win highlighted a powerful alliance built on shared survival against a common foe, not blood ties. Unforeseen challenges—emotional, political, and generational arose from the battle's destruction; The shadows of the future loomed large, casting long and ominous shadows over the blood-soaked ground. Cole expected tough battles, significant risks, and potentially shaky alliances.

Unexpected alliances at Kickapoo Creek heightened the stakes and complicated the coming battle. The war was only just beginning. The peace, achieved through great difficulty, was precarious, reflecting the volatile nature of battlefield alliances. Uncertainty clouded the future, with the landscape proving difficult and the path ahead unclear.

Chapter 34: Heavy Losses

The sun, a malevolent eye in the bruised sky, watched as the last echoes of the battle faded. The air, thick with the metallic tang of blood and the acrid scent of burned powder, hung heavy and still. Kickapoo Creek, once a serene ribbon of water winding through the Texas landscape, now ran crimson, a testament to the brutal cost of the day's conflict. Death and destruction marred the formerly fertile ground; men and horses lay among the debris, their lives violently ended.

Cole kneeled beside a fallen Lipan Indian warrior, his weathered face etched with sorrow. He was barely a man, yet he gripped a broken arrow, eyes fixed on the heavens. Cole closed the boy's eyes, a silent prayer escaping his lips. He'd known the warrior–a mischievous spirit with a quick laugh and even quicker hands. He became another war victim in this seemingly endless conflict. The weight of his death settled heavily on Cole's heart, a chilling reminder of the fragility of life and the brutal realities of this unforgiving land.

Losses were incredibly high. Among the Lipan Indians, friends and allies were absent. Grief etched deep lines into Chief Chayton's face as his haunted gaze swept across the scene of destruction. Among the fallen warriors lay his son, a promising youth. His life tragically ended. A silent grief, born of immense loss, momentarily broke the Lipan Indians' stoic resilience, vibrating in the surrounding air. Amidst the devastation, women, faces stained with tears and dirt, hunted for their loved ones among the corpses, their cries reverberating across the ruined land. A haunting counterpoint to the battlefield's eerie silence was the sound of mourning cries.

Silas, his weathered face grimmer than Cole had ever seen, surveyed the battlefield with a detached gaze. Even the experienced Texas Ranger seemed shaken by the extent of the bloodshed. The unflappable veteran who had witnessed countless battles showed visible signs of strain. The deaths of his fellow rangers, men he had known for years, scarred him. His silence was heavy, broken only by the occasional groan as he helped carry the wounded to makeshift shelters.

The U.S. Cavalry had also endured significant losses. Despite their combat skills, these soldiers felt the heavy emotional burden of war. The camaraderie and shared purpose that had united them during the fighting were now replaced by a somber silence, broken only by hushed conversations and the grim tasks of tending to the wounded and burying the dead. The soldiers' faces were marked with weariness and sorrow; the harsh reality of their sacrifices dulled their once-vibrant spirits. Their uniforms, which had once symbolized authority and power, were now stained with blood, mud, and the silent sorrow of battle.

Victory came at a steep price. The elation of winning quickly gave way to the grim understanding of the heavy cost. The battlefield's grimness served as a stark reminder of war's brutality and the human cost of victory. What followed was a silence deeper than the battle's turmoil.

Cole walked among the wounded, offering what comfort he could.

Many suffered injuries, their survival uncertain. He saw faces contorted in pain, heard the gasps for air, and felt the chilling weight of their suffering. He tended to their wounds, his hands moving with practiced efficiency, but his heart ached with a sorrow that no amount of skill could ease. The faces of the fallen and the suffering of the wounded alike hammered home the horrific reality of war. It wasn't a glorious spectacle, but a messy, heartbreaking tragedy that left its scars upon both the victor and the vanquished.

As dusk settled, casting long shadows over the ravaged landscape, a profound sadness settled over the survivors. A somber reflection on the heavy price paid replaced the celebration of victory. Bonfires flickered, casting dancing shadows that seemed to mock the stillness of death that pervaded the battlefield. Weeping and soft prayers filled the night air, creating a symphony of grief that resonated with the sorrow felt by all those present.

The following day, the people buried the deceased. More blood, a somber addition, stained the already soaked ground. Through haunting chants and mournful dances, the Lipan Indians ritually expressed their grief. Rangers and cavalry alike, the soldiers stood in respectful silence, acknowledging their shared loss, which surpassed their differences. Despite their different roles, the shared grief over their loss brought them together in a somber funeral procession. Crosses and small mounds of earth marked the ground, now a graveyard; a desolate scene of quiet grief.

For days afterward, the impact of the severe losses at Kickapoo Creek lingered. The celebrations were subdued, the joy of victory offset by the sobering reality of the losses. The faces of the fallen, their youthful energy cut short, haunted Cole. War had reshaped him, granting him a profound understanding of its brutality and the devastating impact of loss. The pain of the bereaved, the agony of the wounded, and the destructive force of conflict were all witnessed by him.

Silas, too, carried the weight of his losses. He had lost men he considered brothers, whom he had fought alongside for years. Their deaths weighed heavily on him, intensifying his resolve. This loss only fueled his determination to bring Beaumont to justice and prevent future tragedies. His eyes, hardened by years of observing violence, now reveal a profound understanding of life's delicacy and the importance of choosing battles carefully. The unspoken camaraderie shared in the wake of this shared experience forged a silent understanding between the Ranger and the trail boss.

The hard-won peace remained fragile, a stark testament to the unpredictable nature of alliances forged under duress. Fallen memories persist as a stark reminder of the cost and complexities of Western survival.

The future remained uncertain, yet the memory of their shared loss would continue to bind them.

Chapter 35: A Turning Point

Following those days, a profound and unsettling silence enveloped the valley, stifling all previous sounds and activity. In the place where the sounds of rifles cracking and the cries of warriors once echoed, now only the wind whispers and memories linger. No longer did the air reek of the recent battle; the lingering scent of powder and blood had vanished, leaving behind an unnerving, sterile purity—a silence so profound it was as though the land itself held its breath, waiting. Once a scene of utter chaos and deafening noise, the battlefield fell silent, the sounds of even the smallest movement swallowed by the thick layer of ash and churned-up earth.

Even before the sun had fully risen, casting only a faint light upon the land, they had already begun the solemn task of burying the dead. With reverence and in silence, the Lipan warriors moved among the fallen, carefully lifting the bodies of their relatives. Following suit, the Texas Rangers then undertook the same actions. A single person gave no directives or commands of any kind. It wasn't necessary for anyone to take part. The cost of survival was horrifically apparent in each body that lay before them, a stark and sobering reminder of the terrible price paid.

Working in proximity, Cole collaborated with them on the task at hand. His hands, already irritated by the first day's work, became terribly raw and sore by the second day. Although he hadn't planned on staying so late, the sight of the burial grounds kept pulling him back every time he considered leaving. The man in question was definitive and certainly not Lipan. Note that he was not a Ranger. Although he had fought alongside them both during the battle, now in the grim and quiet aftermath, he mourned with them as well.

With low, rhythmic chants, the smoke of smoldering sage rising in the air, and dancers circling the burial mounds in slow, deliberate movements, the Lipan people performed a ceremonial honoring of their dead. Their rituals were of a time long past, predating any map ever created, their antiquity surpassing any cartographical record. Initially, Cole remained at a distance that conveyed respect for the situation or person. At that moment, an elder, one of the most respected in the community, signaled for him to come inside.

With a heart heavy with grief and respect, and with no pretense of understanding the dance, he joined in. With each powerful drumbeat, he felt his own heart hammer in his chest, the rhythm a perfect mirror of the music. As the chanting swelled, it surrounded him, a suffocating shroud that pressed down on him with an immense weight. Although he was an outsider, and didn't truly belong amongst them, they still allowed him to walk among them. The implications of that were far-reaching and impactful, carrying a weight of meaning that I couldn't ignore.

Reaching the young warrior, who had single-handedly broken the enemy's cavalry line, occurred on the third day of their journey. It was he who, charging alone into the hail of gunfire, displayed unmatched bravery and shattered the enemy's formation, single-handedly turning the tide of the battle. After his death, they transported his body up the hill and carefully placed it on a blanket to lay him to rest beneath the expansive sky. Several of the village elders kneeled down next to him, their voices murmuring in the unfamiliar Lipan tongue, words that Cole could not understand or comprehend. Although the languages differed, the meaning transcended language, so no translation was necessary.

With a graceful step forward, Cole elegantly bent his knees, kneeling down before them. With painstaking care, he retrieved the warrior's tomahawk, noting the cracked wooden handle and the crimson stain of a recent battle still clinging to the blade, before gently laying it across his chest. Throughout the duration of the event, he did not speak, choosing to remain silent and not uttering a single word. With a slow bow of his head, he surrendered to the intensity of the moment, letting its weight sink into the marrow of his bones.

From a distance, Silas stood with his arms crossed tightly against his chest, his expression remaining inscrutable and unreadable, as if a mask covered his true feelings. Since the battle's conclusion, his words have been few, a stark contrast to his previous loquacity. Heavy weights seemed to bind his chest, laboring and slowing his every movement and breath. Nobody gave any orders at all. The interrogation concluded without a single question being posed. The soldier spent his days digging graves, meticulously cleaning his rifle, and often gazed at the distant horizon, lost in a silent vigil for an arrival that never materialized.

As the sun dipped low one evening, casting a golden light across the land, he discovered Cole seated beside the creek-bed, which was now dry except for a thin, muddy stream meandering between the stones. Are you planning to stay? Following a lengthy period of silence, Silas finally posed his question. Cole kept his gaze lowered, refusing to meet anyone's eyes. It seemed to last forever.

Silas gave a single, decisive nod of his head. "That is good news." That concludes everything I wanted to share with you. In the silence between them, however, lingered the reverberations of their shared experiences—the haunting images of what they had witnessed, the weight of their actions, and the profound sense of loss that clung to them.

As the week concluded, the makeshift cemetery, a grim testament to recent losses, stretched its length along the ridgeline. Scattered across the landscape were crosses and carved stones, some etched with the names of the departed, others bearing only a simple token or a fragment of worn cloth as a marker of their passing. Following ancient tradition, the Lipan people meticulously arranged the graves with the deceased's heads facing the sunrise. With a somber precision, as if attempting to impose order on the chaotic scene, the Rangers had meticulously arranged their fallen comrades in neat, measured rows, a testament to their dedication in the face of profound loss.

Regrettably, there was a complete absence of any celebratory parades. There were no proclamations made during the meeting. There was a shared understanding, a silent acknowledgment amongst us all, that something profoundly sacred and significant had transpired in this very place. It was something that neither side could quite explain, a mystery that left an indelible mark on the memories of everyone involved, something none would ever forget.

The victory at Kickapoo Creek was not a decisive or clean victory, achieved through questionable tactics and a high cost in lives. The situation remained unresolved, and in reality, nothing definitively settled the matter. However, the battle irrevocably altered the situation, profoundly affecting everything.

No one had erased the Lipan. They had endured. They had stood their ground, fought with courage, and lived to mourn their dead on their own terms. The Texas Rangers, once sent to peace and containment, had fought beside them. Some out of necessity. Others out of something deeper.

Following a quiet period, new understandings developed, not through spoken words or written agreements, but through lived experience, shaping perspectives and fostering deeper rooted kinships. Near the old mission's former location, a person whose identity is unknown has reopened a trading post. The northern trails became the focus of shared patrols, who, instead of acting as invaders or enforcers, began acting as guardians of the area. Initially, suspicion and slow progress greeted cooperation, but eventually, gestures of cooperation replaced the old, brittle standoffs, a process marked by hesitant and gradual steps. Cole persevered and remained steadfast throughout the entire ordeal.

Contributing to the rebuilding of the village, he help patch the damaged walls of the shelters and hauling the timber. When signs of rustlers appeared, I immediately rode out with my scouting parties to investigate and pursue them. As night fell, he would sit around crackling fires, captivated by the age-old tales shared, some conveyed in a language beyond his comprehension, others communicated through the eloquent silence that resonated as deeply as any spoken word.

As dusk settled, he traversed the ridgelines, his eyes following the graceful movements of deer as they ambled through the cottonwood trees, and a profound silence enveloped the world. Throughout his journey, he engaged in shared meals with Lipan elders, partook in bread-breaking ceremonies with Rangers, and persistently attempted reconciliation with the haunting specters that relentlessly pursued him on every path he trod.

In the stillness of the late-night hours, sometimes, as sleep evaded him, his mind would wander, inevitably returning to the memory of Tala. The way her voice sounded was extraordinary and unlike any other. Her eyes, windows to a powerful soul, possessed a strength that was both awe-inspiring and deeply moving; a strength that transcended the visible. Her love for this land was fierce and unwavering, a deep and passionate rooted kinship that had bound her to it for many years. And now, in some small way, a dawning comprehension illuminated the reasons behind it all, a feeling he hadn't had before.

One morning, as the sun peeked over the horizon, he rode his horse out to the far edge of the valley where ancient burial grounds solemnly overlooked the creek-bed below. Dismounting from his steed, he strolled through the rows. I paused, my eyes lingering on names that were very familiar to me. Kneeling solemnly, I paused at the unmarked stones, contemplating the lives lost and the stories untold. He approached empty-handed, without the customary flowers or any other offerings. All that remains is the heaviness of memory.

The wind picked up, rustling the grass. A hawk called overhead. He stood there for a long time. Then he turned and rode west. He didn't leave a note. Didn't say goodbye. He knew the thread of trusts he'd formed here wouldn't break just because he crossed a hill. Some threads, once woven in blood and fire, hold through anything.

As time went on, many would recount and remember the epic and dramatic story of the Kickapoo Creek battle, passed down through generations. Certain individuals might choose to focus their conversation on the key elements of both effective leadership and strategic thinking. There were others who, despite the risks, showed great bravery and defiance. However, those who had endured the hardships of digging graves, laying their brothers to rest, and tending the nightly fires to keep the spirits near would recall the experience with a vastly different perspective, a perspective shaped by their intimate involvement in these solemn tasks.

Following the commotion, they would recall and cherish the ensuing quietude and stillness that followed. Across the lines etched by time, hands reach out, symbolizing rooted kinship and bridging divides. People perform these songs as a tribute to the departed, a melancholic and poignant expression of grief and remembrance. The youthful warrior, whose courage was unmatched, was the one who bravely broke through the enemy lines. The ranger, kneeling beside him, observed the situation with a keen eye.

Even the land itself would keep a memory of the events that took place.

The grass, slow and stubborn in its growth, stubbornly pushed its way back to the surface. In the springtime, the creek flowed with a noticeably higher volume of water than it did during other times of the year. Nearby, children played at the edges of the ancient burial ground, watched carefully by parents who understood the hard-won peace, its fragility, and its immeasurable worth.

Kickapoo Creek, over time, developed into something far greater and more significant than just a battlefield; it became a place of historical significance. Over time, it transitioned into a destination to which many would make their way back. It was a place where former enemies, though not always easily, would meet with a mutual respect that transcended their past conflicts. It was a place that did not bury the past, but treated it with the respect and honor it deserved.

Although Cole never returned physically, his living memory and memory lived on through the stories told about him.

Within the community and culture of the Lipan people, he transitioned from a simple traveler to someone far more significant and integral to their lives.

Chapter 36: Counting the Cost

With a slow and deliberate rise, the sun cast a harsh red light across the scene, unveiling the battlefield's quiet devastation to a silent observer. The recent catastrophe ravaged the area, turning Kickapoo Creek—once a lively, vibrant waterway flowing through the valley—into a sluggish stream of dismal red water stained with churned earth and ash. The silence was so profound, so heavy, so intensely palpable that it felt like a physical presence pressing down, its gravity exceeding the mere absence of sound and possessing a weight far beyond the ordinary. In the sky far above, scavenger birds circled silently, their shadows stretching long and dark across the blood-soaked ground where the motionless forms of both men and horses lay as grim testament to the battle that had just concluded.

Cole, appearing to be in a trance-like state, moved with an ethereal grace, each step guided by an unseen, almost mystical force that directed his movements. The same young Lipan warrior who had fought alongside him, whose lighthearted jokes about marriage were a fond memory, and whose songs had filled the long night watches with their cheerful melodies, now lay still, lifeless, a single arrow piercing his side and ending his life tragically. As Cole kneeled next to the still form of the boy, he gently closed the child's eyes, a soft feather placed delicately in the lifeless hand before he rose to his feet, the profound numbness settling over him completely.

The grim task of gathering the deceased was a process that spanned three long days. As both the sun rose and set, the Lipan people would solemnly intone their mourning chants, their voices weaving together in a slow, harmonious crescendo and decrescendo that mirrored the gentle sighing of the wind. Showing their utmost respect for the gravity of the occasion, the rangers stood at attention, their hats respectfully removed, their gazes lowered in a somber and reverent posture. In place of the expected speeches, the only sounds present were the gentle rustling of brushes and the soft, murmured prayers emanating from a population deeply affected by overwhelming grief.

On the fifth day, the commencement of the rebuilding efforts marked by hardship and renewal marked a significant turning point in the recovery process. Having completed the arduous and lengthy journey from Fort Worth, Silas at last arrived, his many wagons heavily laden with essential supplies and the much-needed medicine. As he stood in the camp's heart, the man rubbed the dust from his face, his eyes moving reverently over the wounded soldiers and the grieving families who mourned their losses.

Lowering his voice to a near whisper, the man spoke directly to Cole, quietly conveying a message of unity and collaboration with the simple, yet powerful, statement, "We rebuild together." You and I have both observed the catastrophic repercussions of our failure to act, seeing firsthand the lingering devastation of what, with timely intervention, we could have easily prevented. Along the creek's edge, a makeshift hospital overflowed with the sounds of people recovering from their injuries, their collective groans a testament to the healing. Lipan women brewed herbs and laid poultices with practiced hands. Cole, awkward but willing, cleaned wounds and carried firewood, earning nods of approval from those who had once eyed him with suspicion. He slept little, ate even less.

In the quiet moments, he sat with the injured. One Lipan elder, her leg wrapped in a thick bandage, shared with him the wisdom of her father. "Pain is an animal," she said. "It stays as long as you feed it fear. When you stop, it grows tired."

As darkness descended, the community members came together, congregating around the warm, crackling fires that dotted the landscape. Rather than staying quiet, they shared their stories, not tales of warfare, but accounts of new life, successful hunts, and precious memories they wanted to preserve and pass on. Although it only provided a short-lived reprieve, it served as their means of recovering some measure of happiness. At first, laughter was hesitant and infrequent, but it gradually gained momentum and became more copious and unrestrained. Although a heavy weight settled on Cole's chest, a smile still graced his lips.

KICKAPOO CREEK

The resumption of trade was gradual, with transactions occurring at a reduced rate compared to previous levels. With his well-known reputation preceding him, Cole journeyed to a nearby settlement in order to negotiate and buy the supplies. In his appeal, he did not rely on pity, but on a sense of decency, outlining a proposal for fair trade practices and establishing a long-term collaborative partnership. Despite some traders' voicing doubt, most of them successfully completed their transactions. Into the camp rolled many wagons, heavily laden with supplies, including sacks of corn, rolls of cloth, containers of salt, and an assortment of bullets. With quiet gratitude, the residents of Kickapoo Creek accepted each delivery that arrived.

As the afternoon sun cast long shadows, Cole, while working alongside a Lipan carpenter on a broken corral gate, lifted his gaze to see Tala walking toward them. With her braid hanging loose, a curtain of dark hair partially obscuring her face, her expression remained an enigma, betraying nothing of her inner thoughts or feelings. Addressing his persistent labor, she remarked, "Your dedication has been unwavering; you've toiled ceaselessly."

Cole's voice, sharp with a sense of both urgency and necessity, conveyed the gravity of his statement, "I need to." Similar to how the most powerful trees need periods of rest to regain their strength after enduring severe weather events, we humans also require periods of rest and recuperation to recover from the stresses and strains of our lives.

They silently proceeded toward the creek, a tranquil waterway where dragonflies, with their graceful movements, skimmed across the surface of the water. Tala, comfortably situated upon a flat rock, offered Cole a meticulously carved wooden fox, the tiny creature's face subtly oriented toward the setting sun in the west.

My father put the finishing touches on his carving just as the battle was about to begin. With extraordinary care and the gentlest of touches, he handled the object, demonstrating a remarkable level of delicacy and respect for its fragility. Are you suggesting that I need a high level of intelligence to navigate this situation successfully?

You must let go of the belief that you need to satisfy every role and expectation at the same time; it's an unrealistic and potentially harmful expectation to place on yourself. As the evening wore on, Silas, feeling the weight of the future and searching for a clear path forward, gathered a select group of influential leaders—among them respected Lipan elders, seasoned Rangers, Cole, and Tala—beneath the comforting light of a torch-lit canopy to engage in serious discussions about their next steps. Because of orders given by a high-ranking officer, the United States Cavalry received the command to withdraw their forces and vacate their current locations immediately. Despite the absence of any official victory declaration, the participants readily acknowledged and deeply understood the conflict's catastrophic and devastating consequences. Employing his substantial influence, Silas dedicated himself to the active pursuit of establishing new treaties, while diligently advocating for both international recognition and the provision of crucial aid to those in need.

With a burst of excitement, he proclaimed the long-awaited opening of a window of opportunity, a development he had eagerly expected. The item, which was the subject of our discussion, was surprisingly diminutive. Although the Lipan people maintained their cultural traditions and practices, the settlers in the area faced significant challenges—emotional, political, and generational in accessing fair and fair legal systems. Every taking part group could unilaterally block any proposal through the use of their veto power; this ensured that no single entity could force a decision. Although it wasn't perfect by any means, it still represented a significant improvement over anything they had ever possessed or experienced previously. In the weeks following that momentous occasion, the valley underwent a complete and dramatic transformation, changing in ways no one could have predicted. The Rangers' efforts complemented the shared labor of rebuilding homes in digging wells, a combined operation that benefited the community. Using reeds and nets as tools, Lipan families patiently instructed settler children in the art of fishing, sharing their ancestral knowledge and skills. In the late summer, a terrible fever spread rapidly through the camp, but it was the skill of a Lipan healer that ultimately saved half of the population from succumbing to the disease.

One morning, Cole opened his eyes and was surprised to see Chayton awake, sitting by the warm glow of the fire, meticulously sharpening a deadly blade. "The guilt," Chayton pointed out, his voice low and steady, "remains with you still." "I lost too many," Cole replied. Every one of us contributed.

As Cole nodded, the firelight glinted off the small wooden fox that he always carried carefully tucked away in his pocket.

By the time fall arrived, the creek, which had been muddy and murky, had finally cleared and returned to its natural, pristine state. Along the river's edge, where the water flowed gently, children played with sticks, their joyous laughter echoing once more throughout the land, a welcome return to happier times. Though the event left its mark, both physically on their faces and emotionally in their memories, an even stronger force remained—the shared labor, the shared suffering, and, most importantly, the shared hope for a brighter future. Beneath it all, Cole remained steadfast, not as an outsider observing or a hero intervening, but as a man who had persevered through hardship, shouldering his burdens, and showing the wisdom to listen when necessary.

Chapter 37: Healing and Recovery

Amidst a makeshift cluster of tents erected beside a creek and serving as a temporary hospital, the women of the Lipan Indian tribe moved about. With gentle hands, they bathed the wounded soldiers, and as they worked, their soft songs, like wisps of smoke, drifted through the thin canvas walls of the makeshift hospital. Guided by the accumulated wisdom and experience passed down through countless generations, they skillfully splinted the shattered bones and meticulously stitched the torn flesh, their movements precise and practiced.

Although awkward and unskilled in his movements among them, Cole was eager to lend a hand and assist in any way that he could. Although his rough hands fumbled with the task initially, his lack of technical skill was more than compensated for by the meticulous care he took in completing the task. Through diligent study, he mastered the art of identifying yarrow and distinguishing it from rabbit tobacco; he learned to ground bark into powder for medicinal to reduce fever; and he became adept at applying salves to treat burns effectively. With keen observation, he watched everything that happened, listened intently to every word spoken, and as a result, completely understood the situation. During the chaotic battlefield, the women's quiet strength and tireless devotion shone through, creating a powerful contrast between the brutality of war and the resilience of the human spirit. Although their sorrow was profound and immeasurable, their songs contained subtle yet persistent notes of hope that hinted at better times to come. Strangely, the pain and hardship that life presented seemed to diminish in their presence, their being softening even the most tough experiences.

Silas, his face etched with the deep lines of exhaustion and coated in a layer of fine dust, meticulously organized and oversaw the complex logistical requirements of the recovery operation. Driven by a relentless urgency, he moved with the speed and efficiency of someone who had no time to waste on grief. From Fort Worth came a delivery of blankets, bandages, and canned food; he managed the supplies with his characteristic terse efficiency. However, it was apparent to those around him that his demeanor had undergone a subtle but significant shift. In the place where his voice once barked commands with the force of a drill sergeant, it now spoke with a newfound consideration and gentleness. To gain insight, he engaged in consultation with the wise Lipan elders. He showed deference to their superior knowledge and experience for matters of care, allowing their wisdom to guide his decisions. Over time, the roles of conqueror and conquered shifted as the two groups, bound by both necessity and something deeper than mere practicality, collaborated.

The days ran together in an indistinguishable, hazy blend, losing their individual identities in a monotonous stream of time. They laid the dead to rest in rows, transcending tribal and military boundaries. As markers for the graves, they used stones, feathers, and rifle barrels as they drove firmly into the ground. Under the starry night sky, the elders sang ancient songs, recounting stories of the challenges their ancestors had faced and conquered in the past, their voices carrying through the darkness. The young people, captivated by the speaker's words, listened intently to every syllable. Overcome with pain and sorrow, the injured soldiers wept openly, their tears a stark contrast to the harsh realities of war. Under the cloak of night, a sense of bravery previously unknown began to emerge and strengthen.

Cole sat by many campfires, harking to the captivating stories being shared, though he only partially understood the language being used. Despite the difficulties or ambiguities, the storytellers successfully conveyed, and the audience understood the intended meaning. Resilience is the capacity to recover from difficulties and obstacles. Reflecting on the past and cherishing memories. Embracing renewal allows for positive transformation and evolution. He discovered they welcomed him not as a miraculous problem-solver or a distant observer, but as a silent witness to their lives and struggles. His help was crucial in the process of fixing the damaged walls, making them whole once more. Unselfishly, he shared some of his allotted food supplies. Clutching the hand of a scout who was on the verge of death. Through these minor acts, he perceived a change not only in the Lipan people's perception of him but also in his own self-perception, a profound shift in his understanding of his identity.

Lingering effects of the trauma caused long-term emotional distress and affected their overall well-being for quite some time. Although the physical wounds had healed, the emotional scars and painful memories lingered and festered within. Roused abruptly from their nightmarish sleep, the warriors awoke with a start, their fingers involuntarily twitching as if reaching for weapons that were not there. As the thunder cracked, making a loud boom that filled the sky, the children instantly fell silent, their playful sounds ceasing abruptly. Lost in their grief, some people walked alone for hours, their silence broken only by the sound of their own footsteps. The rangers stood with a newfound stiffness in their shoulders, some laughing far too boisterously, others not at all. Despite the suffering they endured together, a peculiar and profound intimacy developed between them, forged in the crucible of shared pain.

Cole, in a surprising turn of events, unexpectedly transformed into a bridge, a remarkable and unbelievable change. In his work, he collaborated with Lipan healers, providing not just physical wound care but also addressing and tending to the spiritual well-being of their patients. With rapt attention, he listened to the speaker, his focus unwavering. Listened with genuine attention and understanding. We dedicate this to fathers who grieve the loss of their sons. To the women who stitched garments for the dead. To the men who questioned whether they'd lived through the battle or died somewhere in it. In those moments, he offered no answers—only a presence. And that, somehow, was enough.

Rebuilding began with simple tasks. Workers repaired the old communal hall using salvaged beams. Children painted new designs on its walls—sunbursts, animals, and abstract symbols of renewal. Families pooled their resources to feed one another. The Lipan resumed their hunting, while the Rangers protected their borders without interference. Tension gradually gave way to a cautious peace.

Cole rode out to Fort Worth twice that season. He advocated for the Lipan, bartered with traders, and wrote letters to men who owed him favors. Supplies trickled in: seed corn, nails, and flour. He did not ask for credit or thanks; the work itself felt like an act of atonement.

KICKAPOO CREEK

Silas remained steady, tired and grizzled, but softened in ways few had expected. He no longer kept his distance from the Lipan scouts. He shared coffee with them, nodded to their elders, and occasionally laughed using the language of gestures and glances, helped the Rangers under his command follow his example. Slowly, trust took root. Seasons passed. The grass returned to the scorched hills; the creek flowed more clearly, and deer reappeared at the treeline. Life, stubborn and miraculous, resumed.

By fall, a harvest festival emerged—part Lipan, part Texan, and part something entirely new. Children ran barefoot through the fields. Women hung woven tapestries along the rebuilt chapel, while Rangers brought salted pork and lively fiddle songs. Cole stood with Silas at the edge of the gathering, watching it unfold. "Never thought I'd see this," Silas muttered. Cole nodded. "We earned it. Every single inch."

They spoke little else; there was nothing more to prove. Over time, Cole built a cabin of his own near the creek, close to the village, but not entirely within it. Just close enough. He planted corn, raised chickens, and learned to mend fence posts. Children often visited him, bringing stories or asking questions, and he never turned them away.

Sometimes, when the wind shifted just right, he could hear songs drifting from the village. At other times, a thick silence, rich with memories but free of sorrow, filled the air. He still rode, scouted, and carried a rifle across his back. Yet, he also carved wood, taught a boy how to track deer, and showed a girl how to clean a wound.

The Lipan elders said little about his presence, but they looked at him differently, with recognition and even a sense of kinship. The land healed more slowly than the people, bearing the scars of conflict: shattered trees, burned brush, and trenches filled with collapsed timbers. But even those scars faded. Roots broke through the old fortifications, and flowers grew where blood had soaked the ground.

The story of Kickapoo Creek spread in fragments. Some called it a battle; others, a truce. But for those who had stood in the fire, it was harder to define. It was a blend of pain and grace, all tangled together.

Years later, Cole would walk its fields and remember each grave, each fire-lit night, and each pair of eyes that had looked to him for strength. He would remember how, amidst the ruin, people chose not to remain broken.

Chapter 38: Grieving the Fallen

Although the battle had concluded, the valley remained a solemn testament to the fallen soldiers who lay scattered across the ground. With the first light of dawn, the silt and ash stirred into Kickapoo Creek gave its waters a shimmering red appearance. High above, crows circled in the sky, their movements silent except for the whistling wind that rushed past. With heads bowed low, men moved solemnly among the fallen, gently brushing the dirt from the lifeless faces and carefully lifting the bodies onto makeshift litters fashioned from rawhide and branches. Although a cloying scent of death permeated the air, even outdoors, the Lipan women ceremonially burned bundles of fragrant sage and juniper, their mournful songs carried aloft on the drifting smoke.

Their work was quiet and purposeful; they washed the deceased with water from the river, wrapped them in animal hides, and added a final touch of feathers and beads to their hair. In a display of respect that transcended the traditional boundaries of conflict, they paid tribute to every individual who had perished in that dusty landscape, friend or foe alike. With remarkable composure, their hands stayed perfectly still, a testament to their control and focus. They were not strangers to grief; it was a feeling they knew all too well and had felt many times in their past.

Though his movements were clumsy, Cole moved among them with a willing spirit, eager to take part. His duties involved the physically demanding tasks of carrying pails, clearing away brush, and digging graves. Just weeks after he had painstakingly taught the young warrior to ride, the warrior now lay wounded on the ground, an arrow still embedded in his side, a grim testament to the harsh realities of war. It was still there; no person had removed it. Just days prior, a Ranger captain with whom he'd had a heated argument had perished on a steep incline, his lifeless body lying there with his mouth frozen in a mid-shout. Cole knew that these things, which had taken hold of him, were not temporary, not things he could escape, now or ever.

Above the creek, a burial ground slowly took shape, marked only by simple cairns, weathered wooden crosses, and the low, rounded mounds of earth. Individually, each body was carefully and solemnly laid down, one after another, in a deliberate and measured manner. Deep, cracking voices carried the chants of the elders, their tones resonating with age and experience. Far and wide, the sound traveled, its journey aided by the wind, a gentle breeze carrying it to distant places. Echoing and resonating throughout the expansive valley, the chants filled every corner and crevice of the landscape, leaving no space untouched. So captivating was the sound that even the typically restless horses stood motionless, mesmerized, and completely absorbed in listening.

Silas, distinguished from the others, stood apart, his hat respectfully held in his hand. Despite the provocation, he displayed remarkable composure and didn't shed a single tear. With his jaw clenched tight, he continued to stare out at the distant horizon, lost in thought. Although he had not lost his nerve during the chaos of battle, the violence of war undid him not but by a quieter grief that slowly and subtly unraveled the strongest of men. Cole watched as the man carefully folded his hands, a gesture that suggested an attempt to restrain or conceal something within.

They undertook the arduous task of burying the deceased over several days. With the last person having fallen to the earth, the singing of the Lipan women persisted, these now being soft and guttural old lullabies. In a manner that suggested a desire to bring peace to the land itself, the action appeared it was an attempt to calm the very ground beneath their feet.

Time marched on, and after several weeks, the appearance of Kickapoo Creek changed significantly. Children's laughter, once again filling the air, was this time muted, softer, and quieter. The men toiled quietly, their efforts marked by a profound and heavy silence. The reduced amount of meat brought back by the hunters wasn't a consequence of dwindling game populations; instead, it reflected a shift in their priorities, as the previous abundance had lessened their drive to hunt extensively. Although the land appeared unchanged to the eye, a subtle sense of violation pervaded the atmosphere, whispering that nothing remained truly pristine.

Various factors delayed the Rangers' departure, resulting in a longer stay than expected. Driven by a strong sense of duty, Silas resolutely dedicated himself to home repairs, the strengthening of fences, and the excavation of new water wells. Collaborating closely with the Lipan men, they shared both tools and meals, working side by side throughout the project. Their words were few, but as time passed, the quiet that followed became more peaceful and less awkward. It was respect, not trust, that initially developed between them.

Cole divided his time equally between the two camps. His significant contributions rebuilt the bridge, which suffered catastrophic damage during the raid. Using the bone-setting techniques passed down by the Lipan women, he gained the skill of mending broken bones. He translated the elders' and Rangers' messages, ensuring accurate conveyance of intent and nuanced meaning.

As the night deepened, he settled down next to Tala beside the gently flowing creek, with the quiet solemnity of the memorial providing a backdrop to their shared silence. Encircling a small space were stones and cedar, tastefully decorated with wildflowers and beads, forming a pleasing and rustic arrangement. She remained silent, offering only a few brief words. It wasn't necessary for her to do that. She carried herself with an air of importance.

The memorial transformed into a site not simply for mourning, but also for the preservation and reflection upon cherished memories. As they approached the large tree, the children carefully gathered a collection of feathers and gently placed them at the foot of its majestic trunk. To add a personal touch, and bring a bit of home with them, the rangers carved their initials into the trees. Every evening, without fail, a person would ignite a tiny blaze and sit silently by it, lost in thought or simply enjoying the warmth and quiet of the firelight.

Under the cloak of night, Silas found himself alongside an aged Lipan man, who clutched something mysterious and concealed within layers of cloth. Intricate etchings depicting powerful storms and the vast expanse of the sky adorned a pipe meticulously carved from rich, red clay. Without uttering a single word, he silently passed the item to Silas.

Chayton finally stated, with a sense of weight in his voice, that this pipe had been a cherished heirloom passed down through his family for four generations. The intended purpose and goal of this is to promote and establish peace.

For a long time Silas continued to hold the pipe, perhaps contemplating something or maybe just enjoying the feel in his grasp. Following that, he gave a nod of approval. He refrained from smoking it, choosing not to partake smoking the substance. I have not done that yet. He kept it securely fastened to his saddle, close at hand and readily accessible.

Time seemed to slow to a crawl; what began as mere weeks slowly and inevitably expanded into months. As the landscape softened, people re-sowed the previously burned fields, and repurposed the fallen trees to construct homes, marking a significant shift in the environment. Wildflowers, having survived the harsh winter, bloomed once more, their vibrant colors a testament to nature's resilience. The sound of axes was no longer heard.

The pain of loss continued to cast a shadow, a persistent reminder of what had been. Deep down, Cole had a powerful, unshakeable feeling that he couldn't ignore. Waking with a start, he found himself jolted from a deep sleep plagued by horrific dreams of intense flames and piercing screams. Awakening, he not only found the delightful aroma of freshly baking bread, but also heard a child's distant laughter and felt the comforting weight of Tala's hand upon his chest.

The recovery process was not straightforward; Setbacks, including heated arguments and the unintentional reopening of old wounds caused by careless remarks, unfortunately marred the event. Despite the setbacks, there was also some progress made during that period. A young girl from the Lipan tribe, moved by compassion, presented a blanket to a grieving Ranger, a gesture of solace offered in memory of the Ranger's fallen brother who had perished at his side. Tears streamed down the man's face as he held the item close, his silence amplifying the depth of his sorrow. In that moment, a profound and sacred silence reigned, a stillness that held a reverence for all its own.

Rumors and whispers spread, weaving their way through the community and captivating the attention of all who would listen. It wasn't just the large-scale battles of war that mattered, but also the minor acts of kindness, such as a Ranger protecting a Lipan elder amidst the chaos of battle, or a Lipan warrior rescuing a wounded Ranger from harm's way. Whispered in both camps, these tales transformed into the new legends that everyone talked about.

Cole understood that the pain was not something that would simply disappear or go away on its own accord. However, its dominion over them had ceased. It had become a significant element within the larger narrative, although it did not encompass the entire story. That narrative remained unfinished, its conclusion unwritten, a story continuously developing and developing.

Chapter 39: Reconciliation and Remembrance

As the season changed, fall slowly and quietly entered the area surrounding Kickapoo Creek, settling over the landscape like a tranquil hush. The edges of the grass browned, a sure sign that the crisp morning air had arrived and fall had set in. River stones and sun-bleached cedar encircled the memorial, making it stand taller than before. A gentle wind stirred the feathers fastened to the posts, causing them to vibrate and produce a humming sound that resembled faint voices from afar. The intense grief she had felt did not disappear entirely, but became integrated into the routine of her daily existence.

The children, full of energy, returned to the fields to run and play as they had done before. With sticks in hand and joyous laughter echoing all around, boys from opposing sides chased one another, the boundaries initially separating them becoming indistinguishable in their shared play. With guarded eyes, the older men observed the unfolding events, yet they chose not to intervene or stop whatever was happening. I used to enjoy that, but not anymore.

Silas was not the same person he once was; a profound transformation had occurred within him, altering his very being. Although his walk had become slower and his shoulders more bowed with age, a profound sense of peace now emanated from him, a tranquility that was not present before. Each evening, he would visit the memorial, where he would stay for only a short period to light a small fire, speak the name of someone, and leave a handful of earth as a small offering.

One evening, as the sun began to set, Chayton once again joined him for an evening of camaraderie and conversation. As the intricately carved pipe changed hands, Silas, on this occasion, lit it. Taking a deep breath, he then returned the item with a subtle nod of his head, signifying his acknowledgement. Silas declared, in a somber tone, that he had nothing to say today. "Sometimes," Chayton responded thoughtfully, "silence is the most appropriate and effective response."

As the night fell, they began the first in a long series of solemn remembrance ceremonies to honor the departed. This will be an informal gathering of people, sharing their thoughts and ideas under the starry sky, free from any pressure or formality. Proceeding in order of seniority, the elders began the proceedings with their opening remarks. Chayton and Silas recounted a variety of tales, some imbued with a somber tone, while others possessed an oddly humorous quality that was unexpected. In their discussion, they touched upon the themes of courage, the pitfalls of folly, and the importance of friendship. Subsequently, a multitude of others also took part. The Lipan children, each one of them, contributed their own unique drawings to the collection. Before the raid began, a young boy offered a song, a sweet melody his mother used to sing to him, as a poignant memory of happier times. Although the melody played on the tin whistle by a park ranger was slightly off-key, it was a heartfelt performance.

Cole had become a bridge. He helped repair fences not just between homes, but between people. When someone muttered an insult, he pulled them aside—not to scold, but to listen. He shared meals with both sides, and translated not just words but emotion. He helped organize shared hunts, planting schedules, even a harvest gathering.

Tala stayed close. She worked alongside the women, helping to teach younger children to weave. At night, she and Cole walked the edge of the creek, their hands brushing now and then, their silences comfortable. Once, he asked her if she thought peace would hold.

"For a time," she said. "And maybe that's enough."

The harvest was modest, but it fed everyone. Corn, beans, squash. Enough to get through winter. The day they finished gathering, someone brought out a drum. A Lipan boy danced. Then a Ranger clapped along. No one planned it. It just happened. Laughter, music, movement—the first true celebration since the battle. Despite that, at the edge of it all, the memorial waited. Every few days, someone left something new. The necklace she had on was a beautiful piece of jewelry. A delicate feather drifted gracefully in the gentle breeze. A single strip of blue cloth, perhaps from a larger piece. The wind danced around them, swirling and teasing, as if they were fleeting memories brought to life in a whimsical ballet of movement.

Later that winter, a heavy snowstorm buried the fields. Supplies ran low. Cole organized shared storage—grain from the Rangers, smoked meat from the Lipan. No one went hungry. They shared firewood, blankets, and even stories to keep warm. Hardship had returned, but this time, they faced it together.

With the coming of spring, they once again engaged in the important task of planting. As the fields turned a vibrant green, children ran and played freely, their innocence shielding the youngest from any memory or knowledge of the past war's horrors.

The memorial, in the valley's heart, served not only as a place of mourning and remembrance for the losses suffered, but also as a place of profound reflection, reckoning with the events that led to such sorrow. Couples married there, and now, to honor the fallen, people added unfamiliar names, some children's names commemorating the dead. As the anniversary of the battle approached, the community gathered once more, reflecting on the events of that day. They expressed no mourning.

Silas rose to his feet, intending to speak, but his voice trembled not from fear, but from the weight of his memories, which he was about to share with all present. Methodically and deliberately, he recited every name of the fallen Rangers, pausing after each one to ensure proper remembrance. With equal reverence, Chayton followed along, taking the time to name every one of the Lipan warriors. Following that, Cole moved to the front of the group, stepping forward with determination. He remained silent about the departed.

"Peace," he stated emphatically, "is not simply something someone gives or receives as a gift; "It's something we create every day."

He gazed across the expanse of the crowd, a sea of faces both familiar and strange—the weathered visages of Rangers and Lipan Apaches, the wide-eyed innocence of children, and the wise, lined faces of elders, all bound by the unbreakable ties of friendship forged in the crucible of shared hardship and adversity. Although he admitted it wouldn't change what happened, he added that the gesture still served as a tribute to the loss. Once the ceremony had ended, he settled down beside Tala, taking comfort in the calming presence of the nearby water. Once a raging torrent, the creek now gurgled gently over smooth stones, its waters clear and no longer stained red. With a sigh of contentment, she gently rested her head against the comforting warmth of his shoulder. She stated, with a certainty that brooked no argument, that their memories would keep the events of the day. "Yes," replied Cole, his voice clear and concise in its affirmation. Their success directly resulted from our prior efforts to guarantee their capabilities.

As the sun dipped below the horizon, casting long shadows across the land, a hush fell, not one of sorrow, but of quiet appreciation for the day that had passed. Though the physical marks of the Kickapoo Creek conflict, etched onto both the bodies and the landscape, endured, they had transformed into symbols not of the war itself, but of the significant aftermath that reshaped the lives and land. Through their actions, they provided a tangible example of what a hard-won peace might resemble. Although it's imperfect, it maintains a certain genuineness, a quality often lacking in more polished works. That is sufficient.

Chapter 40: Remembering the Past

A comfortable silence fell between Cole and Tala as they sat side-by-side, the moon stretching long shadows across the plains. Tranquility hung in the air, redolent of woodsmoke and damp earth, despite the turmoil they'd both faced. Their unspoken words carried the weight of recent conflict, shared losses, and the hard path to reconciliation. With her dark eyes mirroring the moon, Tala used her moccasin toe to draw patterns in the dust. Though softened by the gentle light, the facial scars—grim mementos of the fight—remained palpable, silently affirming her resilience.

Cole watched her, a wave of tenderness washing over him. He reached out, his hand covering hers. The touch, unspoken yet meaningful, conveyed a depth of understanding that transcended words. They had both walked through fire and emerged stronger.

"It feels... strange," Tala said, her voice a whisper, "to have the quiet after the storm."

Cole nodded, his gaze fixed on her face. "Strange, yes. But also...peaceful." He paused, searching for the right words to express the complex emotions swirling within him. "I never thought I'd see a day when the Rangers and the Lipan Indians could... work together. Share this land, this peace."

Tala smiled, a bittersweet expression that mirrored the complexities of their journey. "Neither did I. Cole, I thought hope was lost. When the hatred and the distrust seemed insurmountable." She looked away, her gaze drifting towards the distant stars. "But your belief... your stubborn hope... it gave me strength. Even deepest darkness yields to sunrise."

Their conversation drifted, weaving through memories – moments of shared fear and courage, as well as unexpected kindness and unwavering loyalty. They spoke of the fallen, remembering individual faces, recalling stories of bravery and sacrifice. They remembered the pain, the grief, the agonizing uncertainty of those harrowing days. However, their memories also recounted stories of resilience, of forming unexpected alliances in challenging times, and of minor acts of compassion that slowly broke down the barrier of hatred.

Cole recounted the moment he'd seen a young Ranger, his face streaked with tears, accept a hand-woven blanket from a Lipan Indian woman — a gesture of forgiveness that'd transcended the deep wounds of the conflict. He described the shared meals, the laughter of children, and the quiet conversations that had rebuilt trust. He spoke of the memorial, a silent sentinel marking sorrow, now a testament to their shared resilience and their capacity for healing.

Tala shared her memories — the quiet courage of the Lipan Indian women tending to the wounded, the unwavering loyalty of the warriors who had fought to protect their families, and the dignity they maintained in the face of devastating loss. She recounted the stories of the elders, their wisdom and guidance proving invaluable in the battle's aftermath. She spoke of the tough conversations, the painful compromises, the slow, tentative steps towards mutual understanding.

Their conversation was not a recounting of events; it was a process of mutual healing. It was an acknowledgment of their strengths and a celebration of the human spirit's resilience. Visible and hidden wounds lingered from the conflict, but no longer defined who they were. They were reminders of the past, yes, but they also served as a testament to the enduring power of hope and the transformative potential of forgiveness.

Stars shone brighter as night deepened. Cole and Tala continued to talk, their voices blending with the sounds of the crickets and the rustling of leaves. They spoke of the future — a future built on the foundations of mutual respect, understanding, and a shared desire to create a stronger, more peaceful community. They discussed the challenges—emotional, political, and generational that lay ahead and the lingering tensions that still needed to be addressed. But their voices held a newfound confidence, an unwavering determination to overcome any obstacles that stood in their way.

As dawn approached, painting the eastern sky with streaks of gold and rose, Cole and Tala fell silent. They sat close together, their hands intertwined, the unspoken understanding between them as strong as any spoken word. The journey had been arduous, filled with pain and loss. But it had also been a journey of profound personal growth, a testament to the power of love, resilience, and unwavering hope. They had faced unimaginable horrors, witnessed unspeakable grief, and yet, they had emerged from the ashes stronger, their thread of trust deeper, their commitment to a better future unshakeable.

Their love story, a tapestry woven from threads of adversity and triumph, had become intertwined with the history of Kickapoo Creek.

The sun rose high above the plains, casting its warm light on the newly awakened community. Past wounds marked both the land and its inhabitants. A new energy filled the air, carrying a hopeful vibe reflected in the children's laughter, the friendly exchanges between the Lipan Indians and the Rangers, and the quiet confidence on the faces of the elders. Reconstruction efforts were incomplete. Cole and Tala, their hands clasped together, stood as silent witnesses to this dawn of a new era, their hearts filled with hope for the future and the quiet satisfaction of knowing that they had played a pivotal role in forging a lasting peace in the heart of Texas.

The future was still uncertain, but together, they faced it with a newfound courage, their love a beacon of hope in a land still struggling to find its way. The journey had been long, but their path, now clear and illuminated, would lead them to a future they had fought for, a future of peace and shared prosperity in their cherished Kickapoo Creek.

Chapter 41: Shifting Power Dynamics

The aftermath of the battle hung heavy in the air, a palpable tension replacing the cacophony of violence. Dust still swirled in the weak morning sun, settling on the silent forms of the fallen, both Lipan Indian and Ranger. The landscape, scarred by conflict, mirrored the fractured state of the community. Yet, amidst the wreckage, a new order emerged, fragile yet present. The old power structures, once rigid and defined, were crumbling, giving way to unexpected alliances and shifting loyalties.

Colonel Jackson, the steely-eyed commander of the Texas Rangers, found himself unexpectedly humbled. The sheer determination and tactical brilliance of the Lipan Indian warriors had shaken his unwavering belief in the superiority of the Rangers' methods. He'd witnessed firsthand their courage, their resilience, their steadfast commitment to defending their land and their people. The battle had not been a decisive victory for either side; it had been a brutal stalemate, exposing the limitations of conventional warfare against the Lipan Indian's intimate knowledge of the terrain and their guerrilla tactics.

This realization, though bitter, was also transformative. He saw the Lipan Indians not as adversaries, but as skilled warriors deserving of respect. Not all his men readily accepted this shift in perspective; resentment and distrust still simmered beneath the surface. However, Jackson, a man known for his pragmatism, understood the necessity of forging a fresh path — one built on mutual respect and cooperation.

Chief Chayton, his face etched with the weariness of battle but his eyes gleaming with a newfound resolve, emerged as a powerful force in the new order. The struggle had solidified his position among his people, demonstrating his strategic acumen and unwavering dedication to their survival. His leadership, once challenged by factions within the tribe, now stood uncontested. He understood the need for cautious diplomacy, while still maintaining the Lipan Indian's fierce independence.

Difficult treaty talks progressed slowly as each side grudgingly conceded points. Reluctant to negotiate, the U.S. Cavalry faced growing pressure from Washington, D.C., to find a peaceful settlement with the Lipan Indians. Heavy losses of life and resources in the war made the government keen to prevent more fighting. Unlike his more aggressive colleagues, the practical General Armstrong understood the need to cooperate with the Rangers and Lipan Indians to secure the area.

The resulting agreement was far from perfect, but it represented a significant step towards a fairer distribution of power. The Lipan Indians received a larger reservation and greater autonomy over their affairs. This was a crucial concession that acknowledged their rights as a sovereign nation and their legitimate claim to the land. The agreement also established mechanisms for joint protection of the region, with both the Rangers and the Lipan Indians sharing responsibility for maintaining law and order. This collaboration, while uneasy, proved effective.

Cole, bridging the cultural divide through his unique relationship with both the Lipan Indians and the Rangers, played a pivotal role in facilitating the negotiations. His understanding of both cultures, his unwavering commitment to peace, and his relationship with Tala made him a trusted mediator. He acted as a bridge, smoothing over misunderstandings, interpreting conflicting statements, and patiently nudging both sides towards compromise.

The shift in power dynamics also had a significant impact on the burgeoning cattle trade. The conflict had disrupted the usual routes, and the new alliances created new opportunities for cooperation. Cole, known for his skills as a trail boss, played a vital role in guiding the cattle drives along safer, more established routes, working with both the Lipan Indians and the Rangers to protect the herds from cattle rustlers and hostile elements. The economic advantages of this collaboration soon became apparent, solidifying the nascent peace.

Implementing the new order proved challenging. Hardliners on both sides remained resistant to the changes, clinging to outdated prejudices and resentments. The momentum towards peace was undeniable. A stronger understanding and deeper appreciation of mutual dependence between the communities arose from shared experiences of loss and struggle.

Fort Worth, a rapidly growing and chaotic town, experienced the impact of these changes. The Lipan Indians and the Rangers' new partnership eased the town's concerns, boosting trade. Despite the ever-present threat of violence, the vibrant nightlife thrived. Initially, saloons and dance halls provided a space for Lipan Indians and Anglo-American to interact. Despite initial difficulties and misunderstandings in the cultural exchange, it gradually reduced prejudice.

Shared mourning and reflection filled the memorial, a somber tribute to those lost. The Lipan Indian and the Rangers, their grieving side-by-side, paid their respects to those lost in the conflict. The memorial represented sacrifices and a commitment to peace. It offered refuge; past hurts found acknowledgment, future hope, and embrace.

Tala took on her new role as a link between her people and the wider world. Her courage, wisdom, and unshakeable belief in peace motivated others. She ensured her people's needs and concerns gained recognition in the new political system through her advocacy. Tala and Cole's relationship became a testament to love's power to transcend cultural boundaries.

As the sun dipped below the horizon, long shadows stretched across the plains. The new order was still in flux. Though fragile, hope felt real. It was a long, hard journey, full of violence and loss. Rising stars reflected new constellations of alliances, showing enduring human resilience and transformative forgiveness. Though the future was unclear, a new beginning shone a light on the challenging path ahead. A new order arose from the wreckage of war, hope for its tenuous support against conflict. Cole and Tala, hand in hand, envisioned a future where Lipan Indians and Rangers coexisted peacefully, their differences uniting them in their shared aspiration for peace.

Chapter 42: Rebuilding Communities

Reconstruction's quiet start, marked by countless hands working determinedly, contrasted with the absence of grand pronouncements. The stench of death still clung to the air, a grim reminder of the recent conflict, but the scent of wood smoke from newly constructed shelters and the rhythmic thud of hammers against wood replaced it. Women, their faces etched with a mixture of grief and resolve, sifted through the rubble of their homes, salvaging what they could—a broken pot, a tattered blanket, a child's worn doll. Men, their bodies weary but their spirits unbroken, began the arduous task of clearing the debris, rebuilding shelters, and securing the perimeter of the Lipan Indian village. The landscape, once a battleground, was transforming into a testament to their resilience.

Cole, his hands calloused but his heart full of hope, worked alongside the Lipan Indian men, his knowledge of carpentry proving invaluable. He'd witnessed firsthand the devastation wrought by the conflict, the shattered lives, and broken homes, and felt a deep responsibility to aid in the restoration. Tala, her presence a beacon of strength and compassion, oversaw the efforts, organizing the women and ensuring that everyone had the resources. Her leadership, tempered by recent battles, was unwavering; her quiet competence inspired confidence, even amidst despair.

The rebuilding extended beyond the physical structures. The community's social fabric, torn by conflict, needed careful mending. Chief Chayton, recognizing the importance of unity, started a series of council meetings, inviting representatives from all factions within the tribe to take part. Heated discussions often occurred, bringing lingering grievances and old rivalries to the surface, but Chayton's patient diplomacy and unwavering commitment to unity eased tensions. He emphasized the shared experience of hardship, the need for collective action, and the importance of forging a stronger, more cohesive community.

The Rangers, too, played a crucial role in the rebuilding process. Colonel Jackson, having witnessed the Lipan Indian's resilience and the futility of continued conflict, ordered his men to assist in the construction of new shelters and the securing of vital resources.

This act of cooperation, though met with resistance from some hardened Rangers, fostered a sense of mutual respect. Collaborative work helped erode long-held prejudices and distrust between the groups. The shared labor became a silent testament to the potential for reconciliation.

The U.S. Cavalry, distanced and hesitant, joined the collaborative efforts. General Armstrong, recognizing the strategic advantage of a peaceful and stable region, provided much-needed supplies and logistical support. The Cavalry's presence, a source of apprehension for the Lipan Indians, became a symbol of the government's commitment to fostering peace and aiding in the rebuilding process. Cavalry logistical support, such as medical supplies and provisions, ensured the community's survival and recovery.

The rebuilding didn't stop at physical structures; Cole, leveraging his experience as a trail boss, worked with both the Lipan Indians and the Rangers to establish new trade routes and revitalize the cattle business. The newly established routes, designed to bypass conflict zones and incorporate Lipan Indian knowledge of the terrain, proved safer and more efficient. This collaborative effort not only boosted the economy, but also strengthened the alliance between the different groups. The economic benefits of peace became palpable, providing a tangible incentive for continued cooperation.

The cattle drive, once a source of potential conflict, now represented a symbol of collaboration and shared prosperity. Lipan Indian warriors, renowned for their horsemanship and tracking skills, protected the herds, working alongside Rangers to ensure the safety of the drives. This shared responsibility for the cattle drives engendered a sense of trust and mutual dependence, further solidifying the newfound alliances. Sharing the financial rewards ensured the Lipan Indians benefited from the burgeoning cattle trade. Beyond the practical aspects of rebuilding, there was also a conscious effort to heal the emotional wounds left by the conflict.

A place for shared grief and remembrance replaced the stark memorial. Lipan Indians and Rangers, joined in sorrow and mutual respect, conducted ceremonies together. Built through collaboration, the monument powerfully symbolizes reconciliation, embodying shared sacrifice and a commitment to peace. Shared mourning rituals helped unite cultures, promoting a sense of shared humanity.

Tala's quiet strength and wisdom played a vital role in the community's emotional healing. Drawing on traditional Lipan Indian practices, she organized grief counseling sessions that helped guide others through their pain.

She remembered and honored their sacrifices as she preserved the stories of the fallen. Amidst the suffering, her leadership, compassion, and resilience inspired hope and offered solace. She embodied the Lipan Indians' unbroken spirit and unwavering resolve, becoming their symbol of strength.

The rebuilding process was slow, arduous, and often frustrating. There were setbacks, disagreements, and occasional flare-ups of old tensions. But the shared commitment to a better future, the tangible progress made, and the growing sense of mutual respect provided the impetus to continue. The resilience of the Lipan Indians, the pragmatism of the Rangers, and the strategic support of the Cavalry combined to create a powerful synergy, driving the community toward recovery and growth. Rebuilding involved more than just physical structures. The shared experience of hardship, loss, and subsequent rebuilding forged a thread of trust between the Lipan Indians, the Rangers, and the Cavalry that was stronger than any prior alliance had been.

Although Fort Worth was once a haven for lawlessness and uncontrolled expansion, it to felt the positive effects of the peace. Because the Lipan Indians and the Rangers worked together, the town felt safe and prospered. Once shadowed by violence, saloons and dance halls blossomed into cautious but vibrant hubs of cultural exchange. Lipan Indians and Anglo American interacted, exchanging stories, music, and food. Shared celebrations and a growing community spirit showed that prejudice was slowly fading.

As the days turned into weeks and the weeks into months, the landscape transformed, mirroring the internal shifts within the community. The community's renewal wasn't a physical process; It was a new dawn, a new era, built on the ashes of the past, but rooted in the hope for a shared future.

Chapter 43: Adapting to Change

Dust coated the ravaged Lipan village, changing Cole and Tala's lives. The whirlwind of conflict had subsided, leaving behind a fragile peace, a tentative truce built on shared hardship and a grudging respect. For Cole, accustomed to the solitary life of a trail boss, the sudden immersion into the complexities of a burgeoning intercultural community was a significant change. He traveled through a world distant from the usual rhythms of cattle drives. The constant presence of the Rangers and the U.S. Cavalry, a source of unease, became a comforting backdrop to his new life. The men, once adversaries, were now collaborators; their shared purpose — rebuilding the Lipan Indian village — forged an unexpected camaraderie. He discovered a different leadership was required here, one that demanded patience, diplomacy, and a willingness to learn, traits he was slow, sometimes gaining.

His carpentry skills, a simple means of helping the Lipan Indians, became a source of unexpected social currency. Council meetings welcomed him as a valued member of the community. He learned to appreciate the intricate details of Lipan Indian culture, including their deep rooted kinship to the land, complex social structures, and rich oral traditions. He listened to the elders' stories, their voices filled with the wisdom of generations, and he saw the resilience of a person who had endured unspeakable hardship. Tala, to him, was more than captivating; she was a leader, strategist, and healer. Her quiet strength and unwavering resolve inspired him, pushed him to become a better man, a more responsible partner, and a more effective leader in the process of rebuilding.

Tala, too, faced her adaptations. As an independent plains woman, she found community leadership challenging following trauma. The necessities of collaboration with Anglo newcomers and traditional Lipan Indian ways intertwined, creating a dynamic and challenging environment. She embraced the changes with a cautious pragmatism, balancing tradition and modernity, understanding that the survival of her people hinged on her ability to adapt. She resolved disputes between the Lipan Indians and the Rangers, bridging cultural gaps and safeguarding their shared vision for the future amidst complex cultural differences.

Her relationship with Cole became a symbol of this adaptation. Their love story, a forbidden romance, has now blossomed within the context of the new order, a symbol of the bridging of cultures. Their shared commitment to the community became the bedrock of their relationship. He learned her language, customs, and perspectives, and she learned to appreciate his practicality, loyalty, and strength. Their differences, rather than acting as barriers, became sources of strength and understanding, fueling their shared journey.

The rebuilding extended beyond the physical structures of the village. The economic fabric of the community also required meticulous mending. Cole, leveraging his extensive experience in cattle ranching and trade, became instrumental in revitalizing the Lipan Indian economy. He established new trade routes, handpicking paths that avoided the areas of past conflict, integrating the Lipan Indian's intricate knowledge of the terrain to maximize efficiency and safety.

He negotiated fair deals with traders in Fort Worth, ensuring that the Lipan Indians received a fair price for their goods, and he educated them on the intricacies of the American business world, bridging the gap between traditional practices and modern business dealings. His efforts brought economic prosperity and strengthened the newly formed alliances between the Lipan Indians, the Rangers, and the Cavalry.

The economic success fueled a sense of shared purpose. The cattle drive, once a source of tension and potential conflict, became a symbol of collaborative prosperity and success. Lipan Indian warriors, renowned for their horsemanship and intimate knowledge of the terrain, worked alongside Rangers, protecting the herds and ensuring the safe passage of the cattle to market. This shared responsibility fostered a sense of trust and interdependence, strengthening the newly formed thread of trusts between the cultures. They distributed the financial gains, ensuring the Lipan Indians benefited from their participation, thus strengthening their economic independence and status within the new community.

The social structure required repair, demanding a delicate equilibrium between tradition and modernization. To protect their culture, Lipan elders carefully rebuilt their art forms, teaching the traditions to their younger generations. To preserve their rich cultural heritage, they documented their stories, songs, and rituals, safeguarding them from the impact of change. Despite this, they also welcomed chances of cultural exchange, blending some Anglo-American customs into their lives while protecting their heritage.

Cole and Tala played a central role in this delicate balancing act.

They facilitated dialogues between the different cultural groups, acting as bridges of understanding and ensuring that communication remained open and respectful. They worked to dispel prejudice and misconceptions, fostering a climate of mutual respect and appreciation. Their relationship became a living testament to the possibilities of intercultural exchange,

Demonstrating that love and understanding could bridge the divides created by differences in heritage and culture.

The town of Fort Worth, a symbol of Anglo-American expansion, reflected the changes in the Lipan Indian community. Dominated by a rough and rowdy atmosphere, the saloons and dance halls showcased a blend of cultures. Lipan Indian artisans sold their handicrafts alongside Anglo-American goods, creating a vibrant marketplace where the two cultures intertwined. The music halls now featured a mixture of Anglo and Lipan Indian music, a delightful fusion of cultures. The shared cultural experiences fostered a greater understanding and acceptance between the two communities, eroding the barriers of prejudice and mistrust that had separated them.

The transition was not without its difficulties. There was tension, disagreements, and the occasional resurgence of old resentments. However, the shared experience of hardship, the tangible progress made, and the growing sense of mutual respect provided the impetus to overcome these challenges. The combined efforts of the Lipan Indians, the Rangers, and the Cavalry forged a powerful collaboration.

The rebuilding of the Lipan Indian village was more than just a physical process; it was a transformative journey that redefined the relationship between the Lipan Indians, the Rangers, and the Cavalry. The new order, born from the ashes of conflict, became a testament to the resilience of the human spirit, the transformative power of forgiveness, and the potential for unity amid diversity. New hope, mutual respect, and shared understanding formed a brighter future, replacing past wounds. Cole and Tala, leading this latest order, played a key role in its development. Their love story, a poignant narrative of adaptation and understanding, symbolized this new era, a testament to the enduring power of human rooted kinship.

Chapter 44: New Opportunities

Cole's hammer beat a hopeful rhythm against the new wood, echoing a steady pulse. Though once destroyed, the Lipan Indian village was being rebuilt through the combined efforts and hard work of its people. Charred longhouse skeletons now formed the foundations of bigger, stronger buildings, their shapes more defined, showcasing the community's growing confidence. Despite his calloused hands and weary body, Cole found a strange satisfaction in the rebuilding. It was more than just building something.

Reconstruction went beyond the tangible. Conflict and uncertainty caused a dramatic shift in the economic landscape. Cole leveraged his cattle trading expertise and the Lipan Indians' geographical knowledge to create a new integrated system. To ensure safe and efficient transport to Fort Worth, he established trade routes that circumvented previous conflict areas. By negotiating favorable deals, he secured fair prices for Lipan Indian goods and created a credit/barter system that strengthened the community. Using his water management and crop rotation expertise, he introduced new farming methods to boost agricultural output.

This economic prosperity wasn't just about material wealth; it fostered a sense of self-reliance and agency. The Lipan Indian, once dependent on precarious hunting and gathering, now had a sustainable source of income. Their participation in the cattle drives, hesitant and fraught with mistrust, blossomed into a source of both pride and financial gain. Their horsemanship skills, combined with their deep understanding of the land, made them invaluable partners in ensuring the safe passage of cattle to market. This collaboration wasn't just about money; it was also about building trust and forging a powerful new alliance.

Initially skeptical, the Rangers and the U.S. Cavalry later actively took part in the rebuilding. The Rangers and U.S. Cavalry provided security to protect trade routes and maintain order. Rather than dominating, their presence was one of collaboration. Rebuilding together created an unexpectedly strong thread of trust between us. What had once divided them faded away, replaced by a shared commitment to building a better tomorrow.

The village's social structure also transformed. To preserve their culture, elders created educational programs teaching younger generations ancestral traditions, language, and values. They created a written record of their rich past by documenting their oral histories. They welcomed chances for cultural exchange, adopting helpful parts of Anglo-American culture while keeping their own distinct identity. While staying connected to their land and traditions, they discovered new farming, building, and trade practices.

Tala was essential; Her leadership extended beyond the Lipan Indian community; she became a respected figure in the broader region, facilitating dialogue and understanding between different cultures. Her voice, previously confined to her community, now resonated with the power and authority of a leader who mastered adaptation and preservation. Cultural events organized by her and Cole united Lipan Indians, Rangers, and Cavalry, fostering shared experiences, mutual understanding, and friendships.

The transformation wasn't just confined to the village. Fort Worth, once a symbol of encroaching Anglo-American expansion, reflected the changes occurring within the Lipan Indian community. The saloons and dance halls, once havens for rough and rowdy behavior, were now infused with a vibrant blend of cultures. Lipan Indian artisans displayed handcrafted goods alongside Anglo-American wares, creating a vibrant marketplace where cultures intertwined. Music halls featured a mix of Anglo and Lipan Indian music, creating a unique sonic tapestry that mirrored the growing social landscape.

The changes weren't without their challenges—emotional, political, and generational. There was friction, misunderstandings, and occasional flare-ups of old prejudices. But the shared experience of hardship, the palpable progress made, and the growing sense of mutual respect provided a strong foundation for overcoming these challenges.

Cole's carpentry skills, a simple act of helping rebuild homes, blossomed into a symbol of cultural exchange. He taught the Lipan Indians new construction techniques while learning their traditional methods, creating a fusion of styles and practices in the village's architecture. The result was a unique blend of Anglo-American practicality and Lipan Indian artistry, reflecting the growing synthesis of cultures. He became a skilled negotiator, brokering deals between the Lipan Indians and traders from Fort Worth, ensuring that the Lipan Indians received fair prices and favorable terms. His knowledge of the cattle trade brought economic prosperity to the village, strengthening their financial independence.

Tala shared her expertise in medicinal plants and traditional healing—like mending broken pottery with gold, every scar a story technique, enriching the medical knowledge of the community as a whole. Her leadership extended to the broader social sphere. She helped mediate disputes, reconcile conflicts, and foster unity among the diverse cultural groups. Her calm demeanor and unwavering wisdom were invaluable in navigating the complex social dynamics of the newly formed community.

New opportunities emerged. The transformation extended to the realm of personal relationships. Cole and Tala's love story, a forbidden romance, flourished in this new atmosphere of cooperation and understanding. Once seen as barriers, their differences have now become sources of strength and mutual enrichment. Their shared commitment to the community solidified their thread of trust, creating a powerful partnership that mirrored the unity emerging within the larger community.

Rebuilding Lipan village involved far more than physical structures. Cole and Tala, at the forefront of this new era, weren't mere observers but were active architects of a future where differences became strengths and love transcended boundaries. Their story, a testament to the resilience of the human spirit, became a symbol of the enduring power of unity, forging a path toward a brighter, more inclusive future for all.

Chapter 45: A Foundation for Peace

The sun dipped below the horizon, casting long shadows across the newly rebuilt Lipan Indian village. Once thick with the smoke of conflict, the air now carried the scent of wood smoke from built homes and the earthy aroma of tilled soil. Cole, leaning against a newly constructed porch, watched Tala as she addressed a group of children, her voice a gentle melody that carried the weight of ancient wisdom. She was teaching them the Lipan Indian constellations, weaving stories of their ancestors into the tapestry of the night sky, a vibrant reminder of their heritage. Months earlier, this land lay ravaged; this scene offered a stark contrast. Hope, resilience, and their dedication showed remarkable strength. Individuals—Cole and Tala—who had dared to dream of a different future.

Their efforts extended far beyond the physical rebuilding of homes and infrastructure. They understood that true peace lay in the reconciliation of hearts and minds, bridging the cultural divides that had fueled conflict for a long time. Cole, with his innate understanding of the cattle trade, not only created economic opportunities for the Lipan Indians but also fostered a new sense of collaboration with the Texas Rangers and the U.S. Cavalry. He had crafted trade agreements that benefited all parties involved, ensuring fair prices and fair distribution of resources. This economic interdependence proved to be a powerful force in dismantling the old prejudices and fostering a sense of shared destiny.

He had established a system of mutual support, where the Lipan Indian's intimate knowledge of the terrain and their exceptional horsemanship skills were invaluable in protecting the cattle drives, ensuring the safe and efficient transport of goods to Fort Worth. In return, the Rangers and the Cavalry provided security, protecting the trade routes and maintaining order. This relationship prioritized mutual respect and shared prosperity, not power.

Shared successes softened the once-guarded lines of cultural identity, fostering camaraderie. The rhythmic clang of hammers on wood and the shared satisfaction of a successful cattle drive became everyday experiences that united these different groups.

Meanwhile, Tala had focused on preserving and revitalizing Lipan Indian culture. She established educational programs that aimed to pass down her people's traditions, language, and history to the younger generations. She meticulously documented the Lipan Indian oral histories, preserving a rich cultural living memory that might otherwise have been lost. Tala's influence served as a bridge between cultures. Her leadership was marked by wisdom, compassion, and a deep understanding of the human spirit. She held councils where leaders of all three groups could discuss concerns, iron out disputes, and work toward shared goals. She proved that effective leadership was not about power, but about rooted kinship.

Their joint work resulted in more than just economic growth and cultural safeguarding; Fort Worth, once a symbol of encroaching Anglo-American expansion, now reflected the burgeoning synthesis of cultures. The lively marketplace displayed a successful mix of Lipan Indian and Anglo-American products, highlighting their recent partnership. Once centers of lively activity, the saloons and dance halls now housed a diverse crowd, each group celebrating its own culture while appreciating the others. Anglo-American melodies once dominated music halls, but now a lively blend of Lipan Indian traditional music and modern songs fills them, reflecting the changing cultural scene.

This transformation had its challenges—emotional, political, and generational. Friction, misunderstandings, and occasional displays of prejudice occurred. Cole and Tala, however, anticipated these challenges—emotional, political, and generational. Cole and Tala created conflict resolution systems that used dialogue and understanding to solve disagreements peacefully, instead of resorting to violence or revenge. Their wisdom, peace, commitment, and empathy soothed rising tensions. Their shared struggles and visible progress built a strong foundation to overcome challenges—emotional, political, and generational. Turning past conflicts into growth chances, they created a strong community thriving on shared achievements.

Cole and Tala's influence reached farther than their local community. Their actions inspired hope in other communities facing similar challenges—emotional, political, and generational. Their achievements inspired regional groups to cooperate peacefully. Beyond the physical structures they left behind, their living memory is one of collaboration and understanding, inspiring others to transcend divisions and embrace unity. More than just homes and businesses resulted from their collaboration.

Even with the new social order, conflict continued. Lipan Indian women, previously limited to domestic tasks, thrived in the growing trade, showcasing their exceptional crafting and trading skills, and their strength and resilience became vital to their community's economic prosperity. Celebrated for their riding skills, the tribe's men were essential to the cattle drives, proving their value, challenging stereotypes, and contributing significantly to the region's economy. The children, nourished by Tala's education, grew up with a profound sense of their cultural heritage, embracing the opportunities presented by the fusion of cultures.

Through teamwork, they built a school to teach Lipan Indian children their native tongue and English, preserving their traditions while preparing them for a global future. In shared classrooms, children from different backgrounds built respect and appreciation for each other's differences. The school symbolized progress, demonstrating education's power to overcome cultural divides. The Lipan Indians, Rangers, and Cavalry celebrated together at a newly built community center hosting social gatherings, cultural exchanges, and community events.

Cole's carpentry skills continued to be instrumental, not in constructing homes but also in symbolizing the blending of cultures. His designs incorporated elements of both Anglo-American practicality and traditional Lipan Indian aesthetics, a fusion that reflected the unity and progress of the community. The resulting structures stood as a visual representation of their shared journey toward peace and harmony. Tala, meanwhile, continued to play a pivotal role in the community's health and well-being. Her knowledge of traditional Lipan Indian medicine, combined with the medical practices of the Cavalry, formed the basis of a robust and comprehensive healthcare system for the village.

Their love story, a forbidden romance, became a powerful symbol of intercultural understanding. Cole and Tala's relationship transcended cultural boundaries, challenging long-held prejudices and showing the unifying power of love. Their commitment to each other and shared vision for the future provided a powerful example to their community, a beacon of hope that illuminated the path toward a brighter, more inclusive future.

Their story served as a testament to the possibility of peace and understanding, passed down through generations, a living memory of love that would inspire future generations to pursue peace and harmony.

Cole and Tala's work for lasting peace affected more than just their local area. Their collaborative leadership, mutual respect, and bridge-building across cultures created a model for regional peace. Inspired by their heritage, others will embrace diversity and build a more just and fair world.

Chapter 46: Assuming Responsibility

The weight of their shared accomplishments settled upon Cole and Tala like a warm blanket, comfortable yet heavy with the responsibility of the future. The initial euphoria of rebuilding the village and forging a fragile peace between the Lipan Indians, the Texas Rangers, and the U.S. Cavalry was fading, replaced by the sobering reality of sustained leadership. While still occurring, the celebratory dances and shared meals were now punctuated by long hours spent in earnest discussion, as they navigated the intricacies of governance and the ever-present potential for conflict to resurface.

Accustomed to the independent life of a trail boss, Cole grappled with the complexities of communal decision-making. His previous authority had stemmed from his strength, skill, and ability to provide; now, he needed to learn the art of persuasion, compromise, and mediating disputes between individuals and factions with differing needs and perspectives. The cattle drive, once his sole focus, was now one facet of a far larger tapestry of community concerns: food security, water rights, education, healthcare, and the constant need to reinforce the delicate balance of power between the three groups.

A certain clumsiness marked his initial attempts at leadership. Accustomed to giving direct orders, he struggled with the more nuanced approach required to lead a community with a rich and complex history rooted in traditional forms of governance. He stepped on toes, offended traditions, and sometimes missed the subtle cues that informed Lipan Indian decision-making. Tala, ever patient and insightful, became his quiet guide, correcting his missteps and offering insights into the cultural nuances he struggled to understand.

Tala faced a unique set of challenges—emotional, political, and generational. Her natural authority within the Lipan Indian community was undeniable, but expanding that authority to encompass the Rangers and the Cavalry required a different approach. She had to navigate the delicate balance between upholding her people's traditions and collaborating with a foreign culture that, while increasingly respectful, still held its own ingrained biases and preconceptions. She understood the need to maintain Lipan Indian identity and sovereignty while ensuring the community's participation in the broader economic and political landscape.

Their first major hurdle came as a dispute over grazing rights. An avaricious rancher, emboldened by the initial peace, attempted to claim a significant portion of land used by the Lipan Indians for their horses and livestock. Cole's initial instinct was to confront the rancher, a solution that Tala quickly cautioned against. She suggested a council, bringing together representatives from all three factions—Lipan Indian elders, Texas Rangers, and U.S. Cavalry officers—to discuss the issue and to find an acceptable solution.

The council was a tense affair. The loud and boisterous rancher attempted to bully his way to victory, but Tala dismantled his arguments with calm assurance and impeccable logic. She presented historical evidence of Lipan Indian land usage, backed by the testimony of senior tribal members whose memories extended back generations. Cole, observing her grace and skill in negotiation, learned a valuable lesson in the power of diplomacy. After a heated but respectful debate, the council ruled in favor of the Lipan Indians, setting a precedent for fair resource allocation.

Another challenge arose as a disagreement over the new school's curriculum. Some members of the Cavalry advocated for a curriculum that focused on English language and Anglo-American history, marginalizing Lipan Indian language and culture. Tala opposed this, insisting on a bilingual curriculum that celebrated both traditions. She argued that preserving Lipan Indian culture was not a matter of pride but a crucial element in maintaining their identity and preventing assimilation. This time, Cole's experience in negotiation proved invaluable. He steered the discussion towards a compromise that satisfied both the children's educational needs and the cultural preservation goals of the Lipan Indian community.

Early wins boosted Cole and Tala's confidence; however, much remained. Rumors of dissent were always simmering beneath the surface—whispers of distrust between groups, anxieties regarding the changing social landscape, and sporadic outbreaks of old prejudice. The constant threat of outside interference remained from those who opposed their peaceful coexistence. Cole and Tala realized that their leadership role extended far beyond the day-to-day governance of the community.

A system of regular, open community forums discussed concerns and potential solutions. Shared events and celebrations promoted cross-cultural understanding, fostering a shared identity and common purpose. They implemented a mentorship program connecting young Lipan Apache adults with Texas Rangers and U.S. Cavalry members to foster mutual understanding and respect. Their efforts fostered a sense of community that went beyond ethnicity and heritage.

Leadership's weight differed from its responsibility. Cole and Tala, through their strengths and their unwavering mutual support, were transforming the region. Their leadership built vibrant communities; valuing each voice, respecting every culture, using history to build a better future. The path wasn't always smooth, but with each challenge overcome, Cole and Tala's commitment deepened, their leadership strengthened, and their thread of trust solidified, becoming a beacon of hope in the ever-strengthened Texas frontier landscape. A shared vision, not conquest, forged the community as the rising sun greeted each day.

Chapter 47: Navigating Challenges

The next major crisis arose, a stark reminder that peace, even when hard-won, remained fragile. A severe drought gripped the land, threatening the livelihoods of the Lipan Indians and the surrounding settlements. The meager water sources dwindled, the pastures turned to dust, and the cattle, the very lifeblood of the region's economy, began to weaken and die. The initial harmony, built on negotiated agreements, threatened to unravel under the pressure of scarcity. Sensing an opportunity, the avaricious rancher from the previous grazing dispute attempted to seize control of the remaining water sources, claiming them for his use. This blatant disregard for the agreements reached at the council ignited tensions that threatened to erupt into open conflict.

Despite his experience of hardship, Cole struggled to contain his anger. The drought exacerbated his natural inclination towards decisive action. He wanted to confront the rancher, to force him to share the resources. However, Tala, drawing upon her deep understanding of Lipan Indian conflict resolution, steered him towards a different approach. She reminded him that resorting to force would only escalate the situation, shattering the fragile alliance between the three factions.

Instead, Tala proposed a series of meetings with the rancher and representatives from each community affected by the drought. These weren't formal councils but smaller, more informal gatherings held under the shade of the largest mesquite trees. The meetings were collaborative, focusing on finding creative solutions rather than assigning blame. The discussions were long and arduous, punctuated by intense frustration and despair.

Patiently, Tala heard each side's complaints, validating their worries but stressing their common problem. She made them remember that their shared dependence on the land and its resources was more significant than their disagreements. She called upon their shared humanity and sense of community.

Tala's skill in easing tension and building consensus, despite his initial reservations about her strategy, impressed Cole. His observations showed her knowledge of Lipan Indian traditions, respect for community elders, and diplomatic skills were invaluable in resolving disputes. He developed the ability to control his impulsiveness, improve his listening skills, and seek compromise over conflict. He aided in these casual talks, offering expertise on cattle ranching and resource management. His background gave valuable insight into the discussions, leading to well-informed and more balanced outcomes.

One significant innovation was the sharing of water management techniques. The Lipan Indian, long accustomed to arid conditions, possessed traditional water conservation methods unknown to the ranchers and the Cavalry. Through these gatherings, they shared their knowledge, exchanging techniques for digging and maintaining water cisterns, preserving water through efficient irrigation methods, and managing their livestock during times of scarcity. This proved invaluable in mitigating the drought's effects.

The collaborative efforts also extended to creating a communal grazing plan that ensured fair access to the dwindling pastures. This required considerable negotiation, as individual ranchers, driven by their self-interest, resisted sacrificing any of their grazing lands. However, Tala's unwavering insistence on fairness, backed by Cole's practical knowledge of cattle and grazing patterns, won them over. The ultimate plan involved a designed rotational grazing system that ensured sufficient fodder for all the herds, preventing widespread starvation and ensuring the animals could survive the drought.

This time challenged the rooted kinships between the three groups. Underlying prejudices and distrust became apparent because of the drought's hardships. These hardships forged the strongest rooted kinships. Combating the drought through community efforts yielded unprecedented shared success, highlighting the strength of collaboration. The shared experience forged a stronger sense of unity among the Lipan Indians, Rangers, and Cavalry, overcoming past divisions.

Another challenge emerged as a growing influx of settlers into the region, attracted by the promise of cheap land and the potential for prosperity in the burgeoning cattle trade. This rapid expansion brought with it economic opportunities and new tensions. Conflicts arose over land ownership, water rights, and the allocation of resources. Cole and Tala constantly mediated disputes between the established settlers and the newcomers, ensuring fairness while also upholding the rights and traditions of the Lipan Indian community. This required a delicate balancing act that demanded patience, diplomacy, and a deep understanding of the needs of all parties involved.

They addressed these conflicts by introducing a formal land registration system that defined property boundaries and protected the Lipan Indian's traditional grazing lands and sacred sites. With his knowledge of land surveying and legal practices, Cole played a crucial role in establishing this system. He worked with representatives from the Texas Rangers and the U.S. Cavalry, ensuring the fairness and impartiality of the process. This new system brought much-needed stability to the region, reducing land-related disputes and setting a precedent for future land allocation.

Tala, meanwhile, focused on maintaining the cultural integrity of the Lipan Indian community. She ensured the new settlers understood and respected Lipan Indian traditions, preventing encroachment on their sacred lands and artistic practices. She worked tirelessly to preserve the Lipan Indian language and culture, advocating for integrating Lipan Indian traditions into the educational curriculum and promoting the revitalization of Lipan Indian arts and crafts. Her efforts fostered a sense of pride and self-respect within the Lipan Indian community, strengthening their resilience in the face of external pressures.

Cole and Tala's leadership was not just about resolving immediate crises, but about building a sustainable future for their community. They understood that lasting peace required more than just the absence of conflict; it needed a fundamental shift in mindset, a commitment to mutual respect, understanding, and collaboration. This commitment extended to their relationship as well. Overcoming challenges—emotional, political, and generational together, and their shared leadership — made their thread of trust stronger. As their community grew, so did their love, a testament to their shared dreams and strength. Despite hardship, their inspiring love story blossomed, becoming a beacon of hope for others.

Dialogue, diplomacy, and a shared commitment to peace and prosperity—not conquest—changed the region's landscape thanks to their combined efforts. What was once a heavy burden, the weight of leadership, now feels like a shared responsibility, dream, and commitment. The burden of leadership transformed into a beacon of hope, guiding them toward a better future. Daily, the Texas sun shone on a community showing the power of love, leadership, and understanding.

Chapter 48: Making Hard Decisions

The seemingly endless summer gave way to the crisp air of fall, bringing with it a change in season and a new wave of challenges—emotional, political, and generational. Though easing, the drought had left its mark on the land and its people. Visible damage appeared: the dry land, dying plants, exhausted settlers, and strained relationships between the three groups. Cole and Tala grappled with agonizing decisions, each carrying immense weight and far-reaching consequences.

One thorny issue revolved around the allocation of limited grazing land. The influx of new settlers had increased the demand for pastureland, creating a conflict between the established ranchers and the newcomers. The Lipan Indians, with their traditional grazing grounds, found themselves caught in the middle, their way of life threatened by the encroaching expansion. Someone tasked Cole and Tala with creating a fair solution that wouldn't displace the Lipan Indians while ensuring the new settlers had sufficient resources to survive.

With his intimate knowledge of cattle ranching, Cole proposed a rotational grazing system, dividing the land into sections and allowing different groups to use each section for a specific period. Proper pasture management avoided overgrazing, ensuring access for every group and preventing conflict. However, implementing this system proved to be a Herculean task, requiring intricate negotiations and a profound understanding of individual interests and concerns.

Tala, employing her innate diplomacy and understanding of Lipan Indian customs, facilitated the negotiations. Tirelessly, she bridged the gap between differing perspectives, calming the anxieties of the Lipan Indian elders and reassuring the new settlers that their needs would be addressed. The process was slow and fraught with tension.

Ranchers who had long established their grazing territories resisted sharing their land, viewing it as an infringement of their established rights. The newcomers, eager to prove themselves, also complained about being disadvantaged in the new system.

To address these concerns, Cole and Tala undertook a meticulous process of mapping and surveying the grazing land. They meticulously charted the existing boundaries, identified areas of vibrant vegetation, and assessed the carrying capacity of different sections. This data, presented to all parties, helped to quell anxieties and provided a solid foundation for negotiations. Using his knowledge of land surveying and legal precedent, Cole ensured the accuracy and fairness of the mapping process. His expertise lent credibility to the process, fostering trust and encouraging cooperation.

Once they mapped the land, they began the intricate task of allocating grazing rights. They considered both the size of each rancher's herd and the Lipan Indians' traditional grazing rights, ensuring the Indians' access to critical areas. The negotiations were tedious, requiring countless meetings, compromises, and concessions. However, Tala's patience and unwavering commitment to fairness, combined with Cole's practical insights, proved successful. All involved deemed the resulting grazing plan fair, although imperfect.

Another challenge arose with the burgeoning cattle trade in Fort Worth. The town, experiencing explosive growth, was a magnet for entrepreneurs and speculators, generating a fierce competition over resources and profits. With his considerable experience in cattle drives, Cole found himself increasingly involved in the trade, negotiating deals with buyers, securing transport, and navigating the intricacies of the cattle market. His success in the trade not only benefited him, but also enhanced the reputation of the Lipan Indian community, increasing their bargaining power and economic security.

However, this burgeoning wealth brought its own set of challenges—emotional, political, and generational. Jealousy and resentment arose among ranchers who felt that Cole's success came at their expense. Rumors of favoritism and unfair dealings began circulating, threatening to undermine the hard-won harmony. Aware of the brewing tensions, Cole recognized the need to be more transparent in his dealings. He made a point of sharing his profits, reinvesting a portion in community development projects, and providing economic opportunities for other ranchers, fostering a sense of shared prosperity.

Meanwhile, Tala focused on preserving the Lipan Indian culture in the face of rapid change. The influx of settlers has brought new cultural influences, threatening to erode the traditional Lipan Indian way of life. Tala worked tirelessly to document Lipan Indian oral histories, preserving stories, traditions, and language. She introduced Lipan Indian cultural practices to the newcomers, fostering a greater understanding and appreciation of their heritage. She spearheaded initiatives to revitalize traditional crafts and arts, creating a source of both cultural pride and economic opportunity.

Perhaps the most challenging decision facing Cole and Tala involved a matter of justice. A series of cattle thefts had plagued the region, causing significant hardship among ranchers. The blame fell upon a group of new settlers in the area; thus, they were easy targets of suspicion. Cole, inclined towards swift action, favored a quick investigation followed by decisive punishment. However, Tala urged a more careful inquiry, reminding Cole that their actions could punish innocent people.

This decision pitted Cole's inclination towards direct action against Tala's emphasis on fairness and due process. They chose a middle ground. They established a joint investigation team, comprising members of the Lipan Indians, the Texas Rangers, and the U.S. Cavalry, to ensure impartiality and thoroughness. The investigation was meticulous and time-consuming, requiring careful tracking of evidence and the interrogation of multiple witnesses. The process revealed that the blame for the thefts fell on a notorious gang of outlaws, operating of the accused settlers.

While more demanding, this careful approach avoided a potential miscarriage of justice. It reaffirmed Cole and Tala's commitment to upholding justice and fairness, strengthening the trust of all three communities. Their careful consideration underscored their commitment to ensuring the community's well-being, demonstrating that a balance between decisive action and thoughtful consideration was possible, even in the face of serious threats.

These decisions weighed, testing their patience, diplomacy, and resilience. But they also forged an even stronger thread of trust between Cole and Tala, their shared commitment further solidifying their love. Their leadership style grown into a harmonious blend of Cole's decisive nature and Tala's patient diplomacy. They learned to navigate the complexities of their roles, acknowledging the burdens and rewards of their responsibilities. They understood that authentic leadership lay in resolving immediate crises and building a sustainable future based on cooperation, mutual respect, and a commitment to justice. Though heavy, the weight of leadership was a weight shared, a weight borne together, forging a future brighter than either could have imagined alone.

Chapter 49: Balancing Priorities

The crisp fall air carried the scent of woodsmoke and damp earth, a stark contrast to the parched landscape of the recent drought. Leadership's weight, previously shared, now felt intensely heavy for Cole and Tala. The successful resolution of the grazing land dispute and the cattle theft investigation had brought a fragile peace, but beneath the surface, the tensions simmered. The demands of their respective communities and the burgeoning complexities of their personal lives threatened to overwhelm them.

For Cole, the demands of the cattle trade were relentless. Fort Worth, a whirlwind of ambition and opportunity, had become a second home; yet, it was a home far removed from the quiet serenity of the Lipan Indian lands. The long days spent negotiating deals, securing transport, and navigating the treacherous waters of the cattle market left him weary. He longed for the simplicity of tending his herd, the comfort of Tala's embrace, the quiet rhythm of life on the creek. But the success he'd achieved, the prosperity he'd brought to the Lipan Indian community, chained him to this demanding life. The economic security he'd helped establish was fragile, and any lapse in his vigilance could unravel it all.

He wrestled with his conscience, torn between his desires and his responsibilities. He knew Tala understood the necessity of his work, yet he saw the subtle weariness in her smile. The sacrifices she was making were immense, sacrifices for which he felt a deep sense of responsibility. He'd promised her a life together beyond the endless challenges, yet the reality felt far removed from that promise. The familiar rhythm and predictable cattle trade kept them apart.

Tala, meanwhile, faced her own set of challenges. The preservation of Lipan Indian culture, a task she embraced with unwavering passion, demanded a constant vigilance. The influx of settlers brought with it economic opportunities and the insidious threat of assimilation. She worked, documenting oral histories, teaching Lipan Indian language and traditions to the younger generation, and fostering cultural exchange with the newcomers. Yet, the effort was exhausting, a constant battle against the tide of change.

She felt the weight of her responsibility, the weight of preserving a heritage threatened by the relentless march of progress. She knew that her people's survival depended on their ability to adapt, to embrace the opportunities presented by the new world without sacrificing their identity. It was a delicate balancing act that required strength, diplomacy, patience, and perseverance. She longed for quiet intimacy with Cole when she could be his beloved, not his community's leader. Yet those moments were increasingly scarce, swallowed by the relentless demands of her role.

Discussions of community concerns, economic growth strategies, and cultural preservation plans often consumed their nights, once filled with whispered secrets and shared dreams.

One evening, after a grueling day of negotiations with a disgruntled rancher, Cole found Tala sitting by the creek, her gaze fixed on the slow, meandering water. He sat beside her; the silence stretching between them.

"It feels like we're drowning," Tala said, her voice a whisper. "Drowning in the weight of it all."

Cole reached for her hand, his touch gentle and reassured. "I know," he murmured, his voice rough with emotion. I feel it too. But we're not alone in this. We have each other."

Tala leaned against him, her body trembling. How long will this continue? How much more can we give?"

Cole didn't have a simple answer. He knew the challenges—emotional, political, and generational were immense, the pressures relentless. But he also knew the strength of their thread of trust, the unwavering commitment they shared. Giving up now would negate their considerable effort.

His voice, firm and filled with newfound resolve, declared, "We find a way." "We balance it all. We keep our love alive amidst the chaos, to nurture our community, and to preserve what's precious."

He pulled her closer, holding her, finding solace in the warmth of her body. He knew it wouldn't be easy. Sleepless nights, agonizing decisions, and sacrifices lay ahead. Their shared experience enabled them to surmount challenges—emotional, political, and generational. They would navigate the turbulent waters of leadership, balance their people's needs with their own, and preserve their love amidst the relentless demands of the frontier. They would build a future where their love story was not just a tale of survival, but a testament to resilience, a beacon of hope amidst the chaos of the Wild West.

The path ahead remained uncertain, but they would walk it together, hand in hand, their love a guiding star in the ever-changing landscape of their lives. Shared leadership, despite its challenges—emotional, political, and generational — strengthened and unified them. In the quiet moments, stolen between the demands of their responsibilities, they found strength in their union, a love that promised to endure, a love that would blossom even amidst the harshest realities of the frontier.

Chapter 50: Building Trust

Those next few weeks saw a flurry of activity. Cole, ever practical, focused on strengthening their economic position. In Fort Worth, he secured beneficial trade agreements with merchants, guaranteeing reasonable prices for Lipan cattle and a reliable supply of vital goods for the tribe. By establishing a rotating credit system, he enabled Lipan Indian families to buy goods even during hardship, promoting economic stability and preventing overwhelming debt. By conducting workshops on carpentry, blacksmithing, and basic accounting, he equipped the community with practical skills, reducing their dependence on outside trade.

However, he also pursued other goals besides economic growth. He realized that stability depended on shared goals and collective responsibility. Bridging the gap, he organized meetings between Lipan elders and settlers, encouraging dialogue and comprehension. Patiently hearing the concerns of both the Lipan Indians (anxious about their traditions) and the settlers (apprehensive about the unfamiliar culture), he mediated their communication difficulties. He stressed their common goals: prosperity, security, and peaceful coexistence.

Unlike appeasement, Cole genuinely sought reconciliation. He recognized the Lipan Indians' historical mistreatment, supporting their worries and stressing his dedication to their rights. The settlers' resourcefulness and innovation, along with the Lipan Indian deep-rooted traditions and spiritual rooted kinship to the land, were both emphasized. Through events he organized, he promoted cultural exchange, enabling both groups to share their music, food, and stories. He actively promoted the learning of the Lipan Indian language by the settlers, believing that language was the key to unlocking cultural understanding. It was a slow and often painstaking process, requiring patience, diplomacy, and a willingness to compromise.

Tala was pivotal in keeping Lipan Indian culture alive, meanwhile.

As it adapts to the changing times. To prevent the tribe's oral histories from vanishing, she carefully recorded their stories and traditions. A community center, founded by her, provided Lipan Indian language lessons, traditional craft instruction, and cultural heritage education to children. To protect the tribe's sacred sites and customs from outside influence and maintain their importance, she worked tirelessly within the changing community.

She recognized the necessity of integrating fresh skills and understanding into the Lipan lifestyle. She urged younger people to pursue education, English proficiency, and practical skills for success in a changing economy. Collaborating with Cole, she designed educational programs integrating traditional Lipan Indian wisdom and contemporary skills into a meaningful, empowering curriculum.

Her approach was one of empowerment rather than preservation in isolation. She understood that cultural vitality required a dynamic exchange, not a rigid adherence to the past. She facilitated the creation of a community council that included representatives from the Lipan Indian and settler communities. This council served as a forum for dialogue, a mechanism for resolving conflicts, and making decisions that reflected the shared interests of all members. The council, a symbol of trust, showcased leadership's success uniting a diverse community through cooperation.

One evening, under the vast Texas sky, Cole and Tala sat by the creek, reflecting on their progress. They felt less burdened by past anxieties, now cautiously optimistic. "It's fragile," Tala admitted, her voice soft, "this peace we've built. But it feels real." Cole nodded, his gaze fixed on the stars. It shows what is possible when we collaborate and have faith in one another. "He reached for her hand, his touch gentle, yet conveying a deep affection. "We've shown them, Tala, both sides, that collaboration is stronger than conflict."

Their success wasn't a matter of strategic planning or political maneuvering; it resulted from their ability to build trust—a deep, abiding trust among the diverse factions of their community. They hadn't eradicated prejudice or misunderstanding overnight, but they had established a foundation for a more harmonious future. The shared experiences, mutual respect, and collaborative efforts had chipped away at the walls of distrust, creating space for empathy, understanding, and a burgeoning sense of shared identity.

The trust they'd cultivated went beyond the Lipan Indian and settler communities. It extended to the nearby ranches and even the occasional representatives from the U.S. Cavalry who passed through. The news of the Lipan Indian community's prosperity, of its peaceful and cooperative nature, spread. The initial suspicion and mistrust gave way to curiosity and respect. Traders, once hesitant to engage with the Lipan Indian community, now sought opportunities to do business. The ranchers, once wary of encroaching on Lipan Indian lands, discovered a willingness to negotiate fair deals and create beneficial partnerships.

Cole and Tala's leadership style was remarkable for its success in fostering collaboration and its humility. They sought the opinions and perspectives of others, creating space for diverse voices to be heard. They listened more than they spoke, ensuring everyone felt respected. This approach, coupled with their visible commitment to fairness and transparency, earned them the loyalty and trust of those under their guidance. They showed that leadership wasn't about wielding power but serving the community's needs.

The weight of leadership remained, but it was no longer a crushing burden. It was a shared responsibility, a collective endeavor. The trust they'd built wasn't just a fragile thing; it was a strong foundation, solidifying, a testament to the power of collaboration and understanding, a beacon of hope in the often-turbulent landscape of the American West. It was a foundation upon which they would build not just a community, but a future—a future where love, understanding, and mutual respect could flourish alongside economic prosperity and cultural preservation.

A future where past, present, and Kickapoo Creek life intertwine. Together, they would construct a shared future, showcasing their love as a testament to the resilience of the human spirit in challenging times. Although the journey was far from done, every sunrise made the path ahead clearer and brighter, led by their shared hope and strong foundation of trust. During quiet moments overlooking their flourishing community, they understood leadership's burden—a shared responsibility.

Chapter 51: Passing the Torch

The sun dipped below the horizon, painting the sky in fiery orange and soft lavender hues, as Cole and Tala gathered a group of young Lipan Indian and settler children around a crackling fire. Wood smoke and roasting meat perfumed the lingering warmth. This informal session felt more like a torch-passing ceremony than a lesson held under the stars.

Cole, his weathered face softened by the firelight, spoke. Years spent on the frontier gave his low rumble a resonance of deep wisdom. He emphasized the importance of negotiation, not just in bartering for goods, but also in resolving conflicts and building bridges between different cultures.

He recounted anecdotes from his past, tales of tense standoffs transformed into beneficial agreements through careful listening, patience, and a willingness to find common ground. Understanding others' viewpoints is crucial; he highlighted this before making judgments.

The children, a mix of wide-eyed innocence and burgeoning curiosity, listened intently. Some leaned closer to the fire, their faces illuminated by the dancing flames, while others sat back, their eyes fixed on Cole's every movement. He held their attention, weaving intricate stories of cunning traders, stubborn ranchers, and unexpected alliances, each anecdote laced with a subtle but powerful lesson. He spoke not of survival, but of thriving–of creating a life filled with purpose, meaning, and a strong sense of community.

Tala, her eyes flashing with fierce intelligence, took charge.

She discussed the Lipan Indians' rich history, traditions, and the crucial role of safeguarding their language and customs. Instead of isolating and protecting them, she spoke of adapting and integrating them into modern society. She recounted tales of Lipan Indian women's strength, resilience, wisdom, and unwavering spirit despite facing hardship. Traditional weaving patterns, elegant pottery, and rhythmic ancient chants all showed a tangible rooted kinship to their heritage.

She highlighted the importance of valuing both their Lipan Indian roots and global perspectives, emphasizing English proficiency and cross-cultural understanding while preserving their heritage. By emphasizing their heritage, she inspired pride and encouraged them to value traditions alongside modern possibilities.

As twilight fell, the children contributed by sharing their stories, observations, and hopes for tomorrow. Cole and Tala listened, offering advice and support, gently steering the discussion toward their shared values—respect, trust, cooperation, and resilience—which had fueled their achievements.

These fireside gatherings did not encompass all of Cole's mentorship. Ever the pragmatist, Cole integrated practical skills training into his daily routines. He taught the older boys basic carpentry and blacksmithing skills, which were essential for maintaining and improving the community's infrastructure. His teachings emphasized careful planning and meticulous work, as well as the satisfaction derived from creating something tangible and valuable. He inspired them to take pride in their work and contribute to their community.

Tala, meanwhile, led the younger girls in traditional crafts, teaching them the ancient techniques of weaving, pottery, and beadwork. She emphasized not only the skill and precision required, but also the artistry, creativity, and cultural significance embedded within each crafted item. She encouraged them to express themselves through their art, to find their voice, and to share their stories through the mediums of their heritage.

They fostered a peer mentorship system, pairing older children with younger ones to ensure that Cole and Tala were not the only ones who benefited, but the entire community. This system created a sense of shared responsibility, fostering a sense of community among the children and helping to solidify their understanding of the community's values.

The older children became role models for the younger ones, demonstrating the practical application of the skills and values they had learned. This created a dynamic learning environment where knowledge and wisdom flowed in multiple directions, reinforcing the community's shared identity and purpose.

Beyond the practical skills, Cole and Tala organized group projects that required collaboration, communication, and creative solutions. These projects, ranging from designing a new irrigation system to planning a community celebration, allowed the children to apply their knowledge in real-world scenarios. The emphasis wasn't on competition but on cooperation, on finding solutions that benefited the entire community.

The thread of trust between the older and younger generations wasn't solely based on instruction and guidance. It was a reciprocal relationship, built on mutual respect, shared experiences, and a deep affection. Cole and Tala shared stories of their youth, struggles, and triumphs, forging a rooted kinship that transcended the generational gap. They encouraged the children to share their hopes and dreams, to explore their talents, and to express their opinions. They created a safe and nurturing environment where the children felt valued, understood, and empowered.

The children brought a fresh perspective, a youthful energy, and a boundless optimism that helped to inspire Cole and Tala. They reminded them of the unwavering power of hope, the importance of perseverance, and the enduring beauty of the human spirit. Their laughter and energy revitalized Cole and Tala, reminding them of the reasons behind their tireless efforts to build a better future. Transfer of knowledge and skills failed with the passing of the torch. A generation that understood the importance of heritage, the value of adaptation, and the unwavering power of unity.

Evenings by the fire offered more than teaching; As the stars twinkled overhead, the shared stories illuminated not only the past but also the path forward, illuminated by the enduring light of their shared vision and the firm foundation of mutual trust and understanding. The new generation was ready, eager to embrace the future, and Cole and Tala watched with pride as their community, built on the foundations of love and understanding, flourished and grew. Their work unfinished, the torch's passing kept their vision alive. Their living memory wouldn't be in stone monuments, but woven into the community's very fabric, a living testament to the collaboration's power and the enduring human spirit's strength.

Chapter 52: Mentorship and Guidance

The following year brought the burgeoning spring, and a renewed sense of purpose, to the community of Kickapoo Creek. Cole and Tala, having established a solid foundation of trust and cooperation, turned their attention towards the future, towards the young people who would one day inherit their responsibilities. They did not mentor through a formal program;

Cole grasped the educational value as the West's landscape shifted, highlighting formal education's importance. To guarantee Lipan Indian children equal opportunities with settler children, he and the kind local schoolteacher, Miss Abigail, worked tirelessly. His support went beyond logistics;

Textbooks weren't his only teaching tool for history; He highlighted literacy's significance in understanding the world and handling increasingly complex legal and commercial issues in the expanding town.

His lessons extended beyond the classroom. He organized practical workshops that taught carpentry, blacksmithing, and basic mechanics.

He stressed quality work, pride, and community contribution. The young men learned not just to build but to repair, adapt, and innovate. They built fences, restored homes, and even constructed a new well, learning valuable skills while contributing to their community's infrastructure. The pride on their faces as they completed each project was a testament to Cole's effective mentorship, a visible manifestation of his investment in their future.

Tala established a program dedicated, who was always mindful of preserving their culture. She wasn't teaching. She showed the complex weaving, the fine art of pottery, and the symbolic meaning behind their traditional beadwork. To prevent her people's history from fading, she retold ancient stories, safeguarding their oral traditions. She stressed the need to preserve language, educating youth in their native tongue so they could connect with their elders, history, and heritage. She described traditions, emphasizing their cultural importance, history, and emotional effect. These weren't crafts;

Her teaching extended beyond the tangible arts. She fostered critical thinking and problem-solving skills by creating scenarios that forced the children to think and work together. They planned community events, devising logistical plans, managing budgets, and coordinating tasks. They learned to negotiate, compromise, and work to achieve a common goal. The sense of accomplishment was palpable, a shared pride in their collective efforts. These exercises extended beyond simple problem solving; they instilled crucial leadership qualities and experience in conflict resolution. The children learned to navigate disagreements, find common ground, and work towards solutions that benefited the community as a whole.

The mentorship included more than just Cole and Tala; They fostered a peer mentorship system, pairing older children with younger ones, creating a ripple effect of knowledge and support. Having grasped the skills and values, older children became role models and teachers for the next generation. This intergenerational exchange fostered a sense of community, a strong thread of trust that extended beyond the classroom and fireside gatherings. It strengthened their shared identity as a community working in unison toward a common goal, ensuring that their culture and community would continue.

Practical skills, cultural preservation, and leadership development were all part of their comprehensive approach. They emphasized gaining knowledge, applying it, contributing to the community, and assuming related responsibilities. Instead of competition, they prioritized cooperation and collaboration among the children, believing that a supportive community is the key to success. The children learned the value of adapting and innovating while honoring their heritage, proving modernization and cultural preservation can coexist.

Sundays became a day of community engagement. The children, divided into age groups, took part in various activities. Younger children assisted with tending the community garden, learning about sustainable agriculture and the importance of providing for their own needs. Older children worked alongside the adults, taking part in the building and maintenance of the community's infrastructure. These hands-on experiences solidified their understanding of community involvement and responsibility. They worked alongside the adults, not as passive onlookers, but as active participants, learning practical skills while contributing to the betterment of their shared environment.

Evenings by the fire became richer. They now structured lessons, actively encouraging the children to take part, ask questions, and share experiences and perspectives, instead of just sharing stories. Cole and Tala encouraged critical thinking and open discussions, fostering an environment where children felt comfortable expressing themselves, challenging assumptions, and developing their unique perspectives. They fostered a safe and nurturing atmosphere, encouraging children to share and debate ideas without fear of judgment or ridicule, reinforcing the importance of open communication and critical thinking.

Integrating settler and Lipan Indian traditions into their educational approach was crucial. They recognized the need for the children to adapt to the changing world without losing their cultural identity. They taught the children the history of both groups, helped them understand the complexities of the past, and empowered them to shape their future. This allowed for a mutual exchange of ideas and skills, fostering a sense of unity amongst the community, transcending ethnic backgrounds, and promoting understanding between various groups.

Cole and Tala's commitment wasn't about passing down skills; it was about nurturing future leaders who could navigate the complexities of the changing world while preserving the values and traditions of their community. They instilled in them a deep sense of responsibility, a strong sense of community, and an unwavering belief in their ability to shape their future. Their mentorship fostered skilled individuals who were thoughtful, compassionate, and responsible citizens, equipping them with the skills and knowledge necessary for continued growth and progress, preparing them to step up and become the leaders their community needed.

The noticeable growth directly resulted from their hard work. Community activities' engagement among young people. They led the charge, organizing events, advocating for their community, fostering constructive dialogue, and promoting a shared vision of a thriving future.

KICKAPOO CREEK

Having completed their mentorship, Cole and Tala actively took part in Kickapoo Creek's development, demonstrating its success. Rather than teaching, they empowered children, fostering a future richer in heritage and promise beyond their imaginations. Guided by their elders, the Kickapoo Creek community's shared vision ignited, ensuring a bright and successful future for everyone.

Chapter 53: Sharing Knowledge

The sun dipped below the horizon, painting the sky in fiery orange and soft lavender hues, as the children of Kickapoo Creek gathered around the crackling fire. This wasn't a casual gathering, but an orchestrated lesson in Lipan Indian history and storytelling. Tala, illuminated by the dancing flames, began a tale of the ancient spirits that guarded the land, her voice a mesmerizing blend of strength and softness. She spoke of the sacred mountains, the whispering winds, and the enduring spirit of her ancestors, weaving a narrative that captivated the young listeners. Her words were not just stories; they were a living memory passed down through generations, connecting the children to their roots and empowering them with a sense of belonging. Each child listened intently, their eyes wide with wonder, drinking in the rich tapestry of their heritage. The stories weren't just entertaining; they were educational, imparting valuable lessons about courage, resilience, and preserving their cultural identity.

On the edge of things, Cole noted the children's intense focus. The power of storytelling deeply moved him. He contributed his perspective by recounting the stories of the early settlers, their struggles, and their victories. The Texas plains' vastness, the longhorn cattle, and the arduous journeys across the unforgiving landscape were all described by him. Rather than replacing Tala's teachings, he sought to supplement them, offering a wider understanding of their shared history, illustrating the interactions, conflicts, and eventual collaborations that shaped their present. Respecting diverse cultures, he explained, wasn't an imposed value; it was essential for the survival and success of their shared environment.

In the following days, the boys took part in a series of practical lessons led by Cole, a primary artisan. He taught the older boys the art of woodworking, demonstrating precise wood shaping techniques, the importance of selecting the right tools, and the satisfaction of creating something both beautiful and functional from raw materials. Cole emphasized not only the skill of carpentry but also the principles of design, encouraging the boys to think creatively, innovate, and discover their unique styles within an established framework. He shared stories about various homesteads and buildings that scattered the American landscape, illustrating how these construction techniques adapted to different environments and materials. This experience was not merely about constructing structures; it was about understanding the history of settlement, the resourcefulness of humanity, and their contributions to the development of surrounding communities.

Meanwhile, Tala instructed the girls in the intricate art of weaving. She showed them how to prepare the fibers, dye them with natural pigments, and create patterns that held deep symbolic meaning within Lipan Indian culture. Each thread offered more than mere material. She also taught them beadwork, how to create intricate designs using colorful beads, and explained the deep symbolic meaning embedded within the colors and patterns. Each pattern told a story, represented a specific meaning, and preserved a critical piece of Lipan Indian culture, thus preventing its loss to the changing times.

The lessons included more than just traditional arts and crafts; He highlighted the horse's crucial role in their farming, hunting, and travel. He cultivated their deep respect for these animals, teaching them about humanity's interconnectedness with them.

Tala's lessons extended beyond practical applications. Through discussions of community roles, she fostered collaboration, and a shared sense of purpose in the children. She encouraged critical thinking, questioning assumptions, and open discussion. She explained the inner workings of the Lipan Indian social structure and each member's vital role in community health. Cooperation, mutual respect, and shared responsibilities were highlighted by her as crucial.

The community dedicated Sundays to communal projects. The children, divided into smaller groups according to age and abilities, participated in tasks that benefited the entire community. They helped tend the community gardens, learning the importance of sustainable agriculture, the rhythms of nature, and the satisfaction of producing food for themselves and their neighbors. They participated in the community's upkeep infrastructure, helping to maintain the irrigation system, repair fences, and assist with other tasks that ensured the smooth functioning of their shared life. This practical method gave them real-world experience, building camaraderie and appreciation for teamwork. It reinforced the lessons of responsibility and contribution, teaching them that their roles within the community were vital to its success.

People reserved evenings for storytelling, singing, and dancing. The children learned the traditional Lipan Indian songs, their voices blending, carrying their culture and stories through the generations. They danced in the moonlight, graceful and expressive, honoring their heritage and finding joy in their shared traditions. This wasn't mere entertainment, but a way of keeping their culture alive and vibrant, connecting to their past and securing their future. This continuous reinforcement of their heritage cemented a sense of belonging and identity, creating a deep-rooted kinship to their community and traditions.

Cole and Tala aimed to do more than just impart knowledge; They instilled in the children a deep appreciation for their heritage, a respect for different cultures, and an unwavering belief in their ability to affect the world. A culture of learning, respect, and shared responsibility flourished, creating a safe, valued, and empowering community for the children. Their lasting impact on Kickapoo Creek would shape its future, preserving their heritage for generations. Cole and Tala had prepared the children to lead, protect their heritage, and contribute to their community. Kickapoo Creek's future rested on their elders' wisdom and steadfast commitment to their unique heritage and identity.

Chapter 54: Building Bridges to the Future

The following years unfolded like a slow, deliberate sunrise, painting the landscape of Kickapoo Creek with the vibrant hues of a shared future. Cole and Tala's efforts were the foundation upon which a new generation would build. The children, once wide-eyed listeners, now stood taller, their shoulders squared with newfound confidence. Students became active participants in the life of Kickapoo Creek, their contributions echoing the wisdom imparted by their mentors.

Young gardeners nurtured the communal gardens, formerly symbols of shared work, into flourishing spaces. They experimented with different crops, learned the nuances of soil composition, and even developed innovative irrigation techniques, surpassing the methods of their elders. Their success wasn't just about the abundance of food; it was a testament to their growing understanding of sustainable agriculture, a vital skill for the survival and prosperity of their community. They understood the interconnectedness of their actions with the land, respecting its rhythms and nurturing its bounty. This wasn't farming, but a sacred act — a continuation of the ancient thread of trust between the Lipan Indian people and their ancestral lands.

The woodworking skills honed under Cole's tutelage were clear in the meticulously crafted tools and structures that appeared throughout Kickapoo Creek. The young men, no longer just apprentices, were now contributing artisans, their creations showcasing their talents and their collective commitment to excellence. They built sturdy shelters, repaired damaged fences, and created functional objects, their hands shaped by years of practice and inspired by their heritage. The craftsmanship wasn't just about utility; it reflected their cultural identity, a testament to their ability to adapt, innovate, and stay true to their roots. They didn't follow instructions; they innovated, experimenting with different techniques and adapting their skills to the unique needs of their environment.

The intricate weavings and beadwork created by the young women were more than just beautiful artifacts; they were living narratives, each thread and bead carrying the weight of history and tradition. The young women displayed their designs throughout the community, a vibrant celebration of their cultural identity; these designs drew inspiration from ancient Lipan Indian motifs and their own unique interpretations. They mastered the techniques and infused their work with their creative expressions, ensuring the continuity of their cultural heritage while enriching it with their artistic voices. The vibrant colors and intricate patterns told stories, whispered secrets, and served as a powerful reminder of their enduring heritage.

The horsemanship skills instilled by Cole transformed the children into confident riders, capable of navigating the challenging terrain. They weren't just learning to ride but forging a thread of trust with the horses, understanding their language, respecting their sensitivities, and appreciating their vital role in their lives. The horses seemed to respond to this new level of understanding, exhibiting harmonious movements with their riders, which created a spectacle of coordinated movement and mutual respect. This thread of trust extended beyond mere practicality; it reflected their interconnectedness with the natural world, a testament to their ability to understand and respect all living creatures.

However, the most significant transformation was in the overall atmosphere of Kickapoo Creek. The community grew beyond a group of individuals. The children, now young adults, integrated themselves into the social fabric, actively taking part in the community's decision-making processes. They were not passive recipients of tradition; they were active contributors, bringing fresh perspectives, innovative solutions, and an unwavering commitment to the well-being of their shared home. People heard their voices, valued their opinions, and found their participation essential. It was a community where everyone felt a sense of belonging, responsibility, and shared purpose. Collective determination filled the air, a tribute to Cole and Tala's lasting impact.

Cole and Tala, having witnessed the fruits of their labor, stepped back, not from involvement, but from direct instruction. Their role transformed into that of mentors and guides, offering advice, sharing their experiences, and celebrating the achievements of their protégés. They remained active participants in the community's life, but their focus shifted to fostering the leadership qualities of the younger generation, ensuring a smooth transition of power and responsibility. Their wisdom, once imparted through direct teaching, now flowed through the examples they set, their support, and their guidance. Their influence remained powerful, but it was now a subtle force, shaping the future without imposing on the autonomy of the rising generation. This seamless transition to responsibility highlighted the success of their long-term vision and underscored the sustainability of their efforts.

Annual gatherings went on, but their essence was different. Elders and the younger generation shared their stories, weaving a richer cultural tapestry with diverse perspectives. With renewed vigor, they sang songs; Young people now supported the cultural living memory, ensuring its lasting power. The lively exchange reinvigorated traditions, showcasing the Lipan's cultural resilience and adaptability.

The vision that Cole and Tala had meticulously cultivated had come to fruition. The bridge they had built between cultures, between generations, stood firm, a testament to their unwavering commitment and the unwavering spirit of the Lipan Indian people. Kickapoo Creek's future is secure, thanks to real progress and a strong spirit of cooperation, cultural pride, and unwavering faith.

Chapter 55: A Legacy of Unity

As winter settled over Kickapoo Creek, smoke curled lazily from the chimneys, yet the town itself remained vibrantly awake and bustling with activity. Within the community hall, meticulously crafted from Lipan stone and Ranger timber, elders from both factions sat opposite the younger generation, with maps and trade ledgers between them. Although the tone of the arguments remained gentle, the passion behind them was undeniable and quite moving. Laughter, a surprising and welcome response to the palpable tension, filled the air instead of the expected gunfire.

Positioned at the edge of the room, Mara, a seventeen-year-old granddaughter of Tala, prepared herself to deliver her speech. Across the vast chamber, her voice, though measured in its pace, carried with remarkable clarity, ensuring that her words reached all those present. We don't have to let the cattle trade dispute create division amongst us; instead, let's work together to find solutions and bridge the gap between differing viewpoints.

With a nonchalant air, Silas's son settled back against the chair, his arms crossed firmly over his chest, a clear sign he wasn't in the mood to take part. Effective communication involves more than simply hearing words; it causes actively engaging with and understanding the speaker's message.

Mara responded that fairness meant ensuring everyone expressed their views and be heard, even if a complete consensus couldn't be reached among the participants.

A moment of silence hung in the air before nods of agreement signaled a willingness to seek common ground, hands extending in gestures of compromise.

In the outdoor area, Cole's great-nephew, Jonah, helped a younger child adjust the yoke on the mule team for comfort, safety, and efficiency. With a gentle touch, he corrected the strap's position, murmuring, "Not like that," a soft reprimand. "Do you see what I mean? It was reminiscent of the informal, offhand lessons," Cole imparted casually. Now, the memory of that experience lived on, embedded deep within its primal instincts. The living memory unfolded not in grand monuments or public pronouncements, but in the quiet, collaborative acts of shared harvests, silently repaired boundaries, and peace agreements crafted by the young generation from both sides.

A midday hum of lessons filled the schoolhouse, a vibrant energy buzzing through the classrooms and hallways. On the blackboard, a vibrant display of two languages unfolded, with English occupying the left side and Lipan Apache gracefully taking its place on the right. Ms. Anel, part Lipan and part Ranger but entirely businesslike, paced the room as the students read aloud a story Chayton passed down through generations.

Gazing out the window, one could see rows of hardy winter greens flourishing in neatly raised beds, a testament to the irrigation channels cleverly designed using both ancient river wisdom and modern cavalry engineering techniques. The agreement reached was not merely a compromise, but a complex arrangement born from extensive negotiation and a willingness to meet halfway on multiple points of contention.

Tala had begun her garden many years prior, a small plot of land that was initially no bigger than the area covered by a wagon. During harvest celebrations, Kickapoo Creek residents freely shared their food with neighboring settlements, filling their pantries and hearts and fostering a strong sense of community. Once viewed with suspicion, these visitors now returned annually, ravenous for both food and the valuable lessons offered.

Underneath the wide open Texas sky, there was dancing—spirited, barefoot, and messy, with revelers twirling and spinning with unrestrained joy. The rhythmic thumping of the drums resonated perfectly with the lively melody of the fiddles, creating a vibrant and harmonious sound. Without regard to their respective family origins, the youth enthusiastically took part in a vibrant exchange of dance steps, creating a dynamic and inclusive atmosphere. A boy, extending his hand to a girl adorned with a sash his grandfather might have once deemed frivolous, captured a scene that spoke volumes. Without a second thought, she immediately accepted.

As the evening progressed, an elderly woman, her attire embellished with intricate blue beadwork, settled near the crackling fire and leaned in to speak to her niece. "There was a real possibility that we would have lost these songs forever."

"But we didn't," the girl whispered. "No, we didn't." The council fire remained sacred. Younger members tended it now, but they still used the stones placed by Chayton and Silas. On a cool spring night, fewer elders gathered, but they were no less revered.

They reminisced about the day Cole had stepped between rifle barrels and how Tala had refused to leave wounded strangers to. They spoke of how they had built peace—painfully, stubbornly, day after day. "Don't forget," one elder said, his voice trembling not from age but from emotion. "They chose the harder road so we could walk, the easier one."

Across the valley, homes bore the mark of that union—walls made of pressed earth and pine beams, decorated with carvings and woven hangings. No one built alone. When a new roof needed raising, it didn't matter what blood ran through your veins. You showed up. You helped. When children asked why, their parents told them stories—not of war, but of choices forged in the glow of firelight.

In the weaving hall, Lipan women worked beside newcomers, their looms clicking in rhythm. Trade caravans received some of their creations, while others went to the festival. All bore the same intricate patterns, some old and some new. A circle broken open, then joined again, was the design they repeated over and over. The Rangers didn't leave; some stayed, married, and raised families. Those who didn't visit often, no longer as watchmen, but as kin. They brought books, tools, seeds, and always respect.

Kickapoo Creek's prosperity transcended the limitations of the wagon trails, its influence expanding to a much broader and more extensive geographical reach. Because of articulate and measured letters, penned by those who understood the cost of conflict and written here, policies changed in towns far away. Although newspapers published columns under pseudonyms, it was common knowledge throughout the city that Cole's associates actually wrote these articles.

Yet, people didn't find the heart of the community in print. Action revealed the community's heart—their celebrations of births with blessings and prayers, their shared grief at the enduring memorial, their ready sharing of water, offers of help, and resolutions of conflicts. Even as Cole and Tala grew older, their influence didn't dim. They simply let others take the lead, watching as once-divided bloodlines mingled in laughter and song. They saw their hopes reflected in the eyes of those they hadn't yet met.

When the time came—when the creek ran wide with snowmelt and the town gathered under cypress trees to say goodbye—no one built a statue. Instead, they placed two stones beside the memorial. One bore the symbol of water and wood, while the other displayed a sun cradled by feathers. Around them bloomed wildflowers—planted by schoolchildren and watered by friends. The songs sung that day were not sad; they were full, like the wind after a storm.

The names of Cole and Tala remained in people's memories; Kickapoo Creek endured—not as a miracle, but as a promise kept. Not as a monument, but as a home.

Chapter 56: Life in the Present

The sun, a molten orb sinking behind the distant Texas hills, cast long shadows across Kickapoo Creek's gently rolling land. Warm light touched the garden rows, the eaves of adobe homes, and the worn cedar fences that had seen generations pass. Cole sat on the wide porch of the home he'd built with Tala, a house shaped by two worlds: carved beams with native motifs met with classic western shutters, and inside, cowhide rugs lay beside woven mats dyed with berries and bark. It was more than a home. It steadily proved that something new had been created here.

Tala moved through the garden with the same grace she had as a young woman, though her movements were now slower and more deliberate. A streak of silver ran through her braid, and deep lines curved from her eyes, drawn there by years of laughter, by worry, by wind. With a basket full of herbs and beans, she tucked a blossom behind her ear and glanced up at Cole, offering him her quiet smile.

From the porch, Cole could hear the sounds of life all around them. Children's shouts echoed from the schoolhouse, where a game of stickball had spilled into the dusty field. The rhythmic beat of a Lipan drum drifted from the town square. A dog barked, then fell silent. Somewhere out near the cattle pens, the lowing of calves told him that the spring branding was almost done. It was a sound that once might have meant labor, dust, and long rides; now, it meant something else: continuation.

With a slow, deliberate movement, he brought a tin cup filled with coffee to his lips and took a sip. Tala's unique approach was a fascinating blend of Lipan medicine and the practical habits of a trail boss, a combination that defined her approach to life and work. Only moments before, she had placed the item in his hands, her fingers lingering on his with the same gentle touch she had shown him ever since that day when they had first taken the courageous leap of faith to trust one another completely and implicitly. The weather and the difficulty of their work had etched themselves onto their calloused hands, serving as a testament to a life that, while full of experiences, had certainly not been easy.

Did you see James earlier today, by any chance? As she settled onto the bench next to him, Tala asked her question. He made a brief visit. A chuckle escaped Cole's lips as a fond memory resurfaced in his mind. Attempting to treat her feline companion as if it were an equine, she tried to mount the cat and ride it like a pony.

Tala's laughter was unrestrained and full, a joyful sound that escaped her lips without hesitation or worry. That girl is incredibly energetic and unrestrained, much like the untamed growth of a mesquite tree in the springtime.

Cole declared with a smile that she belonged to him completely and utterly, body and soul. There are so many questions swirling around in my head.

A tranquil hush settled between them, filling the air with a gentle sense of peace and contentment. They watched the sky's dramatic color shifts and mesmerizing blends, their gaze fixed on the heavens. The light illuminated the clouds, causing them to glow and blaze with a golden light. With powerful wings, a hawk soared in a wide circle above the steep, rocky ridge. In the distance, along the path, a sizable group, approximately half a dozen children representing a diverse range of ethnicities, hairstyles, and footwear, ran excitedly toward the town square where the nightly gathering was assembling. Cole fixated his gaze on that spot, unwilling to look away. "In the past, I remember a time where the idea of that was not possible, and it's amazing how far we've come since then." Tala responded quietly, "I do too. I remember when one wrong look could break a day apart. When a mother kept her child indoors at the sight of a uniform."

There was no need for them to say anything further. In every wonderful moment, there was a sense of the past, a feeling that it was always present, lurking at the edge of each auspicious occasion. It wasn't a haunting experience, but a poignant reminder of things past. They achieved peace after a hard-fought and costly struggle. Within the confines of the building, a cacophony of voices swelled and intensified, creating a clamorous atmosphere. Amaya, their daughter, presided over the weekly council meeting, a role previously held by Cole. Possessing both a sharp mind and Tala's remarkable empathy, she had weathered countless quiet storms while remaining under the bridge. Through skillful negotiation, she secured new water rights for her community from the town upriver, a significant achievement that involved persuading a group of initially skeptical ranchers that shared resource management did not equate to relinquishing their individual control. Her voice remained low, yet the room stilled as she spoke, a testament to her commanding presence and the weight of her words.

In comparing her abilities to his own, Cole remarked he had never achieved such a level of expertise, admitting that her skills exceeded his own. Feeling a sense of contentment and peace wash over her, Tala gently laid her head against his shoulder, overcome with tranquility. Unlike many of her contemporaries, she had access to and benefited from a superior teaching staff. As they stood in the side yard, the unmistakable sound of light, quick footsteps reached their ears, familiar and full of youthful energy. Their grandson, Eli, came into view, cheeks flushed a rosy red and a notebook clutched tightly under one arm.

In a breathless whisper, barely audible above the surrounding sounds, the boy excitedly relayed to his grandfather his ambitious plan, a clandestine project to build a chicken coop in the somewhat secluded area behind the imposing school building. Squinting intently, Cole focused his gaze on the boy standing before him, his eyes narrowed in concentration. "I'm curious to know whether you have spoken with your mother concerning this issue." "Her ultimate decision, as she revealed, depended entirely upon my capacity to convince you and secure your affirmative response."

A wide grin spread across Eli's face. "Are you saying that the answer is yes?"

"Please help yourself with whatever you require." As the boy hurried away, Tala called after him, "Remember to put on your gloves!"

As the evening progressed, following supper, a tranquil and peaceful quietude descended upon the house. For a considerable time, they had abandoned all efforts to fill it; the task proving ultimately futile and pointless. As an alternative to whatever they had planned, they gazed out the expansive windows as the stars appeared in the night sky. A gentle,

KICKAPOO CREEK

rhythmic creaking emanated from the porch swing, a sound that blended seamlessly with the persistent chirping of the crickets, each sound echoing and responding to the other in the night's stillness. A gentle breeze softly caused the wind chimes to chime, a gift from a Lipan silversmith who had spent his boyhood with the family and later returned as a teacher.

As a noticeable chill swept through the air, Tala, feeling the sudden drop in temperature, fetched a quilt from her bed and carefully wrapped it around her legs to keep herself warm. With a delicate hand, she reached into the intricately carved box and gently retrieved a recently taken photograph. In the photograph, their children and grandchildren stood proudly before the newly constructed schoolhouse—a striking blend of adobe and timber—where a Lipan Apache flag and a Texas flag flew together in harmonious unity, symbolizing the blend of cultures represented within the community and the school. Occupying the central space within the room was a captivating mural, a collaborative masterpiece lovingly crafted by the local students, which showcased a heartwarming scene of young Cole and Tala, their hands clasped in friendship, standing beneath the delicate blossoms of a majestic flowering pecan tree. Set against the backdrop, the artwork depicted a diverse collection of subjects, including a herd of cattle, a hawk perched high above, and a colorful, semicircular assembly of people representing various backgrounds and walks of life.

Cole muttered in disbelief, expressing his continued confusion and frustration over the inaccurate depiction of his nose.

"That object," Tala explained, "is symbolic." "It's not about you."

A smile touched his lips as he watched her face, illuminated by the dancing light of the flickering oil lamp.

Considering our existence, are we not merely representations or symbolic figures, embodying deeper meanings beyond our immediate perception?

In a pointed statement, she highlighted the enduring and unwavering nature of their function, explaining that they continuously serve as potent reminders. Rather than prioritizing ease of implementation, they concentrated their efforts on realizing the project's potential, undeterred by the obstacles they faced. In one smooth motion, he delicately reached across and clasped her hand within his own. With a speed that belied her grace, she seized the object in a single, swift movement, her hand closing around it with surprising dexterity.

As the wind outside abruptly changed direction, all those present felt a noticeable shift in the atmospheric pressure. A delightful fragrance, subtly combining the fresh, damp scent of the earth with the smoky aroma of burning mesquite wood, gently wafted on the air currents, creating a pleasant and memorable olfactory experience. Once again, children's voices filled the air, their captivating blend of Lipan and English creating a unique and beautiful, unforgettable soundscape. The gentle lullaby was a beautiful composition, masterfully weaving together the calming sounds of flowing rivers and the bright, twinkling brilliance of the starlight above. In school, their great-grandchildren could learn and sing the song, which was passed down through generations of their family.

As the night progressed, a blanket of darkness gradually enveloped everything in its path, obscuring all details and swallowing the landscape whole. Having once boldly risked everything to build a life together, the couple sat on the porch, finding solace in each other's comforting presence as the years of shared experiences and memories settled upon them, heavy yet familiar, like a well-worn blanket offering warmth and comfort.

Following a brief period of contemplation, Cole, with a sigh of relief, announced their successful performance.

Tala squeezed his hand, offering a silent reassurance that transcended words and soothed his worried heart. With unwavering commitment, we dedicated all our energy and resources to the task, tirelessly implementing every solution at our disposal until the very end.

That gentle response, in fact, revealed the genuine reality of the situation—not a flawless, legendary account, but the truth of devoted effort and continuous striving. This is a state of being in which one is eager to take part in something. Driven by an unwavering faith, they navigated a complex path, making a thousand decisions, each one reflecting their deep-seated trust and unshakeable conviction. The combined impact of those decisions resulted in a living memory far exceeding either parent's expectations; not only did it bring about lasting peace, but it also fostered a powerful sense of belonging, creating a home where their children felt secure and empowered to connect with their heritage and explore their future prospects with confidence.

Chapter 57: A Bond Forged in Fire

In the cozy home Cole and Tala had shared for decades, the hearth fire crackled softly, its gentle light casting flickering shadows that danced and swayed across the age-old wooden beams above them, creating a warm and inviting ambiance. With a gentle hissing sound, the logs burned in the fireplace, radiating warmth and filling the room with cherished memories. Upon the mantelpiece, there rested a small, intricately carved turtle, a cherished keepsake Cole had lovingly crafted for Tala during their very first winter as a couple, a tangible symbol of their shared memories. Close at hand, a feather fan used in Lipan blessing ceremonies lay at rest, its dyed tips worn smooth and frayed from countless years of use, a testament to countless blessings given. Bearing the marks of time—scraped and weathered—these two artifacts, similar to their owners, stood as testaments to history's enduring presence, their structural integrity surprisingly preserved.

Settled into his favorite chair, Cole felt the comforting texture of the softened leather, its surface bearing the faint, barely perceptible notches carved by his grandchildren, each marking a testament to their growth and a cherished memory. With a slow, deliberate movement, his hand crept across the intricately carved wood, his fingers gently tracing the familiar pattern, a pattern so ingrained in his memory that he no longer needed his eyes to guide him. Tala, a picture of composure despite her age, sat nearby with her legs crossed on the intricately braided rug, her back remarkably straight. Nestled in her lap was a small woven basket, only about half full, containing fragrant sweetgrass and dried kernels of corn.

A low rumble resonated in Cole's voice as he announced the premature arrival of the storm season, hinting at the tumultuous and unpredictable weather that was soon to follow. Tala nodded slightly in acknowledgment.

Because of the recent rainfall, the creek's water level had already risen to a significantly higher level than normal.

As the sun dipped below the horizon, casting long shadows, and a hush fell over the landscape, Cole, his face pressed against the cool glass of the windowpane, stole a quick glance at the world outside. That event brought back vivid memories of a year when the levee was perilously close to collapse, resulting in catastrophic and widespread devastation across the region. As Tala's gaze settled upon him, he saw in her sharp, unwavering eyes a profound and unspoken emotion.

His response was a single, conclusive word, "No," and then a clarifying, "It wasn't," leaving no room for further discussion.

A heavy silence descended between them, broken only by the cheerful pops and crackles of the pine logs burning merrily in the inviting warmth of the hearth. Outside, a wind whispered and whistled as it moved through the tall, proud cottonwoods. Cole's hand moved a second time, and this time, instead of tracing the contours of the wooden surface before him, it instinctively went to his wrist, where a visible scar, a permanent and stark reminder of a past branding incident, glinted subtly in the ambient light.

He finally offered an explanation, revealing that the source of the trouble stemmed from an earlier disagreement about the subject of beef. In retrospect, the decision appears to have been incredibly ill-advised. Tala stated that when looking back on the past, inevitable disagreements always seemed unavoidable to her.

The event, a significant one in the annals of our history, had transpired a full fifteen years prior to the present moment. Because of a confluence of factors, including lean livestock, failing crops, and the resulting widespread irritability in the region, a volatile atmosphere developed, culminating in the theft of a shipment of meat destined for a nearby military installation. Once directed outward, suspicion now turned inward, focusing intently upon the self and its potential failings. Some settlers made accusations against a group of Lipan youths, claiming that these young people had tampered with, possibly damaged, or even stolen some of their belongings, leading to a significant dispute between the two groups. Despite the boys' vehement denials, past prejudices stubbornly resurfaced, like insidious smoke seeping through a damaged chimney. The boys were not responsible for this. Cole replied, thoughtfully, that while truth is important, it often takes a backseat when fear runs rampant and wreaks havoc.

In that week, Cole unexpectedly and surprisingly found himself during a strained and potentially volatile meeting with the town's council members, a situation that left him feeling quite uneasy. The voices grew louder and louder, their intensity escalating until they reached a powerful, overwhelming crescendo. Old resentments and frustrations unexpectedly resurfaced, reigniting past tensions and conflicts, and creating a renewed sense of animosity and discord. These had previously seemed long buried and forgotten. Someone resurrected and proposed the suggestion to divide the community marketplace, creating separate areas for Lipan traders and settlers—a suggestion absent for years. The ice-cold knife felt as if it had brutally cut down all the hard work and effort over the years.

Cole, overcome with anger, had already gone home. As he arrived, Tala was there to greet him at the door. "Do you really believe that anger solves this problem?" she had questioned, a hint of disbelief in her tone. We are in danger of squandering all the progress and success that we have painstakingly achieved together. She had uttered a decisive "no," her stance unwavering. We are testing the product and we will provide feedback soon.

Returning to the present moment, Tala slowly got up from the floor, approached the fire, and added a few stalks of sage to the flames. As a refreshing and cleansing scent wafted through the air, it filled the space with its fragrance. Turning to face him, she instinctively moved her hands closer to the fire, seeking the warmth of the dancing flames.

"That year," she recalled, her voice tinged with the weight of the memory, "was a close call; we could have easily lost everything we had worked for." "But we didn't."

Cole gave a slight nod of his head in acknowledgement. Our decision to seat them at the same table forced them to sit together again. They were unwilling to take part in the proposed activity, expressing a distinct lack of desire to engage.

"No."

A faint smile touched her lips, barely perceptible but undeniably there. A result of the frybread that I provided to them directly influenced their decision to stay. That statement, or element of the narrative, corresponded accurately with the facts. Instead of hosting the gathering in the community hall, Tala had hosted it in the comfort of their own home. As she cooked, Cole quietly moved from person to person, his attentiveness far exceeding his contributions to the conversations. As neighbors and survivors, they jointly reminded people of the path they had traversed, a journey that transcended mere mistrust to confront the harsher reality of profound isolation. Demonstrating resilience and fortitude, they provided their community with invaluable guidance on how to persevere through adversity once more.

The turning point had come when young Elan, a Lipan teenager accused of theft, publicly offered his wages for the missing beef. It was an act of humility that broke the room open. A settler boy who'd once shouted at Elan walked over and shook his hand. Weeks later, authorities apprehended the actual thieves—hired riders from a passing cattle company. The community didn't erupt in celebration. They sat in quiet relief. The tension had nearly snapped. But it hadn't. That was the miracle.

"Sometimes I wonder," Cole said, "what would've happened if we hadn't stepped in?"

"We don't need to wonder," Tala replied. "We know. Because we've seen it happen elsewhere."

The storms had left their mark; indeed, not all towns had remained completely intact following the storms' passage. People had heard accounts from other places, where a single event destroyed years of fragile, painstakingly maintained peace and calm. Unlike other groups, the Kickapoo Creek community had a unique resilience, not because their inherent nature was superior, but because of their learned ability to persevere amidst challenging circumstances. With a quiet sigh, Tala perched on the arm of Cole's chair, gently leaning her head against his shoulder in a gesture of affection and trust. In a barely audible whisper, she confessed she had never properly expressed her gratitude. "I'm curious about the motive behind this." Thank you for your attentive listening.

A chuckle escaped Cole's lips. If I had tried to leave, you would have certainly pursued me and forcibly returned me to where I was. It is possible that we may consider that option. He gently encircled her waist with his arm, and then, with a tender gesture, he kissed the back of her hand. You possessed

217

an uncanny ability to identify and understand consistently the tasks that required immediate attention.

"No."

Later that evening, their granddaughter Clara arrived, her arms laden with legal documents and her youngest son, clinging tightly to the folds of her shawl, in tow. She gasped for air. She excitedly exclaimed, "Grandma, Grandpa," her words tumbling out in a rush. This is some information of great interest to you that you will definitely want to hear.

Cole, with a subtle movement, raised one eyebrow in a questioning manner. "What is the input from our side?"

The impact of your names, they showed, continues to be substantial and noteworthy. A quick, almost imperceptible exchange of glances occurred between Tala and Cole, conveying unspoken understanding, or perhaps a shared secret. Are you really going to give it to them?

Clara nodded. "But I want to tell them more than just how we shared a creek. I want to tell them how we survived that storm." She paused, looking around the room.

"This house has seen it all. People need to know it wasn't always easy. That unity is hard. Fragile. But worth it."

Cole stood slowly, joints popping. He walked over to Clara and placed a hand on her shoulder. "Then tell them. Tell them everything."

As the fire burned low, the three of them stood together—three generations bound not just by blood, but by choices. Through hard work and perseverance. Sharing stories, resolving arguments, and enjoying meals together strengthens thread of trusts and deepens rooted kinships. As the night deepened, the wind finally calmed, and the house grew still, settling into a peaceful slumber, and in their bed, Cole and Tala lay with their fingers intertwined.

Outside, the moon cast pale light across the land they had once feared would never hold peace. But it had. Not because conflict vanished, but because people chose each other, again and again.

Chapter 58: The Passing of Time

The sun rose and set countless times over Kickapoo Creek, a number too vast for anyone to bother counting. Time relentlessly etched deeper lines around Cole's eyes and progressively stooped his shoulders, but he persisted in his daily ritual, rising early to walk his land, his slight stoop clear as he relied on a sturdy cane fashioned from an aged cedar limb for support. Tala, also, was slower in her movements nowadays, yet there was a defiant elegance in how she swept the porch or styled her braid—as if she was resisting time from taking away more than it already had.

Over the years, their home had grown significantly in size, encompassing many additions and renovations. To make room for grandchildren, then great-grandchildren, and finally to allow for the hosting of council meetings, visiting scholars, and harvest celebrations, they added more space to their home. The walls, silent observers, stood as stoic witnesses to every event that transpired within their aged, sturdy frames. In the hallway, a collection of framed photographs showcased Cole's journey, with one photo prominently displaying him alongside his initial herd. A recent addition to the exhibit was a frame showcasing a mural created by a local student; however, the tranquility of Kickapoo Creek was anything but assured, something that the residents were always keenly aware of. It wasn't something freely given; it demanded continuous effort, sometimes in the quiet background, and sometimes through immense and difficult challenges—emotional, political, and generational. As the town expanded, its infrastructure and social fabric became increasingly complex, reflecting a richer and more intricate societal tapestry.

Some years prior to the current events, a conflict over land ownership had erupted between a recently arrived family of settlers and an established Lipan ranching cooperative. The problem wasn't a recent one; the creek boundaries were informal, passed down through generations by word of mouth rather than officially surveyed, and thus, not clearly defined. In contrast to previous instances, these settlers sought formal dominion, mentioning development schemes and agricultural aid.

It could have unraveled everything.

The co-op, made up mostly of Lipan women and their descendants, felt their heritage was under threat. The settler family claimed ignorance. Still, tensions rose quickly. At one point, angry words flew across the town square. The market shut down for a week. A council elder resigned in protest.

And yet, they didn't fall apart.

A new generation, raised on the legends of Cole and Tala, stepped in, living lives distinct from the past. Noemi, Amaya's daughter, speaking both Lipan and legalese, created a mediation plan that both sides accepted for neutral arbitration. Her meeting place wasn't a courtroom; it was the old pecan tree, a location for community gatherings. With careful consideration for everyone's tastes, they brought an assortment of foods for the gathering. They respectfully sent invitations to the community elders, requesting their attendance. They paid attention to what was being said, attentively listening to every word.

In the end, they redrew the lines, not with ownership, but with stewardship. The creek remained shared. They added a walking trail, naming it after the original Lipan farmer who had tended the land long before maps were made. The settler family stayed—and donated half an acre to a communal garden.

That wasn't easy. But it was real.

Cole and Tala heard the entire story from their porch, watching Noemi walk up the path one evening with her dusty boots and a proud grin.

"You would've been proud," she said simply.

Tala reached for her hand. "We are."

Inside the house, the sounds of life were a constant hum. Children played in corners with hand-carved toys. A distant cousin practiced the flute in the front room. Someone chopped vegetables in the kitchen—preparing a meal for the community elders who gathered every new moon.

Cole moved slower now, but still sat at the head of the table during those gatherings, not to command, but to listen. He spoke less, nodded more.

When asked for advice, he rarely gave answers—instead, he told stories. Not the heroic kind. The kind with doubt. With mistakes. With hard-earned lessons. And it was enough.

One evening, Clara, their granddaughter who taught history in the new schoolhouse, asked him, "Did you ever think it would last? This... peace?"

Cole looked at her for a long time before he answered. "No. But we didn't build it because we thought it would be easy. We built it because the alternative was more dying."

Tala added, "And we stayed because we wanted to see what could live."

The schoolhouse itself was a point of pride. Designed by two students—one Lipan, one Mexican-American—it blended adobe with modern solar panels. The curriculum was bilingual. The school library held books in three languages and a rotating archive of oral histories. Elders came in weekly to speak. The children learned about U.S. history and Lipan cosmology, and teachers encouraged them to question both.

Some newer settlers from larger cities questioned the necessity of so much "cultural programming." A few murmured that the town was "too Indian, not Western enough. But the town responded not with outrage, but with invitations. They received an invitation to help build a sweat lodge. Another led a reading group. And slowly, like a tree leaning toward sunlight, they shifted. The strength of the community was in its adaptability. Not in forgetting the past, but in weaving it into the present.

In the familiar comfort of their home, Cole and Tala discovered a deep sense of contentment and happiness in even the most ordinary activities and rituals. The process of extracting shells from beans. Observing the different species of birds and their behaviors is a fascinating hobby. Relatives who moved to the city frequently sent letters, photos, and updates, including pictures of their stylishly dressed children—many wearing fringe, boots, or both. Among the correspondence, one letter contained a touching PostScript: the Lipan language continues to be spoken on Sundays. Late one afternoon, a young boy, who appeared to be only nine years old, came to their door and knocked.

He stated in a clear voice that his name was Arlo. "They informed me you were the one who constructed this town."

Cole let out a chuckle, a soft sound of amusement. "No, son."

The boy's brow furrowed, his expression twisting into a frown that hinted at displeasure, confusion, or perhaps deep thought. "However, they claimed your actions prevented further conflict between people who were ready to fight."

Tala dropped to one knee, bringing herself down to his level so that their eyes could meet. "We failed to intervene and prevent the altercation from escalating into a full-blown fight." Arlo gave the matter some thought. Following that, he inquired about the possibility of borrowing a story from someone present. Tala, extending a hand towards him, offered a woven bracelet from a nearby bowl with the instruction, "Take two. They last longer when you share them."

Underneath a breathtaking night sky, where countless stars shone brilliantly, the town square was festively lit, preparing for the expected seasonal gathering. The air vibrated with a lively mix of musical sounds, including the cheerful melodies of fiddles and flutes, the rhythmic beats of hand drums, and the beautiful blend of voices in harmony. The weight of the bountiful shared meals caused the tables to groan under their considerable burden, nearly collapsing under the sheer abundance of food. Cole and Tala sat together on a wooden bench, a blanket spread across their laps, and watched as generations of people danced, argued, sang, and stood side-by-side, sharing in the collective experience.

Peace, in reality, was not merely the absence of movement or noise, but a much more dynamic and complex state. It was a decision that required both sides to make concessions and meet halfway.

Chapter 59: A Legacy of Love

The lively chatter of voices suddenly filled the quiet porch as the sun sank slowly behind the tall cottonwood trees. Cole and Tala, reminiscing about their early days together, sat on their old swing, the same swing that had cradled them through countless hours of childhood laughter and youthful dreams.

With joyous abandon, children, their feet bare, raced through the dusty ground, playfully pursuing a hoop crafted from simple sticks. A delicious aroma filled the air, a captivating blend of mesquite smoke from the grill, the sweetness of roasting squash, and the warm, inviting scent of cinnamon-spiced baked apples resting on the windowsill. Sounds of laughter, light, drifted lazily through the open windows, carrying with them a sense of carefree joy. Within the confines of the home, three generations worked together, moving in a synchronized manner as they stirred, chopped ingredients, and recounted old stories, each time adding slightly altered details that reflected the passage of time.

Lena, a young girl, sat perched on a low bench beside the crackling firepit, a notebook carefully balanced upon her knees as the flames danced and flickered before her. Having developed a passion for history by the time she turned twelve, she gave a presentation that evening focusing on Tala, a subject that had captured her imagination. "I'm curious to know, so please tell me; were you completely with no English language skills whatsoever in your life?"

Tala, without uttering a single word, responded to the situation with a warm smile, effectively communicating her message through nonverbal cues. "I had absolutely no intention whatsoever of participating in or engaging with any kind of educational or learning activities of any sort. However, a question has arisen in my mind regarding the accuracy of my previous understanding, prompting me to inquire about whether your grandfather truly spoke the Lipan language."

Lena's pen scratched across the page in a frantic blur, her energy driving her to write with such speed that it was almost a whirlwind of motion. "The question of the very first word, either written or spoken, has always intrigued me, and I am eager to understand its precise nature."

With a burst of laughter, Tala declared emphatically, "Enough!" bringing a sudden end to the proceedings. Beside her, Cole sat quietly, chuckling to himself.

As the children's laughter echoed and filled the room, it drew the attention even of the teenagers huddled in their own little world in a far corner, where they were busy carefully tuning a guitar and quietly sharing a plate of roasted seeds; they looked up from their tasks, captivated by the cheerful sounds. As Lena worked on her expanding oral history project, her notes became integral to the process. Her cousin, Micah, helped meticulously document the interviews using an old, school-donated handheld recorder.

Micah voiced his wish to hear the story. Tala, with the slightest of movements, elegantly arched a single eyebrow, a subtle gesture that perfectly conveyed her profound skepticism regarding the matter at hand.

Lena, remembering the time her grandmother, all by herself, had built the bridge, quoted a story about it, allowing her to reminisce fondly about her grandmother's impressive feat of engineering and construction.

Cole shook his head in utter disbelief. "That project, my dear, did not involve her work or contributions in any capacity."

Tala vividly recounted the scene, describing how she had helplessly watched them nearly drown, standing there as their endless and ultimately fruitless argument over the superiority of their respective plans raged on.

Casting a questioning glance at Cole, she subtly reminded him of their previous conversation, encouraging him to recall the details she had shared with others. "If you had used your ears instead of letting your pride get in the way, we would have already reached our destination," her words still echoed in my mind.

Unable to contain their joy, the children erupted in a cacophony of laughter and shrieks.

Even to this day, that bridge stands as a symbol of strength and endurance, having withstood the test of time. The town brochures and festival banners prominently featured the symbol of Harmony Crossing, a name that beautifully encapsulated the town's spirit. Unaware of the controversy that nearly jeopardized its existence, or of the Lipan woman whose intelligence and courage saved it, tourists eagerly snapped photographs of the landmark.

In their home, Cole's daughter Amaya diligently collected the used dishes, placing them carefully into a basin while being assisted by her young daughter, Clara. A palpable tension lingered between them, originating from Clara's absence at a crucial council meeting. She had attempted to excuse her absence by claiming she was attending a storytelling workshop in a distant town, yet her explanation clearly had not satisfied the person she spoke with.

"You're needed here," Amaya said quietly.

"I'm learning how to help. Just not the way you did."

They didn't speak for a few minutes, working side by side in silence. Then Clara handed her mother a clean bowl.

"I'm not trying to be different," she said. "Just... useful."

Amaya stopped what she was doing, a thoughtful pause descending upon her as she carefully contemplated her next action. She subtly nodded, showing agreement and understanding.

Although the initial disagreement appeared insignificant, it had the latent capacity to escalate into a considerably more serious problem. However, in Kickapoo Creek, even the typically volatile and immediate nature of conflict had been unexpectedly and remarkably imbued with patience.

After supper, the family gathered around the warm hearth; the younger children, content and relaxed, sprawled on handcrafted woven rugs spread across the floor, while the adults settled comfortably into chairs or leaned against the sturdy, wooden beams of the room. As the day transitioned into evening, the outdoor light faded, its gentle hues of dusk deepening gradually before the all-encompassing darkness of night settled in. As the evening approached, the crickets, awakened by the descending darkness, began their familiar nightly chorus, a vibrant and ceaseless chirping that filled the stillness of the night with sound.

Among all the countless moments that had shaped her life's journey, Tala held this moment most dear, a cherished memory that she kept ever close to her heart.

Among the group of boys, one particularly bold and curious lad pressed Cole for details about his first kiss, his questions revealing an intense interest in the experience and all its details.

Cole's eyes blinked once, flickered, and then a sly grin, holding a mischievous glint, slowly spread across his lips. "While I remember trying, the details of my attempt escape me now, lost to the sands of time and the fog of memory."

Tala's unrestrained mirth erupted in a loud laugh, the sound shaking her shoulders as she yielded to the joyful outburst. In his mind, his actions were not only discreet but also undetectable, and therefore, he believed he was operating with no one noticing.

He claimed to have believed that he had successfully caught her attention; however, uncertainty lingered in his mind regarding the accuracy of this belief. "Much to my dismay, I subsequently discovered that my ill-fated choice of seating had placed me in the unpleasant position of being downwind from a skunk."

The joke was incredibly humorous, provoking unrestrained laughter even from the typically stoic teenage attendees.

However, a palpable shift in the atmosphere soon transpired, marked by a transition from the earlier lightheartedness to a mood that was far more contemplative, prompting a period of reflection among those present.

In Tala's hands, she carefully held a photograph, its colors faded and edges softened by passaging time, a cherished relic from their early years as a couple. The painting showed a young Cole, seated rigidly and uncomfortably on a horse, in stark contrast to Tala, who stood beside him with arms folded tightly across her chest, her expression sharp, watchful, and wary.

Letting out a wistful sigh, she spent some time reflecting on the day and its events, finally starting with certainty. "I remember this day vividly. It's unforgettable."

A thoughtful expression settled on Cole's face as he meticulously examined the photograph, paying close attention to every detail in the frame.

"Despite your feelings of fear or apprehension, your actions showed a level of bravery that even surprised you."

"Your patience pleasantly surprised me; it exceeded my expectations."

In that instant, as their eyes locked, the family, the walls, and passaging years all seemed to fade away, leaving only the two of them.

A hush fell over the room, and all conversation ceased. Following a period of silence, Clara then spoke, sharing her thoughts and ideas with those gathered around her.

"Do you believe that the character and nature of this town will remain unchanged in the years to come?"

Cole's brow furrowed in thought, his expression becoming serious and intense as he pondered the problem.

Cole explained that, similar to any other skilled craft, the process involves continuous refinement and reshaping.

As the evening progressed, one teenager, a young man named Mateo, eventually approached Cole while he was sitting on the porch. He paused for a considerable length of time, his thoughts swirling before he finally spoke.

"I believe that running for a position on the council might be something I'd like to pursue," he thoughtfully remarked.

Cole, relaxing against the chair's backrest, leaned back. "I am curious to know the rationale for this."

"My intention is to ensure that my sister receives the attention and consideration she deserves, and to prevent her from being disregarded or overlooked." Cole gave a slight nod of his head in acknowledgement. Mateo shifted his weight from one foot to the other, shuffling his feet nervously. "There are those who harbor the misconception that, because of my age, I lack the experience or maturity."

He paused, a moment of silence hanging heavily in the air before he continued. "One develops skills and understanding in various areas by engaging in and actively participating in those activities."

As the night sky darkened, countless stars emerged, illuminating the heavens in all their glory. Like a celestial river of stars, the Milky Way flowed across the vast expanse of the night sky, its shimmering band acting as a cosmic rooted kinship between our planet and the grand scale of the universe.

Moving quietly and carefully inside, Tala gently placed the sleeping baby into a small cradle positioned snugly next to the warm, crackling fire. With a gentle hand, she rearranged the blanket, a thoughtful gift from a neighbor meticulously stitched with a blend of symbols representing both their unique cultural heritages. Born from the union of a Lipan woman and a Czech settler's son, a recent marriage, the child's background was mixed heritage, representing a fascinating blend of two distinct cultures. Surrounding towns buzzed with rumors and speculation about their union, sharing whispers and conjecture, yet their hometown remained conspicuously silent, offering neither commentary nor judgment on the matter. It is important to note that the location is not, in fact, Kickapoo Creek; it is elsewhere.

In this place, a single defining characteristic did not encapsulate the complexity of each individual.

With the fire's dying embers casting a soft glow and a peaceful quiet descending upon the house, Tala and Cole lingered on the porch, their fingers lightly laced together.

"Is it your considered opinion that, given the passage of time and all that has happened, they will have forgotten the relevant details?" Cole's voice was soft as he asked his question.

"No," Tala said. "Because they'll remember in how they speak. In how they settle arguments. In the questions they ask."

She smiled. "They'll remember by how they love."

And in the hush of that moment, surrounded by the distant thrum of a town they'd helped build, they knew their living memory was not something written. It was lived.

Chapter 60: The Enduring Spirit

As the morning sun ascended, it cast its golden light silently and authoritatively across the fields and rooftops of the quaint little town nestled beside Kickapoo Creek. Near the river, a light breeze rustled the leaves of the cottonwood trees, creating a gentle whispering sound that resembled the murmuring voices of storytellers who were just beginning their enchanting narratives. A rich earthy scent of mesquite filled the air, mingling with the warm scent of fertile soil; it was as if the land itself was awakening in anticipation of the approaching powwow.

From the first light of dawn, a gentle current of purposeful movement flowed through the town, the people proceeding with a steady gait. As they ran their errands, the children carried bundles of sage and feathered ribbons, their steps light and quick. As the elders carefully unpacked the hand-woven baskets, the aroma of dried fruits and the sight of savory venison strips filled the air, promising a feast of traditional foods. A freshly painted banner proclaiming "Annual Spring Gathering–Two Rivers, One Root," fluttered in the breeze along the weathered wall of the old schoolhouse.

As the years passed, what began as a small gathering of Lipan Apache dancers and musicians, the annual powwow evolved and expanded, transforming into a vibrant and diverse event that beautifully blended time-honored traditions with exciting and innovative elements. The Anglo families attending the event brought with them many dishes, including beans and smoked brisket. The settler children, standing side by side, sang their traditional songs, which were distinct in rhythm yet harmonized beautifully with the Lipan chants that were also being performed. Annually, the event served as a poignant reminder of Kickapoo Creek's transformation and the fragile beauty it represented.

But no one mistook it for permanence.

That morning, Cole and Tala dressed slowly. Tala smoothed the folds of her skirt, her hands lingering over the beadwork sewn decades earlier by her mother. Cole buttoned a vest passed down through four generations, each button replaced by someone else's hand. He checked his watch, a gift from a cavalry captain long gone, and nodded to himself. It still ticked.

"Ready?" Tala asked.

Cole gave her a sideways look. I had already prepared before you took charge of this whole town. "Never in charge," Tala stated. "I just kept reminding people what mattered."

"And sometimes reminded them loudly."

She smiled. "Only when they needed it."

They arrived at the square just as the drums began—four slow beats spaced evenly apart, like footsteps coming across the plains. The dancers stepped into place, their regalia brilliant in the morning light: feathers, turquoise, dyed leather, and fringes that flowed like water. The beat sped up, and the circle widened.

Near the stage, Micah stood nervously, a sheet of notes clutched in his hands. He was sixteen now, and this would be his first public welcome. As he stepped forward, a hush fell over the crowd. His voice wavered at first, but then found its footing, the cadence strong as he welcomed everyone in both English and Lipan Apache.

"The past alone does not build a community," he said. "We shape it by how we carry it." His words drew soft murmurs of approval. Tala closed her eyes and smiled.

As the day progressed, the storytelling tent became a place where individuals recounted tales of their ancestors' arduous journeys across rivers to evade raids, contrasting with narratives of settlers who bravely jeopardized their social standing to protect their community members. Some narratives, while engaging, did not conclude with triumphant victories or happy endings. There were some things that were exceptionally messy.

A disagreement, intense and sudden, flared up unexpectedly in a quiet corner of the otherwise peaceful gathering. In a recent market dispute, a long-established vendor of handmade beaded jewelry publicly accused a newer vendor, just arrived in town, of unlawfully appropriating and reproducing traditional Lipan designs without seeking consent or authorization. A subtle increase in the volume of voices momentarily threatened to shatter the day's harmony, rekindling older conflicts and tensions that had been dormant. Before the murmurs of the crowd could escalate into a cacophony of speculation and dissent, two young women, Eliza and Clara—great-granddaughters of the esteemed Cole and Tala and both integral members of the recently established Cultural Stewardship Committee—stepped forward to address the gathering.

Because no disagreement arose, they continued their work. They openly and freely expressed their opinions and emotions instead of remaining silent, ensuring clear understanding. Something utterly captivated their attention. Driven by a desire for complete transparency regarding their sourcing practices, Clara formally requested a detailed explanation from the vendor about how they gain their raw materials and manufacture their products. Eliza painstakingly explained the symbolism inherent in every distinct bead pattern, expanding upon the wealth of stories and historical contexts, each design eloquently communicated. The crowd, typically boisterous, was unusually still and focused, a remarkable change from their normal behavior. With the event's conclusion, the newer vendor, overcome with remorse for any caused inconvenience, extended a formal apology for her actions and, in a gesture of generosity, committed to donating all her event profits to the community center. Their combined efforts resulted not only in the preservation of peace but also in the forging of a strong and decisive peace, a testament to their collaborative spirit.

Noemi stirred a truly enormous pot of thick, savory blue corn stew with steady, rhythmic movements near the cooking fires, whose flames danced merrily. A local farmer, who was of Anglo descent and had been born and raised in the Kickapoo community, worked alongside her, her movements precise and expert as she sliced the squash. Despite their lack of overt communication, their quiet collaboration powerfully conveyed a message surpassing any formal speech. As time went on, they became embroiled in a fierce and contentious argument about the proper distribution and official approval of permits for the use of land. At the present time, they are collaboratively engaged in the management and oversight of the town's crop share program, a vital initiative designed to serve and enhance the well-being of the entire community.

High above, flapping proudly in the breeze, were three flags: the Lipan emblem, the familiar Texas star, and a vibrant new banner, created by children, depicting a majestic creature that was half-eagle, half-longhorn, with a sunrise dramatically rising between them.

With the afternoon sun beginning to set, the rhythmic pulse of dancing picked up again, its lively energy permeating the air and creating a vibrant atmosphere. Beneath a striped canvas canopy, Cole and Tala observed the children, who were whirling in tight circles, their movements a captivating blend of practiced choreography and unrestrained, joyful abandon. As the drums pulsed with a powerful heartbeat, a sound that transcended generations and connected everyone present in a shared experience, the rhythmic clapping of the elders filled the air, creating a powerful atmosphere.

Turning to Cole, Tala spoke, her words a gentle invitation to share a cherished memory of their first powwow together, a moment she hoped they both held dear in their hearts. Giving a slight nod of his head, he silently conveyed his concurrence with the proposal. He added a further point, emphasizing that three families were actively involved in the project's development and execution. Tala explained that, besides what she had already stated, three more supporting arguments lent considerable credence to her main point.

The word "four," a single syllable, escaped his lips and settled between them, pregnant with unspoken meaning and lingering in the silence. If my memory serves me correctly, there was a rather heated disagreement between us concerning the preparation and, more specifically, the quality of the stew we were discussing. Tala responded, stating that although others doubted her assertion, it ultimately proved entirely accurate. With a teasing tone, he remarked that her current emotional state was not unusual for her, implying a familiarity with her emotional patterns.

With the sun descending below the horizon and dusk settling in, illuminating the grounds were the torches lit around the perimeter, casting a warm, inviting, golden glow upon the dancers as their synchronized movements in perfect harmony gracefully performed the traditional Unity Song.

In the town square, a captivating new dance unfolded, its choreography a collaboration between a young Lipan man and a young woman descended from Kansas's buffalo hunters. The steps in the progression, initially showing two rivers meeting in a show of resistance, ultimately told a story of their unification into a single, powerful current flowing as one.

As the event concluded, a profound silence descended upon the square, a palpable stillness hanging in the air. Then, a thunderous eruption of applause filled the space, a wave of appreciation washing over the performers. Gradually, the crowd formed a circle, resembling more a group of people coming together for a shared experience than an audience watching a performance.

As more people joined in, one voice at a time, a powerful and unified chant emerged, beginning with Lipan, the first language spoken, and then continuing in English. They then considered both options. Cole leaned in close to Tala, his body almost touching hers. "Can you describe the sounds you are currently perceiving?" he asked.

With a sigh, she responded, "Memory," letting the word drift into the silence of the room. "Hope and optimism for the future fill our hearts."

Later that evening, once they were back at their house, they relaxed on the porch, their view encompassed by a spectacular star-filled night sky. Long after the powwow had ended, its vibrant rhythms and powerful energy continued to echo in their memories. The fragrance in the air was a potent mix of cedar smoke, mingling with the deep, damp smell of the soil beneath. From the nearby houses, the soft, almost indiscernible sounds of children's laughter floated on the breeze, a gentle reminder of the carefree moments of childhood. Despite the circumstances, life continued all around them—not in a grand or perfect way, but through the quiet, resilient strength found in the everyday choices people make.

"Given the situation's complexity, is it likely they accurately remember every detail?" Cole, taking a deep breath, finally posed the question that had been weighing heavily on his mind. Tala, with a quick flick of her wrist brushing a stray strand of hair from her face, delivered a curt, "No," and added, "but they'll remember enough." As her gaze fell upon him, she paused for just a moment, her eyes lingering on him before she shifted her gaze in another direction.

A gentle breeze, whispering the familiar tune of a child's lullaby from earlier in the day, softly rustled the leaves of the tall cottonwood trees that stood majestically in the landscape. Her voice remained steady and clear throughout her beautiful song. At that very moment, Cole and Tala, who were not only founders and elders but also pivotal historical figures, experienced a profound emotional shift, moving beyond their established roles and into a realm of feeling far exceeding those titles. Experiencing such unity with the river, they felt an intense rooted kinship, as if they were not just observers but integral components of its ceaseless movement, its powerful current, and its vibrant life force. Because they had helped to shape its course, they discovered they were now caught up in and carried along by a powerful, independent force that was now completely self-reliant and followed its own path.

High above, in the vast expanse of the night sky, the stars performed their silent, celestial dance, twinkling softly as if in quiet approval of the events unfolding on the earth below.

Acknowledgments

I would like to take this opportunity to extend my sincerest appreciation to everyone who offered assistance and motivation while I was writing Kickapoo Creek. I would like to begin by extending my sincere gratitude to the members of the Lipan Apache Indian Nation, as well as the citizens of the City of Lipan, whose influence served as the inspiration for this particular novel. The novel was greatly enhanced by their generosity as well as their openness in sharing their rich heritage. I am immensely thankful to those individuals, whose essential direction and specialized knowledge were crucial to my success.

In addition, I want to express my sincere gratitude to the beta readers, editors, and everyone else who contributed insightful feedback. The final manuscript was significantly improved due to your insightful feedback and consistent support. I would like to extend my sincere gratitude to my wife, Karen, not only for her careful editing, but also for her unwavering support throughout the duration of this project.

Throughout the extended and often challenging process of writing this, I would like to express my gratitude and appreciation to my family and friends for the patience, encouragement, and understanding that they have offered me.

Author's Biography

Brett is a book author with a lifelong passion for horses and the western history of the area. Growing up on a farm surrounded by animals, he developed a deep appreciation for the thread of trust between humans and animals, a theme that resonates throughout his writing. He believes in the power of storytelling to inspire and educate young readers, fostering a love for nature and a respect for all creatures. When not crafting heartwarming tales, Wyatt spends time with his horses, explores the outdoors, and shares his love of animals with others.

Brett's journey as an author began in his childhood, where he spent countless hours immersed in the world of books. His favorite stories featured animals as central characters, tales that highlighted the unique relationships between humans and their animal companions. These stories ignited his imagination and planted the seeds of his future career. As he grew older, Brett's love for horses deepened, and he saw them not only as animals but also as friends and confidants. This profound rooted kinship became the cornerstone of his writing, infusing his stories with authenticity and heartfelt emotion.

His farm, a picturesque haven nestled amidst rolling hills and lush pastures, provided the perfect backdrop for his creative endeavors. His daily interactions with his horses, the quiet moments spent grooming them, and the exhilarating rides through the countryside all inspired his tales. Brett's horses were more than subjects for his stories; they were his muses, each with unique personalities and quirks that found their way into his characters.

Brett's love for nature intertwines with his writing process. He often takes long walks through the woods, letting the sights and sounds of the natural world fuel his creativity. Walking provides time for reflection, environmental rooted kinship, and inspiration from nature's beauty. His stories aim to capture the magic of nature's voice for those who listen.

Brett's literature inspires young readers to connect with animals. His stories are not only about adventure and excitement, but also about understanding, friendship, and the special thread of trust between humans and animals. Through his work, Wyatt hopes to inspire the next generation to appreciate and protect the natural world and its creatures.

When he's not writing or spending time with his horses, Wyatt enjoys exploring the outdoors, hiking through the mountains, photographing wildlife, or sitting under a tree with a good book. These activities give him peace and fulfillment, allowing him to recharge and find new inspiration for his stories.

Brett's life is a testament to the power of following one's passions. His love for horses and storytelling has shaped his career and enriched his life in countless ways. Through his books, he shares that joy with others, inviting readers to embark on their adventures and discover the magic of the thread of trust between humans and animals.

www.ingramcontent.com/pod-product-compliance
Lightning Source LLC
Chambersburg PA
CBHW070837030726
47504CB00005B/1124